GALAXY UNDER SIEGE

FORGOTTEN GALAXY
BOOK 3

M.R. FORBES

Published by Quirky Algorithms
Seattle, Washington

Cover illustration by Tom Edwards
Edited by Merrylee Lanehart

CHAPTER 1

The Splinter shuddered violently, the magnetic grip of Caleb's seat straining as the tiny breacher ground through eight inches of alloy, along with a mess of pipes and wiring, before bursting through the bulkhead of the cargo hauler Tonneau. Compressed air pumped into bladders surrounding the back half of the breacher, sealing the hole it had created. Another burst of compressed air, and the Splinter's bow popped open. Caleb deactivated his seat's maglock and dove forward onto the deck of the cargo ship.

He rose to a crouch, rifle leveled to sweep the passageway in both directions. "Clear," he announced over the unit's networked comms. The rest of his boarding team joined him in the corridor as he sent a second message back to Gorgon. "We're in."

"Copy that, Captain. We're almost finished dealing with the escorts. This one is pretty much wrapped up."

"Don't get ahead of yourself, Sarge," Caleb warned. "Ishek isn't usually right about much, but he's right when he says never underestimate the Relyeh."

One of the everything I'm correct about.

"I thought you said this run was clean?" Damian countered.

"I did. That means no khoron. But Iagorth's moieties can be anywhere, and they don't use the Collective. We can't see them."

"It's been three months since the stardock," Damian continued. "If there were more moieties out here, wouldn't we have encountered them by now? Or does Crux not care that we've intercepted over a dozen of his haulers since then?"

Caleb didn't reply. His helmet's sensors detected movement before his ears could. The other members of the Razor's Edge who had accompanied him—Penn, Orin, and Sparkles—all turned toward the sensor hit. Not that he could always trust his helmet sensors. He had learned fast that there was the occasional spoof contact, along with ways to jam sensors. The helmet was an early warning system, but nothing beat human sight and hearing for confirmation.

His doubts were confirmed when the signal should have become visible at a junction a short distance ahead, but nothing appeared.

"Spoofed," Sparkles spat. "I guess they like playing games with us, Cap."

"We know the rules to this one," Caleb replied. "Penn, Orin, go left. Sparkles, you're with me."

"Copy," Penn replied, gesturing to the Jiba-ki, who scratched his armpit before following her down the passageway. All clothes were uncomfortable for him, the tactical gear especially so.

"Granger, sitrep," Caleb said, continuing along the corridor with Sparkles on his six.

"Our bird just landed, Cap," the leader of the Berserkers rumbled. "On our way to secure the hold."

Caleb pulled to a stop a few meters short of the junction,

glancing at the tattooed Edger. "What do you think, Sparky?"

"By the book," Sparkles replied.

They both remained static in the passageway, but not for long. A small drone zipped around the corner ahead, accelerating toward them. Neither man turned their rifle toward the machine. Instead, Sparkles tapped the trigger of the directed electromagnetic pulse device in his hand. The drone immediately powered down, crashing to the deck in front of them.

"By the book," Caleb repeated, shaking his head. They had captured over fifty million coin worth of Legion military supplies over the last three months, and the cargo ships transporting the goods had yet to change up their tactics. It appeared they still didn't expect anyone to have the audacity to attack them. After all this time, they had made no changes to their defenses in the face of Gorgon's increasing raids.

Still, Caleb refused to grow complacent with their assaults, which was why he had continued joining the boarding crews on their missions. Each time they located a transit route for Crux's war machine, each time they went out in the Splinters, he expected beefed up defenses and a more challenging takeover. Once more, those expectations hadn't been met.

He and Sparkles advanced to the corner, swinging around it in unison. A unit of defenders had taken a position near the far end of the passageway. A hardened portable barrier—small gaps allowed for firing through it—separated them from the two men. These were contracted mercenaries, not Legionnaires. Guns for hire that the Legion had decided wouldn't make suitable hosts. They weren't poor fighters, per se. But there were no surprises in their tactics, and the Razor's Edge had come prepared.

Plasma bolts spewed from rifle muzzles resting in the

small gaps of the barrier, across the passageway toward Caleb and Sparkles. Caleb crossed to the other side of the junction to take cover, while Sparkles temporarily pulled back. When the plasma stopped, Caleb laid down covering fire while Sparkles moved back into the open, needing only a second to launch an explosive gel round down the passageway. It hit the barrier and stuck there; the gel spraying out on contact.

"Fire in the hole," Sparkles growled, enjoying the moment as he jumped back behind the corner for cover from the rounds still flying down the corridor. The gel detonated, blasting a hole in the barrier and sending shrapnel into the defenders behind it. Rushing the defenses while the smoke of the blast provided maximum cover, Caleb and Sparkles arrived at the scene uncontested. "This is too easy, Cap."

"I keep thinking that every time we board one of these ships," Caleb replied. "Penn, we're clear in the aft, headed toward Engineering."

"Copy. No resistance so far. ETA three minutes to the bridge."

Caleb and Sparkles picked up the pace, breaking into a run after sweeping their rifles over the downed defenders, making sure they were all out of commission. While the bridge was the brains of the ship, Engineering was its heart. They needed to reach the control room before the hauler's captain could send the order to jump to hyperspace.

Nearing the end of its route, the hauler had been traveling at sub-light speed when Gorgon arrived—the only reason its captain hadn't jumped already. It would take him a few more minutes to reset the hauler's drive, offering Gorgon the opportunity for a quick getaway. They needed the advantage, since the pair of Spectors orbiting their destination, a sparsely populated planet named Callisco, were en route and burning hard to reach the

Tonneau. It was a race Caleb and the others had run, and won, before.

"Escort ships are neutralized," Damian announced. "Specters will be here in sixteen minutes."

"Copy. We're on schedule." Of course, there wouldn't be time to capture and unload the hauler before the Specters arrived, which was the other reason they needed to control both the hauler's head and heart. Once the ship was theirs, they could jump it to a predetermined rendezvous point and take their time transferring as much of the spoils as Gorgon could carry before scuttling the rest.

Passing a sealed hatch on their right, Caleb and Sparkles came up on a pair of defenders coming out of a small passageway on their left. Spaced evenly along the bulk-head, the maintenance corridors were barely big enough for a single man to pass through, but they were the most direct route to their destination.

Caught off-guard, the two defenders barely had time to shift their rifles before Caleb and Sparkles took them down with a quick barrage of energy blasts. Stepping over the still smoldering mercenaries, they ducked single-file into the maintenance corridor, running along the humid and dim corridor.

"Cap, we're two minutes from the bridge," Penn reported. "Light resistance. Orin took care of it."

"Copy," Caleb replied. "Granger?"

"Moving on the primary hold, Captain."

They had added the Berserkers after the last job, when the free-thinking captain had started jettisoning cargo before the ship was fully under their control. Granger would ensure that wouldn't happen again, or if it did, that the bay doors would be shut before too much booty could escape.

Already familiarized with the layout of the hauler, Caleb and Sparkles navigated smoothly through the maintenance corridors, avoiding potential confrontation from the more traveled passageways and reaching the secured hatch to Engineering nearly half a minute early. Turning sideways to give Sparkles access, Caleb watched him hold a small electronic device under the face scanner. It produced morphing holographs of thousands of faces in rapid succession, the projections denser and more detailed than the holotable on Gorgon could produce.

Caleb had been interested to learn from Tae and Naya that as far as these kinds of scanners were concerned, there were only about fifty-six thousand permutations. The odds that the portable projector would match one within a few seconds went up with the system having access to more faces. This time, the LED on the scanner flashed green after only three seconds.

Caleb and Sparkles emerged on the far side of Engineering, taking a pair of mercenaries standing guard near the main door by surprise. Two quick energy bursts, secured the control room in a matter of seconds.

"Penn, we're here," Caleb said, jabbing the end of his still warm rifle barrel into the cheek of one of the seated engineer's. "Deactivate the hyperdrive. Now."

"I... I can't."

"I know you can." Behind him, Sparkles herded the rest of the engineering crew into the corner and began slapping energy cuffs on them. "Cooperate," Caleb told the engineer, "and you'll make it home. Refuse, and I'll keep killing engineers until I find someone more agreeable."

Ohhh, I love it when you talk dirty.

"He can't do it," a dark-haired, heavyset engineer said from the corner, his eyes settling without so much as a blink on Caleb's. "He doesn't have clearance. But I do."

"I take it you're the man in charge," Caleb said, recognizing the man's air of authority.

"I am." He stepped forward.

"Fine, get over here and do it." Caleb jerked the engineer up out of the seat in front of him. "You get over there with the rest of your crew." He pushed the man toward Sparkles.

They switched places. The supervisor opened the controls for the hyperdrive, taking it offline. "There. Happy now?" He looked up at Caleb. "I've heard about you, you know. The Vultures. Pirates? Or rebels without a clue?" He shrugged. "Same difference, right?"

"Can you open the hatch to the bridge from here?" Caleb asked, ignoring the man's sarcastic remarks.

"Sure," the engineer replied, opening a new console and scrolling through a list of doors. He stopped at one of them and tapped on it. "She's all yours. Not that it will get you anywhere. Do you really think you're hurting Crux with these attacks? He has the resources of nearly the entire Spiral at his disposal, not that he needs them with the Specters in play. This ship means nothing to him. The cargo on it means nothing. You might as well be ants trying to carry off a mountain."

Caleb leaned in, getting close. "It means something to the people still fighting for this galaxy. The people who don't accept the rule of a tyrant, or his Master."

The engineer's brow wrinkled. "Wh... what do you mean, his Master?"

"Did you think Crux came into all this power on his own? Do you think the Relyeh came from nowhere? He's their puppet."

"No, the Legion is his. Which means the Relyeh are his."

"You're welcome to keep thinking that. I'd rather be an ant carrying the mountain that's crushing humankind beneath its weight than to get squashed like a pancake."

Was that a mixed metaphor?

"Bridge secured, Cap," Penn said. "Thanks for opening the door for us."

"Anytime," Caleb replied, backing away from the engineer and activating his comm. "Sarge, how long until the Specters arrive?"

"Thirteen minutes."

"Granger, sitrep."

"We're almost to the hold, Captain. Oncoming traffic is heavier than we expected."

Caleb's jaw clenched. He hated complications. "Do you need backup?"

"If you have the time."

"Penn, are we ready to go?"

"Aye, Captain."

He turned to the engineer. "Re-engage the hyperdrive."

"You just asked me to—"

"Do what you're told. Re-engage the drive."

The engineer tapped on the control pad a few times. "Done."

"Sarge, we're about to go hyper. Prepare Gorgon to meet us at the rendezvous point."

"Aye, Captain," Damian replied.

"Sparky, keep an eye on these guys. If any of them look like they're about to do something stupid, kill them."

"Aye aye, Captain."

Caleb left Engineering through the main door, sprinting full speed toward the lift. For all the times they had hijacked Crux's cargo ships in the last few months, this was only the third time the Berserkers had been involved, and the first time they'd needed help.

It seemed the defenders were done responding by the book.

CHAPTER 2

"Still no sign of any khoron on board?" Caleb asked Ishek as he turned the corner, running toward a pair of lifts at the end of the short passageway.

No. The entire ship is clean.

"Why would the enemy focus their defenses on the cargo hold? What good is it if they do that and lose the rest of the ship?"

Perhaps there is something valuable down there. A Sanctifier or crates of Legionnaire combat armor.

"I wouldn't mind pillaging either of those things. But that's not my point. It doesn't make sense for them to focus their defensive energy on the stomach over the head and the heart. You can live without the stomach, at least for a while."

Do you believe this is a trap?

"I always believe there's a trap. I don't know; it definitely doesn't feel right."

Agreed.

The familiar pressure of a hyperspace field washed over him, adding to his unease. At least they wouldn't need to worry about Specters intercepting them inside the protective bubble.

Pausing at the lifts, he summoned a cab, waiting only a few seconds before it arrived. After a quick drop down to Deck One, he emerged into the passageway leading to the hold, rifle at the ready as he made his way across the deck. To focus, he calmed his mind, still certain there was something about this situation that didn't add up.

"Granger, what's your position?" he asked. For all the functionality of his light tactical gear, he still couldn't understand why it didn't include anything similar to the Advanced Tactical Combat System in use when Pathfinder had left Earth. "Granger?" The lead Berserker didn't respond. He hadn't called for help, or left any other sign his team was in trouble. So where the hell had he gone? "Granger!"

More angry than concerned, Caleb charged along the passageway toward the large airlock and service lift used to load and unload the vessel. Turning the corner, he spotted the front of the Berserker's Splinter up ahead, the nose jutting upward, a pair of dead mercenaries sprawled on the deck. He rushed past them without slowing, sweeping through the passageways to the hold.

Almost there, he slowed when Strom came around the corner at a run. The Berserker waved to him, his voice finally reaching Caleb's on the comms.

"Captain, can you hear me?"

"Strom, I copy," he replied. "What's your sitrep?"

"I think they're jamming our comms. It took us a minute to realize it. Granger sent me to find you. We have a… complication, sir." His voice quivered as he spoke.

I don't like the idea of a problem, but I am enjoying his fear.

"What kind of complication?"

"A major one. I can explain on the way."

"Penn, I contacted the Berserkers. The enemy's jamming

comms around the cargo hold. They knew...no, it's more than that. They wanted us to come."

"That can't be good."

"No, it can't."

"Should we terminate the hyperspace field?"

"Negative. Whatever the issue is, we need to deal with it."

"The bridge crew is under control. I can come down to assist."

"I'm not sure that would help either. I'll send Strom back into comms range if I need anything."

"Good luck, Captain."

"Let's go." Caleb broke into a run, Strom pacing him as they headed back the way the Berserker had come. "Okay, tell me. What's the complication?"

Strom quickly explained. "First, after the standard defensive barrier and drone attack worked like it never has before, we cleared the first unit we encountered. Then a second unit ambushed us and ran before we could return fire. We chased them all the way back to the cargo hold. Once they reached the door, they turned and opened up on us until Granger took them out with a second gel round. If they had taken cover they would have had a much better chance of survival, but they didn't. Anyway, we figured it meant they had something extra valuable in the hold. Granger was getting all excited about it. Heck, we all were. We figured we'd see what it was before we contacted you."

Caleb and Strom turned the last corner before the hold. Caleb winced in response to the gory mess the gel explosive had made of the defenders.. "So what's the problem?" he asked, not that he needed Strom to tell him.

At their approach, the large, heavy blast doors to the cargo hold, damaged by the gel blast, complained as they groaned open. Caleb's attention immediately landed on the other three Berserkers, gathered around a tall cylinder resting in the center of the hold. "Strom, is that what I think it is?"

"Yes, sir. It's a bomb. Big enough to vaporize this entire ship."

Ishek began laughing. Caleb wasn't amused, but he also wasn't about to panic. "How long do we have?"

"There's no way to know. We couldn't see a timer."

"So it could go off at any second."

"'fraid so. Somebody must have a detonator. The way those Specters came running, I don't think they knew about the bomb. I don't think anyone did, except the defenders down here."

Strom paused, a shiver of fear running down Caleb's back. He hadn't noticed any silvery liquid metal in the remains of the second defense unit, but that didn't rule them out as Iagorth's puppets. "The Specters would have arrived in eight minutes. Let's figure we have about ten. Run back into comms range and ask the others if anyone knows how to defuse a bomb. Have Sparky question the engineers. It's their lives too, if it blows."

"Aye, Captain." Strom stopped on a dime and raced back toward Engineering.

All three Berserkers around the bomb looked his way as Caleb jogged up to Granger. A mass of muscle beneath his tactical gear, he towered over Caleb. However, his size and strength did nothing to negate his fear, which set his voice to quivering. "What do we do with this damn thing, Cap?"

"First thing, stay calm," Caleb replied. "You can't think straight if you're freaking out."

"I can't think at all," Lilly, one of the other two Berserkers, said.

"How bad are you wounded?" Caleb asked, noticing the stream of blood running down her shoulder from a hole in her armor.

"It might not matter soon," she replied.

Caleb thoughtfully pursed his lips. A cylinder of metal sitting in the center of the cargo hold, there wasn't much to it. No external wires. No countdown timer. A light hum and expelled heat provided the only indication of activity. "How do we know this is a bomb?"

"What else could it be?" Granger asked. "A juicer? No offense, Cap, but maybe we should disarm it first, and then confirm it won't blast us all to dust."

"Strom said it's a bomb," Ilya, the last Berserker, said. "He says he's sure. I believe him."

Caleb saw a round access panel on the side of it closest to Granger. "Do we have the tools we'll need to disarm it?"

"Do you know how to shut it down, Cap?" Lilly asked.

"No, but if we can find someone on board who does, we can save some time by removing the access cover and getting a look at what's inside."

"Here, use this," Ilya said, holding out a multi-tool she'd produced from the hip pocket of her armor.

"Just what we need," Caleb replied, accepting the tool.

"I believe in always being ready for anything, Captain. You never know when you need to open something up. Like a bomb." She chuckled nervously.

Caleb set about removing the panel, keeping an esti-mated countdown in his mind while trying not to think about how the thing could go off in his face at any moment.

Unless it is a juicer. If not, at least we won't feel a thing.

"Captain!" Strom shouted, rushing back into the hold. "Sparkles is on his way with one of the engineers."

"The engineer knows how to defuse it?"

"No one does, but he said he's willing to look at it."

Caleb's hopes sank. There was nothing he could do about it, other than question his boldness in attacking the ship. Maybe they had pressed their luck, sticking too long to haulers. Even so, there were hundreds of Crux's cargo ships moving across the Spiral at any given time. How had he known to set his trap on this one?

Unless he's put a bomb on all of them.

He couldn't discount Ishek's idea. *It would be a very Relyeh thing to do.*

Caleb removed the last screw on the access panel and cautiously lifted it out of the way, peering in at the innards. Seeing nothing out of the ordinary, he tossed the panel on the deck.

"Damn," Granger commented behind him. "Nerves of steel, Cap."

Shaking off a case of hidden nerves, Caleb threw a deliberate look at Granger before releasing the pent up breath.

The interior of the device consisted primarily of wires connecting a pair of small circuit boards to a power supply. Their origins somewhere inside the canister, the wires were all the same color, making it impossible for Caleb to guess which wire controlled the countdown and detonation. He couldn't do anything to disarm the device, so he stepped back to wait with the others for Sparkles and his charge.

A minute passed before Sparkles jogged into the compartment carrying the head engineer on his back. Out of breath, Sparkles stumbled when he reached Caleb, sending the engineer rolling off him and onto the floor.

On his side, an elbow braced behind him, the engineer scowled up at Sparkles. "Clumsy idiot." Sparkles glared back, drawing his rifle back with the obvious intent of smashing the butt into the man's face.

"That's enough, Sparky." Caleb said. "Stand down." The Edger obeyed.

The engineer turned his angry attention to Caleb. "You should tell your inarticulate meathead to be more careful with the only person on this ship who might save your lives."

"What's your name?" Caleb asked, ignoring the man's displeasure."

"Johan Ling," the man spouted. "Engineer First Class. His Majesty's Royal Navy."

"You're military?" Caleb looked the balding man over more closely this time. His sagging slacks and untucked button-down shirt didn't scream enlisted.

"My military service means nothing anymore," he replied. "When the Legion attacked the Stardock near Atlas, they gave me a choice. Pledge fealty to Lord Crux or die. So I bent my knee and gave my oath, and here I am. But Crux doesn't give a damn about his human employees, only Legionnaires. We all get relegated to cargo hauling duty while they get to live it up on the Specters."

I doubt any of the khoron are truly living it up, as he calls it. They're only a grade above slaves themselves.

"And now he's installed explosives on this hauler," Caleb said. "My gut and my Advocate tell me he's probably put bombs on all of his haulers. Crux's master thinks all humans are expendable."

"That's right, you said he has an evil overlord. Damn. I miss the good old days, when the Lo'ane dynasty reigned. Hard to believe that was less than a year ago."

"Enough talking. I figure we don't have much time left before this bomb blows. We have five minutes to disarm it." He motioned to the open panel on the canister. "Do you know which wire to cut?"

"I need to look at the thing first."

Caleb stepped back as Sparkles helped Johan up. Moving to the open panel, the engineer reached into his pocket and retrieved a small light he stuck to his forehead. He went down on his knee, and with a precision screwdriver he took from another pocket, he pulled at the wires, peering down into the gap behind them to see where they were attached.

"It's a bomb, isn't it?" Granger asked.

"I didn't think that was in question," Johan replied. "There's a nuclear explosive device resting at the bottom of this can. Once it goes off, we'll be glad we're at ground zero because the rest of the folks on this ship may have a few seconds more to live."

"You need to disarm it, man," Sparkles said, obviously afraid.

He threw Sparkles another irritated look. "You should have thought about that before you almost smashed me in the face with your rifle. I'm tempted to let it blow just to kill *you*."

"What?"

"Yeah. Anyway, staring at these wires is a waste of time." He stood up and turned to Caleb. "The interface is remote. It was likely armed when the ship went into hyperspace, while simultaneously activating a jamming signal to make sure it couldn't be disarmed. And also to mess with your comms."

"I'll ask one more time. Can you disarm it?" Caleb asked.

"Give me twenty minutes, and I can probably figure it out."

"We have about ten or less." Caleb had adjusted the time left since they'd gone into hyperspace.

"That is a pickle." Johan rubbed at his chin. "We need to locate the jammer. Once we do, I can see about networking with the thing on my pad." He pulled the device from his other pants pocket. It looked like a bomb had already hit it, but somehow it remained functional.

"What does the jammer look like?"

"I don't know. It's probably about the size of a dime. It would need to be relatively close by and putting out a high frequency broadcast to give it the best range."

Caleb looked up toward the top of the hold, nearly

thirty meters overhead. The light pattern on the ceiling made it hard to make out anything in the shadows it created, but the jamming device had to be up there.

Somewhere.

He looked at Sparkles. "How many gel rounds do you have left?"

"Nine, Cap," Sparkles replied.

"The rest of you?"

"Eight for me," Granger said.

"I've got five," Lilly added.

"Add my six," Ilya said. "That makes twenty-eight, plus whatever you have left, Cap."

"I've got five," he said, continuing to scan the top of the hold as he did his calculations. "If we spread our fire well overhead, we could cover at least eighty percent of it with enough heat to melt any electronics hidden up there. Sparky, take the far side. Judge your spread as best you can, our lives depend on it."

"Wait a second," Johan said. "You can't blow up the top of the cargo hold. Falling shrapnel could hit us. Or—"

"I'm open to other ideas," Caleb replied. "But make it quick."

"Blobs of burning gel could hit us. Or—"

"Or a nuke could vaporize us," Lilly interrupted.

"I wasn't asking for anyone's opinion," Caleb said, eyeing her.

"Aye, Captain," she said, running across the empty hold to the far side. Granger smiled as he moved to the port side of the hold and aimed his rifle upward. Caleb and Ilya spread out where they were, all of them triggering their gel launchers. Small shockwaves traveled through the enclosed space as they spread blobs of gel across much of the space, the blobs clinging to the patterned overhead before detonating. Bits of hot metal flew everywhere. Caleb grabbed Johan and pulled him close, smothering the man so none of the debris would hit him.

"This is crazy," Johan cried as they continued the assault, hitting the top of the hold five more times in rapid succession. Flaming pieces of material fell around Caleb. Some of it landed on the canister, Strom quickly brushing it off.

"Penn, do you copy?" Caleb asked. No reply. "Keep shooting!" he ordered. Five more rounds hit the top of the hold. The heat from all the gel extended to the deck, making Caleb sweat beneath his helmet. "Penn, do you copy?"

"Captain?" she answered. "I copy. Loud and clear."

"Hold your fire!" Caleb shouted. Granger glanced over at him, clearly disappointed he hadn't been able to light off all his rounds. "Johan, get to it!"

Johan tapped furiously on his pad, entering commands at breakneck speed. Lines of code rolled down the semi-transparent screen, indecipherable to Caleb but clearly meaningful to him. "I found it," he said. "Connecting." He continued tapping on his pad before freezing suddenly, his entire body shaking.

That is more fear than I have dined on in quite some time.

"Johan?" Caleb asked tentatively.

"We have forty-seven seconds," the engineer replied.

"Can you do it?"

Johan tapped the screen, paused a moment to wipe the sweat from his brow, and tapped some more. Caleb counted down from forty-six. He felt strangely calm, a benefit of Ishek sucking up all the pheromones from all the people present, especially the engineer.The intoxicating effect left him feeling immortal, not vulnerable, and he had to fight to keep the unnatural elation in check.

"Got it!" Johan cried in victory as Caleb reached thirteen

seconds. "Disarmed! Woooo!" The engineer threw up his hands, dancing comically for a moment.

"Are you sure?" Strom asked. "It's still warm."

"Uh. Yeah," Johan answered unconvincingly, looking at his pad again. After a moment he nodded his head more vigorously. "I'm sure."

Caleb continued counting down. "Three. Two. One." Johan clenched his eyes closed. The others tensed as well. "Boom. We're all dead."

Except they weren't. The bomb remained undetonated on the cargo hold floor while the last of the ash and debris from the overhead fires drifted down around them. Caleb put his hand on Johan's shoulder. "Nice work."

Johan's breathing remained heavy, but he looked back at Caleb. "Thanks. You know, this might seem like a strange question considering the circumstances, but are you hiring?"

CHAPTER 3

Less than a minute after the hyperspace field dissipated, Gorgon lumbered into view off the starboard bow of the cargo hauler Tonneau. The randomness of the compression put the pirate ship nearly twenty minutes away, though Orin quickly changed the hauler's vector to trim the distance between them in half.

Caleb had spoken to many of Tonneau's remaining engineers and bridge crew by the time the two vessels had matched velocity and aligned for both linking and retrieval of the Splinters. Many of them were unhappy with the way the Legion had used them as both bait and sacrifice, leaving them eager to join Gorgon's once depleted crew. Foremost of all was Johan Ling.

With no true love of Crux's Empire, and a longing for the return of the Lo'ane Empire, Caleb felt certain he would be a positive asset. The engineer had already shown a knack for operating under pressure, and for quick, logical thinking. Maybe he could even help Naya finally crack Graystone's bank accounts.

Damian waited at the other side of the primary interlink as the airlock doors between the ships opened. He nodded respectfully to Caleb before his eyes shifted to Granger and Sparkles, who had carried the disarmed explosive up from the hold.

"Captain," he said, motioning to the bomb. "Are we keeping that?"

"It's a nuclear explosive," Caleb replied. "I imagine it has to be worth something."

"We can probably get a million in coin for it," Damian confirmed. "If we can find a buyer."

"Not all the dark markets are under Crux's control yet. If we can't find a buyer, we'll deliver it to the Dromedary," Caleb said, referring to the hauler they'd commandeered for storage and had parked in the middle of nowhere for later pickup.

"The Dromedary is nearly at full capacity," Damian reminded him. "We'll need to drop some of our booty off with the rebels sooner or later."

"We can always name this hauler Dromedary Two and leave it parked with Dromedary One. In any case, we have to find the rebels first," Caleb said. "Haas believed I could locate them when the time came, but I think he overestimated my ability."

"Elena will get a message through. I'm confident of that."

"She's been trying for weeks and has gotten no response."

"That doesn't mean she won't eventually succeed. We just have to be patient."

Caleb nodded. "Let's get this thing aboard and secured. We have a lot of work to do before we're ready to leave." He gestured to Granger and Sparkles, who carried the explosive past them and onto Gorgon. "Put it in the hold. I want Tae to look at it."

"Aye, Captain," Granger replied.

"I can't believe Crux would booby-trap hundreds of

ships just to destroy *us*," Damian said.

"I can. It's easier and cheaper than having Specters escort every hauler crossing the Spiral."

"But the number of lives he'd put at risk..."

"You know he doesn't care about that. And neither does Iagorth."

"The mercs you killed?" Damian asked.

"Clean. No khorons, regular or otherwise," Caleb replied. "At least as far as Ish could discern, and he's the expert. We didn't waste any time jettisoning them though, just in case."

Caleb turned when he heard footsteps coming from the adjacent passageway. A moment later, Penn and Orin strode into view, two dozen men and women trailing behind them. Johan stood at the head of the line, and he offered a slightly awkward wave.

"Haverblaad should be here any moment to test their blood," Damian said.

Caleb nodded. The only surefire way to detect Iagorth's infection was to draw blood from every member of the hauler's crew. He had learned the trick from Ishek, who pointed out that the oddly structured cells of the moieties clustered around nerve endings, especially the brain stem. The clusters easily stood out when examined beneath a microscope. When the host organism died, the moieties would coagulate and almost literally run for the nearest exit. It was one of many things Ishek knew about the powerful Ancient, most of which made Caleb's blood run cold.

"Any moment is here," Haverblaad said, reaching the passageway. A hover cart floated ahead of her, a small black box resting on it, along with enough replacement needles to stick all the potential new crew members. She guided it to the interlock, glaring at the hauler's crew on the other side. "What a motley-looking bunch."

"This is what Crux's non-Legionnaire military looks like," Caleb replied.

"You're all an embarrassment. You should at least take personal pride in your presentation," she huffed at them.

"Our apologies, ma'am," Johan said. "But if you were on this side of the airlock, you would understand. Our own Emperor was ready to blast us into space dust."

"He's no Emperor," Haverblaad spat. "He's a puppet. Nothing more."

"Aye," Johan agreed. "That's what Captain Card says, and all of us here agree. We want to help bring him down."

"Then come on forward for a poke," she said. "We need to make sure you aren't compromised."

"And if we are?" a crew member near the back asked.

"I've got a bullet with your name on it," Penn replied.

Caleb put his hand on Damian's shoulder. "I'll leave you to it. I need to pay Junior a visit."

"Do you think he had anything to do with this?" Damian asked.

"I don't think so, but I want to be sure."

Caleb made his way past Haverblaad and across to Gorgon. Making his way through the corridors, every member of his crew he passed offered him nods of respect, which he returned in kind. Even the pirates who had stayed on with him for the coin appreciated his no-nonsense approach to leadership and the strict but fair rules he had put in place. It also didn't hurt that they had sold enough of their stolen surplus to keep all of them well paid for some time to come. While some of the pirate culture remained, including the endless jockeying for position within the ranks and the racks, Gorgon functioned now more like the Marine units he had commanded in the past. Giving them the Vulture moniker he often bestowed on the units under his command had further cemented their cohesiveness, camaraderie, and morale.

And again, the coin doesn't hurt.

Not one bit, Caleb agreed.

Despite the day's setback, his Robin Hood mission remained mostly on track. They had an entire cargo hauler laden with an assortment of military equipment, from small arms to millions of rounds of ammunition, tons of MREs and other imperishable sundries — ammunition and replacement parts for various types of ship-mounted cannons, shield conduits, transformers, and other supplies a small, rebel army might need to fight.

While Crux and the Royal Armed Forces demonized the Pirate Captain Card, word of their exploits spread across the Spiral in back channels and underground networks, reaching those still loyal to the true Empire. A nice start, but only a start, and if nothing else, the nuke on Tonneau had served as a wake-up call to Caleb that they needed to move into a new phase of guerilla warfare. As Johan had alluded, the cargo was small potatoes compared to bigger, better targets. Even the capture and ultimate destruction of the hidden stardock dealt a more painful blow to Crux than taking Tonneau.

It was time to push the limits, and to focus more on his other mission objectives. Not only did they need to locate the Guardian's new base, they still needed to track down the Empress' daughter and also do something about the khoron replication facility, which he knew was being run by Relyeh loyal to Iagorth. Or perhaps Iagorth himself. As Ishek put it, the Ancient was both nowhere and everywhere, able to split his consciousness into infinite pieces, his influence limited only by the strength of his reach. Caleb didn't know yet if Iagorth had entered the Spiral with Pathfinder or if the new settlers had found him here. He was both worried and certain the Ancient had a secure foothold.

For now, anyway.

When Caleb reached the brig, Jack was sitting on his bunk, staring at the wall. He glanced over at Caleb as he approached, his expression flat.

"What do you want?" he asked.

"To talk," Caleb replied. "How are you doing?"

Jack nodded. "As good as I can be, given the circumstances. Did the mission go well?"

"No."

"Is that why you're here?"

"Yes."

"Gareshk is still subservient to me. Just like he's been since you almost killed me three months ago." Jack spit out the last sentence in an accusatory tone.

Caleb didn't blame the kid for his anger. Three months was a long time to remain locked up in the brig, especially when the combination of Gareshk's knowledge of Crux's logistics and the data Naya recovered from the stardock had led them to this point. While this robbery had gone sideways, it didn't outweigh the success of the other missions.

"I'm sorry," Caleb said. "You know we can't let you loose until we have no doubts that we can trust you to remain in control of Gareshk."

Jack looked down at his hands before turning his eyes back on Caleb. "It's okay. I understand why I'm still in here, but that doesn't mean I like it. And if things are going wrong..."

He trailed off, leaving Caleb to fill in the blanks for himself. He knew Junior wanted to be free again, but he was also afraid of what would happen once they let him out. By every indication, Jack had Gareshk under control. But the Advocate had already proven how wily he could be. It was a tricky situation all the way around.

Still, Jack had a point. Three months was a long time, and every bit of intel he'd shared had turned out to be accurate. Without Jack's ability to force Gareshk to give up what he knew, they might still be looking for their next target.

"Tonneau didn't have any cargo on board," he said. "Only a bomb. I would be dead if not for one of the hauler's engineers. What do you think about that?"

Jack shrugged. "I had nothing to do with it. Neither did Gareshk."

"We have two theories. Either Crux planted a bomb on every hauler crossing the Spiral, or someone on Gorgon tipped him off as to our target."

"It wasn't me or Gareshk. I would know if he used the Collective to contact any other Relyeh."

"I want so much to believe you."

"Then believe me, Captain. Even though I'm still in this cell, you freed my mind from the monster. That's more important than physical freedom. Why would I want anything bad to happen to you? And why would I want Crux or the Relyeh to succeed? They killed my father, and then taunted me with it. I'm on your side. I just don't know how to convince you of that from in here."

Caleb's thoughts quickly turned to the sabotage of the ship's sensors during their escape from Aroon. While nothing similar had occurred since, suggesting that crew member had departed the ship, he suddenly questioned the accuracy of that assumption. Blood tests had confirmed none of the crew were under Iagorth's control through moieties. That didn't mean none of them remained loyal to Crux. At a minimum, he needed to reduce the number of potential leaks.

Are you sure this is a good idea?

No, but I'm going to do it anyway, Caleb replied to Ishek while locking eyes with Jack. "You just convinced me you're on my side," he decided. He couldn't keep Jack locked up forever.

Junior smiled. "Thank you, Captain."

"But you aren't completely free yet. For now, you'll have a guard with you at all times, and a tracker integrated with your comms patch. "

"That sounds reasonable. I'll take whatever you're willing to give, Captain."

Caleb moved to the cell controls, tapping on the interface and opening the door to Jack's prison. At first, Jack remained on the mattress as if afraid to leave the small chamber. As if he wasn't sure he could trust himself. Then he smiled and hopped to his feet, stepping over the threshold and up to Caleb.

"Captain Card, I'm at your service."

"Please don't do anything to make me regret letting you out."

Jack smiled. "Aye, Captain. I won't."

Caleb motioned Jack to follow him while tapping on his comms patch. "Bones," he said, reaching out to the deckhand.

"Aye, Captain," Bones replied. "What do you need?"

"Meet me outside my quarters. I need you to find a berth for Jack on the officer's level."

"Err, Captain, sir, that's a problem. There ain't no berthing available on Six. She's all full up, stem to stern."

Caleb glanced at Jack. He had already suspected the quarters were fully occupied considering the addition of more crewmen. But he didn't want Junior too far out of sight. "Bring two other crewmen with you. I need you to rearrange some furniture."

"Aye, aye, Captain," Bones replied before Caleb disconnected the comms.

"Furniture?" Jack asked, confused by the side of the conversation he'd heard.

"Follow me. I'll show you around your new quarters, roomie."

CHAPTER 4

Caleb had already finished giving Jack the quick tour of his quarters by the time Bones arrived, a pair of lower-deckers in tow. Having taken it upon himself to learn the names of everyone on board, he greeted Malthus and Ian by name as he let the pirates inside.

"Captain," Bones said, eying Jack warily. They had never met in person, but everyone on board knew about Leighton's son and his situation. "What can we haul for ye?"

"We're going to move my desk into my bedroom." Caleb pointed at the small office area. "Then we'll take the bar out altogether. Neither Jack nor I can get drunk, even if we wanted to. We'll put a mattress where the bar is, and a storage locker where the desk is. Or vice versa. Whichever Jack prefers."

Bones' eyes shifted from Caleb back to Jack. "Aye, Captain," he replied hesitantly, turning to Jack. "I'm Bones."

"Jack. Good to meet you, sir."

Bones cackled. "Sir? I ain't never been no sir. I like that."

"Bones is our elder statesman," Caleb explained. "No one on the ship has been at it as long as him."

"I knew your father when he was just a boy," Bones

added. "Even then, I had a feeling he would be something special one day. I respected him quite a lot. I hope you'll live up to his memory."

Jack swallowed hard at the mention of his father. "I'm going to do my best." He looked at Caleb. "I have to be honest, Captain. Before all this happened, I wasn't much of a spacer. I spent all my time drinking and playing games in Recreation, and using my father's legacy to lure women into my bed. I took a lot of things for granted."

"You aren't the first, and won't be the last," Caleb replied. He had only known Leighton briefly, but he was sure the self-ascribed pirate king had a darker side as well. After all, he made a living by theft and assault. It wasn't exactly noble. "The important thing is to define yourself in the present, and not to dwell on the past."

"Aye, Captain," Jack answered.

"Aye, so true," Bones added. "You're wise for your years, Captain."

"You'd be surprised how old I really am, Bones. I've spent a lot of years in stasis and Ishek keeps me looking young. Something Gareshk will do for you, Jack." he said, winking at him.

"Really?"

"Really," he confirmed. "Malthus, Ian…" He glanced at each of them. Both men were short but muscular with the same dark hair and eyes. It was easy to tell they were related. Brothers or cousins, he wasn't sure which. "Go fetch a mattress from storage. If Hank gives you any trouble, have him contact me."

"Aye, Captain," both men replied in unison. They offered him a quick nod and left the quarters.

"Jack, help me move the bar," Caleb said, walking over to the cabinet. He had cleared the bottles and glasses from its top weeks ago, and would have removed the entire thing sooner if he had needed the floor space.

"I can get it," Jack replied, eagerly putting his arms on either side. He smiled as he strained, lifting the entire thing on his own. "Should I drop it outside?"

He's boosted.

Clearly, Caleb replied to Ishek while staring at Jack. "Did you ask Gareshk to boost you?"

"I didn't have to. He knew I needed more strength, so he pumped me up. I guess Ishek does that for you?"

Caleb nodded. "You need to be careful though. Using it too often, too quickly, and you risk destroying your body and you'll both die."

Ishek laughed in the back of his mind, amused by the warning Caleb rarely heeded himself. *Do as you say, not as you do.*

"He says he can heal any damage it does. He's not surprised Ishek can't, since he's a lesser Advocate."

Lesser advocate! What? There is no such thing.

Gareshk is mutated and Sanctified, Caleb reminded him. *He's bound to be stronger than you.*

Whatever advantage he might have in strength, I can certainly make up for in experience.

Caleb grinned. "The last thing we need is for our khoron to get into a pissing match."

Jack grinned back. "Agreed, Captain."

"And yes, you can drop it outside. Bones, help me with the desk."

"Aye, Captain," Bones replied.

Jack easily carried the entire cabinet, loaded with booze and weighing close to a hundred kilos out of the quarters and into the corridor.

"What are you doing here?" Caleb heard Damian say, his voice gruff.

"I'm moving into Captain Card's quarters," Jack replied. "He released me from the brig."

"I can see that. I hope you won't give him cause to regret the decision."

"No, sir. I'm not Gareshk anymore. I'm just Jack."

"That remains to be seen," Damian answered. He and Jack entered Caleb's quarters together. "Captain," he said, nodding respectfully. "Doctor Haverblaad is finished testing the recruits from Tonneau. They're all clean."

"That's great news," Caleb replied. He could tell Damian wanted to say something about Jack's presence out of the brig. He also knew the other man wouldn't raise any concerns until they were alone. "Bones, go down to storage and pick up some bedding, and see if you can get some more clothes from surplus that'll fit Jack." While imprisoned, Junior had been forced to wear whatever Penn or one of the Edgers had brought him every morning. It seemed fitting to give him a choice now.

"Aye, aye, Captain," Bones said. "What about the desk?"

"Sarge can help me move it."

"Aye." He nodded to both Caleb and Damian before exiting the room.

Malthus and Ian had returned by the time Caleb finished disconnecting the terminal on the desk, preparing it to be moved. "You can put the mattress there," he said, pointing where the bar had been. "Then go get a storage locker."

"Aye, Captain," Malthus said, pushing the mattress up to the bulkhead.

"Jack, make yourself comfortable. Damian, take the other end of the desk."

Damian picked up his end. The desk wasn't that big or heavy, but it was easier to maneuver with two people. They carried it into the bedroom, squeezing it into a corner.

"Do we have any spare terminals for Jack?" Caleb asked. "And he'll need a comm patch."

"I can check with Hank on a terminal, and I'll send

someone up with a comm patch. But why move Jack in here with you? I take it, you don't want to leave your desk out here in the common area with him living here too?"

"Exactly. I don't need Jack peeking over my shoulder when I'm checking finances, crew records, and all of those things that are better left private. And that goes double for Gareshk."

"You must trust Jack a little more, to let him out of the brig. I know you aren't asking me, Cal, but I think it's a bad idea."

"Ishek agrees with you. What's the alternative? Keep him locked up forever?"

"Or at least until Crux is dethroned."

"That could take years."

Damian shrugged. "It's not his fault, just bad luck. But..." he trailed off.

"Jack says he has Gareshk under control. I know how it works, so I mostly believe him. But I'm not exposing sensitive data to his eyes that his Advocate could pass on to Crux. I also don't intend to let him wander the ship without an escort."

"A wise idea."

"At the same time, I want to continue building his trust. Jack can be valuable to us. He has the same ability to overpower khoron I do, and he's probably better at it. There's no denying Gareshk is a more powerful Relyeh than Ish."

I hate you for saying that.

Sorry, Ish. But facts are facts.

"Are you sure Gareshk can't regain control?"

"Not at all. He's more powerful, which means he might reverse the bond again at some point. That's my biggest concern, but when it comes down to it, the benefits outweigh the drawbacks. We need to be careful how we position him as an asset. We can't give him too much information, at least not too far ahead of time."

"Agreed. I'll make sure an Edger is always with him."

"I had a thought while I was talking to Jack. My initial impression was that Crux might have booby-trapped all the haulers in the Spiral hoping to kill us. But what if someone on board tipped him off?"

"We thought we got rid of the saboteur."

"What if we didn't?"

Damian considered the scenario. "It's definitely possible. I can talk to Naya about comms records. If someone sent a suspicious transmission, we can find it."

"Unless Naya is the spy."

"Naya?" Damian shook his head. "I don't think so."

"Why not? She has the skill set to sabotage the sensors. She can use the comms with no one ever knowing. And she's been stalled on Graystone's accounts for weeks. What if she cracked it a long time ago, and she's just sitting on it to reap the rewards from multiple angles?"

"Is this an official accusation?"

"Of course not. Pure conjecture. I'm just saying, the pieces fit."

"Tae can do the same things. Just because he's military doesn't make him honest."

"You're right. It looks like I already have a job for Johan."

"The recruit?"

"He's the only one with the skills we need that we know can't be a suspect. Set him up to audit our systems. I want him to look at everything, top to bottom. Don't mention sabotage or mutinous comms to him. It'll only prime him to find something. Let's see what he gets on his own."

Damian nodded. "Aye, Captain."

Caleb smiled. The conversation had gone better than expected. He knew Damian was loyal and trusted him completely. They had become close friends in the past few months, but he also understood where some of his friend's hesitation came from. If Jack turned out to be a threat,

Caleb would be responsible for it, and they all could pay for his poor judgment with their lives.

Bones had returned pushing a hover cart laden with bedding and clothing by the time Damian and Caleb returned to the front of the suite. Jack looked happier than Caleb had seen him as he made up his mattress. It may not be a bed per se, but it had to beat the six-inch pad he'd been sleeping on in the brig.

"You have your orders," Caleb said to Damian. "We'll have a briefing to discuss next steps in one hour. Whoever you send to keep tabs on Jack, they can stand guard outside the door."

"Aye, Captain," Damian replied.

"Dismissed."

Damian nodded and left the quarters. Malthus and Ian returned a few minutes later, straining to carry a large storage locker. Jack jumped to help them. Still boosted by Gareshk, he easily assumed most of the weight, helping them put the locker in position.

"Thank you again, Captain," he said, looking at Caleb. "I'll make you proud. I give you my word."

He's a bit naïve, isn't he?

You're just sore about what Gareshk said. He might be a little green, but I think he's a good kid. He has a lot of potential.

I agree that he has potential. But will he end up helping us? Or destroying us?

CHAPTER 5

As usual, Caleb arrived at the briefing room last. He had showered, changed, and grabbed a bite of Atrice's favorite gripplin stew and still had a portion of a baguette in his mouth. All eyes turned his way, but his senior crew members had already learned to remain as they were when he arrived.

"Captain," Elena said. "I was just telling the others about the message I received from a contact of mine. A former comrade-in-arms named Sang. We served on board the Yoko together. He's in hiding, but he keeps his eyes and ears open, and he's loyal to the Empress."

"What did he tell you?" Caleb asked, voice slightly muffled as he finished chewing the baguette.

"I pinged him almost two months ago, asking for a meet. Just like I did with a dozen other former contacts. He was the first to respond, and he used a coded message to tell me where to find him."

"Do you think he knows where the Guardians are hiding?"

"Honestly? No. But he might know someone who does.

It would be easier if we could communicate remotely, but..." She shrugged, trailing off.

"Unfortunately, we don't know who we can trust on this ship right now," Caleb finished for her, eyes shifting momentarily to Johan. "I'm working on that. What can you tell me, without being too specific?"

"Sang is currently working as a dockmaster at a small space station near one of the outer worlds in the Spiral. The planet itself isn't habitable because it's too close to its star, which means there's no real reason for anyone else to go out that far. Sang says the outpost is small and mostly self-sufficient, so they've avoided Crux's attention, but I'm sure his hand will reach them eventually."

"His hand will reach everywhere in the Spiral eventually if we do not chop it off first," Orin said. "It is true."

"Agreed. Damian, what do you think?" Caleb asked.

"I agree with Elena about Sang not knowing where the Guardians are hiding," Damian said. "Which makes me wonder if it's worth the risk to make contact, for him and for us. But it could be worth it to meet him face to face on the off chance that we could get valuable information from him. It's the first lead we've had in months."

Caleb sighed heavily. "I just don't want to be responsible for bringing the Legion down on the outpost and a bunch of innocents. What happened in Aroon's orbit was bad enough. But I'm also tired of sitting here waiting for another opportunity like this one to present itself. We pressed our luck by hitting too many cargo haulers in a row, and we were nearly burned to a crisp because of it. One reason I called this meeting was to discuss our next steps. We need to move away from these smaller hits and start pushing our full agenda forward."

Johan raised his hand. "Captain, if I may?"

"Go ahead."

"What is our full agenda? I mean, I know you've been attacking cargo ships and making a name for yourself to the people still loyal to the Empress. And clearly, you've become enough of a thorn in Crux's side that he unquestionably wanted you dead. But if the robbery isn't the point, then what is?"

"I'm glad you asked," Caleb replied. "First, by attacking Crux and surviving, we're proving to the loyalists in the Spiral that the Legion isn't invincible. We can stand against them, and we can succeed. We're also gathering supplies for the resistance. Second, we aim to reconnect with General Haas and the rebellion's leadership as soon as we can find them. Third, I have reason to believe Empress Lo'ane has a daughter. We're trying to find her. I think you might help immensely with that."

"I hope so, sir. I'll certainly try."

"Fourth, I already told you Crux is dancing to the tune of a master. That master is bad news. He mutated Crux into a stronger, more twisted version of himself, and he's supplying the Legion with khoron to continue growing their ranks. We need to find that reproduction facility and shut it down."

"And by shut it down, you mean—"

"Blow it to smithereens," Caleb answered. "Yeah."

"It seems to me like we have a lot on our plate. Does the order matter?"

"As long as Crux and Iagorth are out of the Spiral by the end, nothing else matters."

"You left one other objective out, Captain," Damian said. "You want to find a way back to your part of the universe, and deliver your friend Ham back to his family."

"Yes, that too. Speaking of which, have you made any progress on the algorithm, Tae?" Caleb turned his attention to the engineer.

"Wait," Johan said. "What do you mean your part of the universe?"

"Caleb is from billions of light years away, and about two hundred years timeline-wise," Tae answered. "From Earth. The planet the founders really came from."

Johan eyed Caleb as though he were insane. "How is that even possible?"

"Math," Tae answered. "I'm sure Cap will order me to share my work with you before the meeting is over, so I'll volunteer it now. I'll explain everything as soon as we're done here." He glanced at Caleb. "It's complicated."

"Yes or no is a binary choice," Caleb said. "It isn't complicated."

"I've made some progress and deciphered some of the methodology, but I'm not about to crack it."

"But you have an idea how to do it?" Elena asked.

"Theoretically," Tae replied. "The problem is, there are too many unknowns for me to say definitively if I know what I'm talking about."

The comment drew laughs from the others in the room.

"I'll take that as a no for now," Caleb decided. "And yes, I'd like you to share your work with Johan."

"Aye aye, Cap."

"Bringing this conversation back around," Penn said. "A meeting with Elena's contact sounds like the most efficient way forward. And I don't think it's as risky as it may seem."

"Why not?" Damian asked.

"Because as far as the universe is concerned, Tonneau's nuke went off and killed Captain Card and his boarding crew an hour and a half ago. Crux has no reason to believe anything to the contrary, as long as we lie low for a while."

Orin's laugh came out as a halting growl. "If that is the case, then my contract to kill Captain Card is void. I am only sorry that I cannot keep my reputation within the Dark Exchange by ripping your intestines out, Captain."

"Yeah, that's a real shame," Caleb deadpanned back. "If Crux believes we're dead, that can buy us some time. But Gorgon is hardly inconspicuous. We need a different ship if we want to make it all the way to Sang without drawing attention."

"I have just such a ship," Orin replied. "She is not the newest or fastest. But she will get you there."

"Kitana only seats two," Caleb said. "And no offense, Orin, but being spotted with a Jiba-ki is the opposite of inconspicuous."

"I am not offended. I am beautiful. But it is true. I regret I cannot accompany you. But I will teach you to fly Kitana. It is easy, and you are a smart human."

"Kitana's your ship. You don't need to do that."

"I desire to do it. Despite my intention to kill you prior to our deaths in a cargo hauler explosion, I consider you a friend." He laughed again, freely enough that the others in the room couldn't help joining in.

"Johan, I know I'm giving you a lot of work right off the bat," Caleb said, turning his attention to the engineer. "But I want you to work with Elena to enter the coordinates of the space station into the hyperdrive. I want you to do it so that no one else can see them or know what they are, including me. That way, if trouble finds us there, we can narrow the source down to two suspects."

"Aye, Captain," Johan agreed. Caleb glanced at Elena to see her reaction. She nodded approvingly, rather than showing any hint of upset that any hypothetically treacherous plan she might have would be foiled.

"I also want you to lock down external comms to Sasha's station on the bridge, and keep it monitored full time by your team from Tonneau. That includes hypernet access or any other forms of transmission off the ship. If anyone sends anything, I expect you to know about it immediately."

"Captain, if I may," Damian said before Johan could answer. "Many of the crew make calls home when we're out of hyperspace. Are you suggesting we cut them off?"

"No. They can come to the bridge to contact their families, one at a time." It was clear from Damian's expression that the idea wouldn't be popular with the crew. At all. "I understand your concern. I'm not trying to separate the crew from their families or infringe upon their privacy. I really don't want to do this, but we came within a hair's breadth of dying today because someone might have tipped the Legion off to our movements, whether on purpose or by a slip of the tongue. I can't chance that happening again."

"I know, Captain. But we have no proof anyone gave away our plans. Your initial assessment was that Crux might have rigged all the cargo ships. I worry we may be overcompensating, given our lack of concrete evidence."

If it had been anyone other than Damian raising the objection, Caleb might have found it suspicious. He trusted his second more than anyone else on the ship. "We need to catch up to Haas, the Guardians, and my friend Abraham. That makes Sang a high value lead. One we can't afford to have compromised by a potential mole or even by someone calling home and saying something they shouldn't. There's an old saying from Earth...*loose lips sink ships*. My decision stands. I'll reconsider once we've completed our meet with Sang. I don't expect us to be out of the hyperspace field for long. Let's move on. Have we made any progress identifying the Empress' daughter?"

"None, Captain," Elena replied. "With billions of people in the Spiral, and not a single lead, anything we came up with would be a guess or a rumor."

"Have you heard any rumors?"

"No, sir. Even if she knows she's Lo'ane's child, she's

not saying anything. And why would she, especially now? It would be equivalent to inviting your assassin to dinner."

"True," Caleb agreed. "How else might we pick up a lead? Any ideas?"

The group remained silent for nearly a full minute in contemplation before Tae spoke up. "This is going to sound crazy, but I figure since we're brainstorming I should throw it out there."

"Go ahead," Caleb said.

"Someone had to know Lo'ane was pregnant, right? It's not something you can totally hide. So if we find that someone, we can find the child. And before you ask how we find that someone, the answer is that we work to pinpoint the time when she disappeared from public view long enough to have been pregnant and given birth. Once we've narrowed the timeline down, then we just need to know all the places she traveled during that time, and if there was one place in particular she returned to or spent more time at, especially at the tail-end of her pregnancy."

"Where are we going to get those records?" Penn asked.

"The Royal Archives should have it," Tae answered. "They keep track of everything the Royal Family does. They can probably tell us what toilet in the Palace Cruxie-pie crapped in last night."

"That's your idea?" Johan said, laughing. "You're crazy, man."

"I didn't hear you coming up with anything," Tae shot back.

"What's crazy about it?" Caleb asked. "It sounds like we need to access a datastore. I assume it's encrypted, but we have some brilliant engineers on board."

"Captain, if you hadn't already told me you aren't from around here, I would know that now," Johan said. "The Royal Archives are on Atlas. In the military facility they call the Imperium. We're not getting in there, under any circumstances. And if you somehow got in? You aren't getting back out."

"I said, we're brainstorming," Tae said. "One crazy idea is better than no ideas."

"Not that crazy idea," Johan countered.

"Okay, that's enough," Caleb said when Tae's mouth opened to rebut the other engineer. "I appreciate every idea and angle. Keep thinking about it. I'll spend some time learning more about this Imperium and the Royal Archives. If nothing else, you reminded me I need to work harder to better understand the history of the Spiral. Does anyone have anything else?"

"Captain, does this mean we're done attacking Legion assets?" Penn asked.

"At least until Crux knows we aren't dead," Caleb answered. "We have an opportunity to move a little more freely. We need to take it."

"Aye, Captain."

"If there are no other questions, you're all dismissed."

The others nodded to him, filing out of the briefing room. Caleb remained behind so he could use the holotable to look up the Imperium on the hypernet.

"You were awfully quiet," he said to Ishek.

Sometimes, it is better to listen and observe.

"What do you think?"

If you had made any horrible decisions, I would have tried to stop you. Of course, you wouldn't have listened.

"I might have."

No, you would not. But you didn't make any horrible decisions. You're learning from experience, with my help.

Caleb ran a hypernet search for the Imperium. The holotable displayed text about the location, while a holographic projection of the place appeared above the surface. Constructed into a mountainside ringed with fixed gun and missile batteries, with walls of thick metal and only a single access road leading up from lower elevations, it was immediately obvious it would be a tough nut to crack.

"What do you think?" Caleb asked.

Let us hope someone comes up with a better idea.

CHAPTER 6

After ten days in hyperspace, Caleb sat at the command station on Gorgon's bridge, staring out at the compressed space at the leading edge of the distortion field. They were about to arrive near Sang's space station, though he wouldn't know where in the universe that was in until they were actually there. None of the rest of the crew, except for Johan and Elena, would know that either. While Caleb had designed that outcome by preventing anyone else from knowing the coordinates ahead of time, that didn't make it feel any less strange.

At least the transit time had passed quickly while training with the boarding crews and spending time with Orin learning how to fly Kitana. He'd also spent a good deal of time working with Jack to improve their rapport and to draw out the fullness of Jack's bonded abilities with Gareshk. Now, as Caleb prepared for the compressed field to expand again, he suddenly felt as though he hadn't prepared at all for the mission at hand.

We are prepared. I should know. I was there. We have nearly arrived. I hunger.

The bomb scare only bought us ten days, Caleb replied.

At least now, Jack and Gareshk can work effectively together in the Collective. A decision which I still question. Gareshk was already formidable, and now you have made him stronger by developing his prowess with Jack.

You told me they're no match for us.

Right now, but only because Jack does not have your experience, determination, or courage. Those are all traits he can learn.

I hope he does. He'll be a formidable ally. Besides, he's a good kid. Teachable, unlike you.

I am teachable.

No, you really aren't.

Ten days had also given Johan plenty of time to get settled in and to set up the communication monitoring Caleb had requested. Placing the only accessible comms terminal on the bridge had had a chilling effect on the crew, both in their overall morale and in their willingness to communicate with friends and family without privacy. When they had come out of hyperspace to deliver Tonneau to the same stretch of vacant space where they'd left Dromedary, only a handful of the pirates had stepped onto the bridge to send messages. Caleb was certain that if he hadn't built such a good relationship with his crew over the prior months, they might have mutinied over his decision to monitor their outside communications.

The time had also allowed all of his senior crew to think more about how to locate Empress Lo'ane's daughter. At first, Caleb had thought the extended opportunity would result in at least a few approaches other than the impossible mission Tae had suggested. Instead, the passing days had only solidified the fact that there was only that one option. The outcome forced Caleb to consider a plan that didn't include rallying the loyalists around a blood member of their true Royal Family.

Ten days, and Tae still had nothing useful to report on Benning's algorithm. Even with Johan's help, the engineers hadn't been able to make any headway in breaking down the calculations beyond bits and pieces they couldn't translate into a whole. The best they could offer was confirmation that the wormhole wasn't stable in spacetime. Depending on how one traversed the spiraling vortex, one could wind up as much as a million years off course in either direction. That Caleb had lost only two hundred years was testament to Benning's intellect and calculation. Considering how Ham had loaded the algorithm into Spirit's computer and relied on the ship's AI to work out the kinks, they had been incredibly lucky to come out where they did on the other side.

Neither had Naya pierced Graystone's bank accounts. She only had a few tries left before being locked out completely, and her efforts at social engineering hadn't gone as smoothly as she'd hoped. Graystone had paid extra for multiple layers of authentication, trusting no one, and rightfully so, not to rob him blind.

"Captain," Rufus said from the helm. "We're coming out of hyperspace."

Caleb looked forward again. A small section of space directly ahead began to shimmer and change shape. Gorgon's sensors updated the view as the compressed light stretched out into normal spacetime. First came stars—thousands of them, all different colors and sizes—followed by a nearby nebula, its colorful and abundant gasses creating a heavenly glow under the light of the closest star.

"Jump complete," Rufus added. Gorgon remained in motion, vectoring toward the seemingly endless nebula.

Johan had made the shift to keep Gorgon close, but not too close to Sang's station. Elena would enter its final coordinates into Kitana's hyperdrive interface, and they would make their way the final twenty light years to the station in Orin's ship.

Caleb stood up. "Sarge, you have the bridge."

"Aye, Captain," Damian replied. "I have the bridge."

"Good luck with Sang, Cap," Rufus said.

Elena rose from her station as well. Nodding to Damian, she joined Caleb at the base of the command station, and they walked off the bridge together.

"I'll meet you in the hangar in fifteen minutes," Caleb said as they reached deck six and the doors opened.

"Aye, Captain."

Caleb stopped by his quarters to grab his gear—a long red leather-like coat with anti-ballistic properties, Hiro's sword, and a blaster he strapped to his hip. Not wanting to repeat the mistake he'd made at Aroon, he had already checked with Elena to ensure they permitted weapons on the station. Afterward, he continued down to the main hangar where Orin and Elena waited for him at Kitana's side hatch. Despite the thousands of coin in repairs they had done on it, the small hyperspace-capable starship still looked like it had seen better days.

Orin smiled at Caleb as he approached. "You are sure you do not want me to come along?"

"You'd have to shave off all your hair," Caleb remarked.

"Then I would not be so beautiful."

"No, you wouldn't."

"I will pass. Perhaps another time. It is fortunate I no longer need to kill you, is it not?"

Caleb smiled. Orin had been joking about that change of plans ever since the meeting. In some ways, it seemed to Caleb as though the Jiba-ki was disappointed that he no longer had a reason to murder him.

"Very fortunate," Caleb replied. "I don't want to be killed yet."

"Then you will be cautious. It is true." Orin reached out and patted him on the shoulder.

"Definitely," he replied, returning the gesture.

"You will also be cautious with Kitana. She is a fine ship,

and she will treat you well if you do the same to her. But…"
He wagged his finger at Caleb. "…she will not suffer
mistreatment."

"I'll be as gentle as a kitten," Caleb replied.

Orin growled in laughter. "There you go again,
suggesting I resemble a feline." He threw his shoulders
back and haughtily posed, hand on hip.. "I am far more
beautiful."

"Just keep telling yourself that," Caleb teased, elbowing
him before he turned to Elena. He hadn't seen her out of a
uniform before. She cut a much more feminine figure in her
coat, slacks, and a blouse that hid her armored underlay.
"Are you ready to go?"

"Aye, Captain. Ready when you are."

"You said that Sang is a dockmaster. I assume he'll be
easy to find."

"There are only two dockmasters on the station, so that
should be the case."

Caleb turned back to Orin. "Thank you again, my
friend."

"You are most welcome, Captain." Orin nodded to him
and backed away from the ship as Caleb and Elena climbed
through the hatch.

While Kitana's exterior looked beaten and worn, the
ship's interior was anything but. Decorated in thick
carpeting and bright colors, it was barely large enough for
the two person flight deck, a head, and a sleeping area
ahead of the reactor and thrusters. The first time he had
boarded the ship with Orin, he had joked about finding a
litter box instead of a toilet. It would have been more
amusing if it hadn't gone completely over the Jiba-ki's head.

Entering the flight deck, Elena took the copilot seat
while Caleb settled in on the pilot's side. He had spent
enough time with Orin over the last ten days learning,
without too much trouble, how to fly Kitana. The controls

were similar enough to the Splinter's flight systems it was mostly a matter of getting used to the interface being displayed in Orin's native Jibariki hieroglyphs. Thankful the hyperdrive interface was available in English, he had at least memorized the most important glyphs.

Activating the small starship's reactor, it hummed softly behind them as he tapped his control pad to close the hatch. Igniting Kitana's thrusters, he lifted off; the ship rising to float on an anti-gravity cushion.

"Captain, you're clear for launch," Moss, the hangar boss, said. "Hangar doors are opening now."

"Copy that," Caleb replied.

Warning lights flashed for a short time before the large doors parted, needing only a handful of seconds to open far enough for Caleb to guide Kitana through. At that point, he activated the main engines, shooting away from Gorgon and out into space.

Tapping on a series of hieroglyphs, Caleb opened a comms channel to Gorgon. "Kitana is away. Keep your comms open and standby."

"Aye, Captain," Damian replied. "We'll be waiting to hear from you."

"Elena, prep the hyperdrive."

"Aye, Captain."

She brought up the interface, navigating through it before entering the coordinates. Even though Caleb could see the numbers she input, they still meant absolutely nothing to him. "Hyperdrive is loaded and ready," she said once the system finished its calculation.

"In that case, punch it."

CHAPTER 7

The hyperspace field around Kitana expanded less than thirty minutes later, releasing the small starship back into uncompressed space. The space station Sang worked at immediately came up on the craft's sensors, while the forward viewscreen zoomed in to give them an immediate look at the location.

"It's called Dragonfire Station," Elena said while Caleb stared at the structure. It resembled the axle on a horse-driven carriage, with a pair of wagon-wheel hubs at either end and a short central column in the center. Bigger than he expected, the entire station compared well in size to a single dome on Proxima, which held nearly forty-thousand people.

Nestled in a field of dust and debris, the station orbited a red giant star currently in the process of ejecting additional atmosphere. Matter and energy spread from the core of the star across space, reaching out as if to impact the station. Beyond the star, unknown gasses created endless whorls of red and orange.

"I see where it gets its name," Caleb said. "How many people live here?"

"About five thousand," she replied. "The station is one of the first built in the Spiral and originally orbited Atlas. A private buyer purchased it and moved a little over a century ago, brought here as an orphanage of sorts. Do you see that ship docked to the upper wheel?"

Caleb's eyes shifted to where she suggested, locating the medium-sized starship in question. A standard cargo ship, rectangular and uninteresting. "Yeah, I see it."

"All the cargo vessels going in or out of the station are owned by the station. They have agents around the spiral who find or purchase the children and bring them here. The ships also export Lanium, a rare metal used in hyperdrive production."

"Did you say purchase?" Caleb asked, barely hearing the last sentence.

"Aye, Captain. Pirates are an important part of the human trafficking chain."

"And you're okay with that?"

"Not at all. While some members of the Consortium deal in trafficking, Leighton never did. He was more like you regarding his morality."

"So they export Lanium and import children. What do they want the kids for?"

"They educate them, raise them, and send them out into the Spiral as highly functioning adults. Believe it or not, Dragonfire graduates have a reputation for being some of the smartest and most well-rounded people in the galaxy."

"What does the station get out of it?"

Elena seemed confused. "Captain, I'm not sure what you mean."

"They're putting a lot of time and effort into these children. How do they benefit?"

"They benefit by providing opportunity to youth who would otherwise never have it. Isn't that enough?"

"I think my experiences and a long time bonded to Ishek

make me highly cynical. I didn't think there was much good in the Spiral. I'm happy to be wrong about that."

"It's understandable, considering the group you fell in with. Though as you know, some pirates may be lawbreakers, but they haven't fully abandoned all their scruples. It was smart of you to keep the station's location secret from everyone except Johan and I. Dragonfire station's reputation is relatively well-known across the Spiral."

"And yet Crux has taken little interest in it."

"Four of the five thousand people living on the station are under the age of sixteen. Maybe that's why."

"I don't think Crux would have any qualms about destroying a station full of children. But you're right that he probably doesn't see them as much of a threat."

As Caleb guided Kitana closer to the station, Elena tapped her control pad to open comms with station operations. "Dragonfire Station, my name is Elena Shirin, aboard the starship Kitana, requesting permission to dock."

A gruff voice replied almost immediately. "Kitana, what business do you have here?"

"We're here on personal business," Elena said. "I'm meeting an old friend."

The stationmaster laughed. "Now that's a line I haven't heard very often in relation to Dragonfire. We don't have many old friends for anyone to meet."

Elena laughed with him. "Nevertheless, he sent me a message and asked me to meet him here."

"How many souls are on board your ship, Elena Shirin?"

"Only my husband, Creb and I," she replied.

Caleb glanced at her, mouthing *husband*?

Creb? Ishek chuckled at the name.

Elena smiled back playfully.

"Docking fees are five hundred coin per night for your ship. Occupancy on the station is two hundred per night, per person. Or you can stay on your vessel. There are no restrictions on the station save one. I will put anyone caught harming any of our children to death without due process. Do you understand?"

"Yes," Elena replied. "And we agree wholeheartedly with your approach. We only plan to stay for a few hours."

Caleb noticed the weight of his sidearm on his hip. Now that he knew the composition of the station's occupancy, he intended to leave both it and the sword behind. Again.

"You traveled all the way out here for a few hours?" the stationmaster commented. "Your old friend must be very important to you."

"He definitely is."

"You're cleared for docking on Spoke Nine. I'm activating the docking light now."

A bright green light flashed on at one spoke on the lower wagon-wheel, showing where Caleb should park. He changed Kitana's vector, guiding the ship toward it.

"You can pay the dockmaster once you've arrived. Enjoy your stay."

"Thank you," Elena replied before cutting the comms and glancing at Caleb. "We'll suffer less scrutiny and distrust if we travel as a married couple."

Caleb nodded. "But, Creb?"

"It seemed as good a name as any. Have you ever been married, Captain?"

He already knew Elena had and that her husband had died on Atlas fighting Crux. "No. I've been in the Marines since the day I became old enough to enlist. They shuffled me around a lot, which made it more challenging to settle with someone. And then the trife came."

"The trife?"

"Relyeh infantry. Nasty things. They multiplied faster than we could kill them, and within a few years Earth was theirs. That's why ships like Deliverance and Pathfinder were built. To get humankind off Earth to somewhere safer.

Looking at the state of the Spiral and knowing that humankind originated here with Pathfinder, I suppose we're destined to repeat the sins of the past."

"You know what they say. Absolute power corrupts absolutely."

"I had hoped to find Pathfinder's descendants living in a Utopia. Instead, I'm trying to fight a war we've already lost."

"We haven't lost yet, Captain, and we won't lose. Not as long as people like you continue fighting. You never know what could happen until it happens."

Caleb didn't reply. Following the green docking light, he guided Kitana into position beside Spoke Nine, slowing the ship until it came to rest against the docking clamps. After he turned off the reactor and thrusters, the dockmaster extended an umbilical connector to Kitana's hatch, providing the ship's occupants with not only access to the station but also with oxygen, fresh potable water and waste tank drainage if needed.Once a green light blinked on in front of Caleb, showing that the umbilical was securely maglocked to Kitana's hatch, they left the flight deck, pausing at the hatch for Caleb to remove and leave behind his weapons.

A boy of only fourteen, with dark hair and a friendly smile, waited for them at the station side of the umbilical. "Welcome to Dragonfire Station," he said. "My name is Liam. Stationmaster Klim wants me to look after you while you're here. I understand you're looking for an old friend?"

"That's right," Caleb said. "He's a dockmaster here. His name is Sang."

Liam's grin widened. "You're friends with Sang? I didn't think that mean old cuss had any friends."

Caleb glanced at Elena, who shrugged. "He's never been mean to me," she replied.

"Maybe he just doesn't like kids," Liam suggested. "He's

always yelling at us. 'Stop your messing around. You're too loud. Get lost.' Things like that."

Caleb couldn't hold back his amusement, smirking at Liam's impression of the man. "Do you know where we can find him?"

"He should be up at Spoke Three looking after the cargo ship that just docked," Liam said, but I bet he's In Control. I'll show you the way."

"Thank you," Caleb said.

"It's no trouble at all. We don't get a lot of visitors, so it's always nice to see fresh faces. Right this way."

Liam led them through the station's corridors toward the lift. The interior was clean and well-maintained, with bright lights and plenty of open space. They passed other children on their way, most of whom were younger than Liam and dressed in plain clothing that reminded Caleb of pajamas. He couldn't help noticing how happy they seemed as they ran around playing games or reading from data-pads. It made him feel better about his decision not to bring his weapons onto the station.

"Where are all the adults?" Caleb asked, taking in the scene.

"The adults run the station," Liam replied. "There aren't enough to keep watch over all of us, so the older ones take care of the younger ones."

As if on cue, a group of four teenagers came around the corner ahead. Dressed the same as the others but with a red sash across their chests, they looked more serious and official than any of the other kids they had passed. The oldest of the group, a girl of fifteen or sixteen, eyed Caleb warily as they approached.

"Jillie, this is Creb and his wife Elena. They're here to see Old Man Sang."

Her expression didn't soften at the introduction. "I see. Where are you from, Mister Creb?"

"Atlas," Caleb replied.

"You came a long way. Why didn't you just use the hypernet?"

"It's been a long time. I wanted to see Sang in person."

"Where do you know him from?"

"Why do I feel like I'm being interrogated?" Caleb replied, locking eyes with the girl.

She looked away, her face flushing. "Nevermind." Still refusing to regain eye contact, she led the group past them and down the corridor.

"Monitors," Liam explained. "They keep an eye out for trouble. All of us over twelve have rotations as monitors. Don't mind Jillie; she's usually much nicer, but that sash goes to her head when she has it on."

They boarded an elevator, taking it up to the middle of the central column before getting off again. "Control is this way," Liam said, leading them down another corridor past three crowded classrooms that all looked identical to Caleb. Rows of seats faced toward the teacher at the front of the room, with projections displaying various images and videos related to whatever was being taught. The kids all seemed attentive and engaged, their eyes glued on the instructors while they spoke.

"Here we are," Liam said, guiding them into a large room just past the classrooms. Caleb craned his neck, searching for Sang among the older children and adults manning the terminals and workstations. Elena looked too, but neither of them had any luck finding him.

"Liam," said the oldest man Caleb had seen on the station so far. At least sixty years old, with thinning white hair and a kind face, he stood behind a raised workstation in the back of the room, keeping watch over the other workers. "What are you doing here?"

Caleb recognized the man's voice. The stationmaster they had spoken to on the comms. This had to be Klim.

"Liam thought Sang would be here," he explained before the boy could answer.

"You came here to see Sang?" Klim questioned, obviously surprised. "Why didn't you say so over the comms?"

"We were hoping to surprise him," Elena replied.

"Do you know where he is?" Caleb asked.

"In his quarters, I imagine. He's written out ill for the last three days." Klim turned his attention to Liam. "Please show them to Sang's quarters, will you, my boy?"

"Of course, sir," Liam answered.

Klim smiled at Caleb and Elena as they left Control.

"He seems nice," Caleb said when they were back out in the corridor.

"Everyone on Dragonfire Station is nice," Liam replied. "Well, except maybe for Sang. That's why they built it this way. To give kids a chance at something better than what they had before."

Caleb couldn't help noticing that while all the children seemed happy enough, there wasn't much emotion behind their smiles. It made him wonder if some of those grins might be forced. Or maybe he was just being cynical again. He didn't have any experience with orphanages or foster care.

They continued through the corridors until they reached another elevator, taking it up a few decks. The station felt more industrial here, though still clean and well-maintained. There were fewer people around too, and a greater proportion of them were adults who smiled and nodded to them as they passed by.

They turned one corner after another until Liam brought them to a stop outside a plain metal door. With all the twists and turns they had made on the way, Caleb had completely lost his bearings.

"This is his quarters," Liam announced, pointing at the door. "I'll wait out here for you."

Caleb glanced at Elena, who stepped up to the door and banged her fist against it. Waiting a short while, she banged again, adding her voice this time. "Sang? It's Elena!"

There was still no answer. She pounded a third time, achieving the same results.

"We need to get through that door," Caleb said to Liam. "Sang may be in trouble."

Liam nodded. "I'll get Stationmaster Klim. Wait here."

The boy hurried off, leaving Caleb and Elena alone outside Sang's quarters. Caleb considered forcing the door open, while Elena tried knocking again, more likely because it gave her something to do than because she expected an answer.

They were both surprised when the door suddenly unlocked and slid open.

"Sang," Elena said. "It's about—"

A dark form burst through the doorway, shoving Elena aside and shooting past Caleb before he could react.

"Sang, wait!" he shouted instead, wondering if their banging had spooked the man.

"Captain," Elena said. "I got a glimpse of his face on the way past. That wasn't Sang."

CHAPTER 8

Caleb spun around an instant after the man fled past him, catching just a glimpse of him as he ran around the corner in the corridor outside Sang's room. He looked back at Elena. She was already getting up after the man charged out of Sang's door and knocked her into the wall. "I'm fine," she said, realizing he had hesitated pursuing the man out of concern for her. "Go!"

He nodded and took off after him, following him deeper into Dragonfire Station. A ways behind but pumping hard to catch him, Caleb wasn't about to give up. The man kept looking back at him, obviously realizing as much. He picked up speed, desperate to escape.

The chase continued through corridors that all looked alike, with Caleb slowly gaining. Up ahead, the man collided with a young girl of about ten as she came out of one of the rooms, bowling her over as he stumbled and fell to the deck. By the time Caleb helped the girl up, the man was back up and racing away. Caleb took time to straighten the shoulders of the girl's coveralls and then clasped her arms. "Are you all right?" he asked her, gazing into her eyes. Giving him a dazzling smile, she nodded. He returned her smile, patted her shoulder and was off again, chasing the unidentified man through the passageways.

After turning several more corners, he caught sight of the man bolting inside of the elevator at the end of the corridor. Caleb turned on the jets, but he was a hair too late. The doors slid closed just ahead of his grasping fingers, leaving him to pound angrily against the metal surface. He stepped back from the lift and glanced up at the floor indicator. The cab was descending.

He had an idea.

This one isn't completely terrible.

Thanks for the vote of confidence, Caleb replied. *Boost me.*

For once, Ishek didn't argue. He sent the chemical mix into Caleb's bloodstream, offering an immediate boost to his strength and stamina. Stepping forward, Caleb pried his fingers between the elevator's outer doors and pulled. They groaned with resistance before giving way, opening just enough for Caleb to wedge himself between them and look down into the shaft. The cab was already nearly thirty meters down.

Do you think I'll break my legs or go through the top of it? he asked Ishek.

You'll break more than your legs. It's too far down.

"Captain," Elena said over comms. "Are you still in pursuit?"

"Affirmative," he replied. "I'm in the lift shaft. What's your status?"

"You're where? Nevermind. Captain, we're too late. Sang is dead."

"And I'm sure that bastard I'm chasing killed him," Caleb spat, angered by the news. How the hell had Crux beaten him to Sang? It made no sense. He again glanced down at the descending cab.

And then he jumped.

Unlike elevators on Earth, this one ascended and

descended using gravity plates affixed to the bottom, leaving the top of the cab devoid of cables, the roof flat. Caleb plummeted toward it, laying himself out as he dropped in the dead center of the shaft. The collision would hurt, he had no doubts about that. But he wasn't about to let Sang's murderer, and only lead on Ham, get away.

He hit the top of the elevator with an echoing bang, denting in the metal top. His enhanced muscles absorbed some of the shock from the impact, and the give of the ceiling helped a bit more. It wasn't enough to prevent him from breaking bones. The air exploded from his lungs, a pained grunt escaping him as both his shoulders dislocated and his right kneecap shattered.

Still more pissed off than in pain, thanks to Ish flooding him with adrenaline, he slammed his shoulders, one and then the other, into the metal, driving them both back into place. Ishek quickly responded, sending additional chemicals into his bloodstream to heal the cartilage and bone.

The cab slowed, preparing to stop. Caleb lifted himself up on one leg and jumped on the crumpled roof, further caving it in, until a bullet blasted up through the crumpled metal, nearly hitting him in the groin. More followed as he hopped to the cab's edge, the slugs turning the top of the cab into Swiss Cheese barely missing him.Off balance, he had to lean forward to catch himself with his hands. Palms flat on the shaft wall, he walked his hands down the wall as the cab finished descending.

At the bottom, he stepped back onto the riddled ceiling of the cab. Softened by the bullets, it gave way, dropping him to the cab floor. Unfortunately, the doors had already opened, and his adversary was making a run for it.

Caleb gave chase, limping along as quickly as his still healing knee allowed, the kneecap still binding some movement of his knee. There were more children in the passageway here, most of them less than ten years old.

They watched him with gaping mouths as he shambled past, lamenting that he had left his blaster behind.

"Captain?" Elena said over his comm. "Did you get him yet?"

"Working on it," he growled back. *Damn, Ish, fix my leg.* The assassin was getting away.

This isn't magic. It still takes time to heal.

We don't have time.

Ishek didn't reply, but the pain in Caleb's knee began fading almost immediately. He could almost feel the displaced patella mending as his knee moved more freely, allowing him to pick up the pace. He turned the next corner in time to see the door at the end of the corridor slide closed.

I hate this bastard.

Caleb pushed himself harder, racing for the door. It opened ahead of him and he bounded through, coming within centimeters of losing his life as he ducked away from a long, glittering blur at the corner of his peripheral vision. The blade clanged off the frame of the metal door as Caleb threw himself to the floor, rolling all the way to his feet. Sang's murderer stood in front of him, his face finally visible.

"You're just a kid," Caleb said, staring at a boy. Though big for his age, the kid couldn't· be more than twelve years old.

He didn't reply, instead rushing forward, driving the knife toward Caleb's stomach. The kid was unnaturally fast, but he wasn't a trained fighter. Caleb grabbed his wrist before the knife could connect, twisting hard enough that he heard bone snap. The boy cried out in pain, releasing the knife and stumbling backward. He glared at Caleb through angry eyes.

"Who are you?" Caleb asked. "How did Crux find us here? Where is Ham?"

He doesn't know anything useful. He's infected with moieties. There's no other explanation.

Caleb stared into the boy's eyes. There were no emotions there beyond anger. No fear or sadness or remorse. It reminded him of how Junior had looked when Gareshk controlled him.

The boy lunged forward again, throwing a punch with his uninjured arm. Caleb caught it easily, grabbing the kid by the collar and slamming him face first into the bulkhead.

You need to kill him.

He's just a boy.

Whatever he was before, whoever he was before, that's all gone. Now he's an extension of Iagorth. Nothing more.

The boy still glared at him with feral, angry eyes but didn't speak or struggle against Caleb's powerful grip.

Why would he kill Sang? What does Iagorth stand to gain by preventing me from reaching the Guardians?

Perhaps he understands your plan, and the thought of its success frightens him.

It was a nice sentiment, but Caleb doubted that. "Why did you kill Sang?" he asked the boy.

"It suited my purpose."

"What purpose?"

The kid responded with a menacing grin. "Distraction."

Before Caleb could ask him what he meant, an alarm blared.

CHAPTER 9

"What did you do?" Caleb growled, gripping the boy by the throat. Red lights flashed around him, the wail of sirens echoing in the passageway.

The boy didn't answer. His eyes rolled back in his head, his body falling limp in Caleb's grasp. Dead.

Do not let the moiety escape.

Caleb stared at the boy's suddenly serene expression. Ishek wanted him to see the kid as nothing more than a vessel. It was easier said than done. He was too young to get caught up in all of this. War never spared the innocent.

"What am I supposed to do to stop the moiety?" he asked. "I don't even have a gun or a helmet this time."

We passed an airlock a short way back.

"Captain, are you there?" Elena said, her voice panicked.

"I'm here. What's going on?"

"According to Liam, a Specter just came out of hyperspace. It's nearby and heading for the station."

"Son of a bitch," Caleb spat while gently lowering the boy to the deck. "Iagorth knew we would come here. I don't know how, but he knew."

"Jack?" Elena questioned.

"He didn't know about Sang. No one did except you and Johan knew. And only Johan had access to the comms."

"Do you think Tonneau was a setup to plant him within our ranks?"

"It seems impossible, but we can't rule anything out right now."

It's also possible Sang had nothing to do with the message Elena received. The moiety is already here. It could have sent the message as Sang before moving to the child.

Another setup?

You are a threat to the Relyeh. Perhaps their greatest human threat. Is it a surprise that they would go to great lengths to kill you?

"Elena, how long before the Specter arrives?"

"Six minutes before they reach optimal firing range. The children are evacuating to the hardened core. The station isn't defenseless, but it can't hold out against a Specter. Little can."

The central core of the station was no doubt more protected than the wheels, with heavier shields and a denser grouping of gun batteries. It was probably enough to repel a regular starship or two, even military warships. But the Specters changed the equation. If he didn't do something, a bright spot in the galaxy would be wiped out, and thousands of children would die.

"Get to Kitana," he replied. "Send a message to Gorgon. We need them here, asap."

"Aye, Captain. I'm on my way."

"I'll meet you there."

If Iagorth infected Sang, and Sang contacted any loyalists who know where the Guardians are hiding...

Then Crux knows where they are, Caleb finished for Ishek. *This keeps getting worse.*

You know as well as anyone how difficult it is to outmaneuver my kind.

Caleb looked down at the dead boy. "I'm sorry," he said. It was his presence in the Spiral, his attacks against Crux that had led to this. But what other choice did he have? Giving the galaxy up to Iagorth wasn't an option.

That doesn't mean we stop trying. Guide me back to the lower wheel.

The alarm continued blaring as Ishek guided his steps toward the lift he had come up in while children rushed past him. Some were crying, others walking with stoic expressions, all headed for the lifts.

He reached his target elevator, taking it down to Spoke Nine. The area had been alive with activity only an hour earlier, but the evacuation left it deserted. Scenes of abandonment were visible all around in the discarded tools, computer tablets, and toys.

"Cap, I'm on Kitana's flight deck," Elena reported. "Gorgon is on the way."

"Copy." Caleb sprinted through the corridors at full speed. "Stay there and warm her up. I'm almost there."

The station shuddered, the lights flickering and going out. The instant silence of the alarm unnerved Caleb more than the alarm itself. "They're firing on the station!" Elena cried as the backup power source kicked in, the LEDs in the passageway coming back on at half power.

A second hit quickly knocked the power out again, along with the charge to the gravity plates. He activated his magboots, clamping them to the deck. Crouching, he released the maglock to spring forward, grab onto the pipes running along the ceiling and pull himself at an ever-increasing speed. Ricocheting around the corner, he sped toward the umbilical like a bullet.

He activated his magboots again to drop to the deck and board Kitana. Elena's flushed face told Caleb what to expect when his eyes shifted to the scene she was watching on the front surround. A single Specter, still out of optimal firing range, had already destroyed part of the lower docking wheel. The station's batteries fired back, but of course they were insufficiently powerful to do more than tickle the warship, especially with the ship still thousands of kilometers away.

"What's our plan, Captain?" Elena asked as Caleb dropped into the pilot's seat.

"If that ship is here for me," he said, buckling in, "then we need to lead it away from the station." As he'd ordered, Elena had already started the reactor and ignited the thrusters. With the station's power out, he would have to disconnect the umbilical by force. He didn't waste any time. Opening the throttle, Kitana strained to break the link as he gradually increased thrust. The ship shuddered, the umbilical refusing to disconnect as the spoke's structure bent under the force.

"You're liable to rip a hole in the hull," Elena cautioned.

"We have no choice," he replied, adding even more thrust. Kitana shook violently as it remained anchored to the spoke.

A bright flash blinded Caleb, the Specter's energy beam missing them by less than a meter. It sliced through the spoke, inadvertently severing the link for them. Kitana shot forward, shoving Caleb back in his seat as it rocketed away from the station.

Debris from the wheel smacked off the small ship's shields as Caleb guided it away, putting some distance between Kitana and the station. He watched the Specter, waiting for it to stop attacking the station and come after them. It didn't take him long to realize the warship wouldn't change its course. Energy beams continued pounding the station shields, intensifying as the Specter reached the optimal maximum firing range.

"Damn it!" Caleb cursed. Iagorth knew enough about him to know he wouldn't leave a station full of children unprotected. Furious, he guided Kitana in a sweeping one-eighty and sent the small craft hurtling toward the Specter.

"What are you doing?" Elena cried. "Are you insane?"

"I can't live with myself if I let those kids die," he replied. "So we might as well die trying to save them."

She didn't argue, her expression tight. "Fire control system activated," she said, tapping on her control pad. "Not that it'll do any good."

"Fire," Caleb replied.

Kitana's guns opened up on the Specter, energy blasts pulsing from the cannons like spittle from a gnat. At first, Caleb thought the warship would continue to ignore him. Then some batteries ceased firing on the station and redirected at Kitana. He banked hard to port, rolling over inverted. The beams didn't stop tracking them, staying close but not quite hitting their target. Caleb kept juking Kitana, diving and rolling while Elena continued firing on the Specter. It was all for nothing. Their guns couldn't hope to penetrate the warship's armor.

"Kitana, this is Dragonfire," Klim said over the comms, a slight quiver in his voice. "Our shields are at fifty percent. We can't take much more of this."

"Elena, how long until Gorgon arrives?" Caleb asked.

"Ten minutes," she replied.

"They won't last ten minutes."

"No," she agreed. "But there's nothing we can do."

Caleb cursed under his breath, dodging another energy beam as they crossed beneath the Specter, momentarily out of range.

I have an idea. And unlike yours, it is good.

I'm listening.

It is time to put Jack to the test. You need to put Kitana in a position to enter the Specter's hangar.

I don't even know where the hangar is on that thing.

They are launching Nightmares. That is your answer.

Caleb looked at the sensor grid, quickly scanning the feeds from Kitana's cameras. He spotted four tiny objects shortly after they breached a square of light bounded by the Specter's dark armor near the bow.

Got it, he said to Ishek before realizing his symbiote's presence had faded.

"Captain?" Elena asked curiously as he cut the thrust, firing vectoring thrusters to stay as close to the Specter as possible. The Nightmares were changing course as well, turning and redirecting to attack them.

"Tell Klim we're doing the best we can. It isn't over yet."

She relayed the message as Caleb threw Kitana into a tight rotation, spinning quickly to bring its guns around toward the oncoming Nightmares. It would still take a lot of firepower to take any of them out, but at least he stood a chance against the smaller craft.

Evading as best he could, he fired on one of the enemy ships, energy blasts pounding its shields. The Nightmares shot back, hitting Kitana twice as hard. The shields held up to the first pass, but like Dragonfire Station, they couldn't take another round of that.

Ish, whatever you're doing, do it faster.

Ishek's presence returned from the Collective. *It's up to Jack and Gareshk now.*

CHAPTER 10

"Captain!" Elena cried out as two of the four Nightmares broke off their approach, hoping to achieve a better angle to attack. Caleb didn't have time to watch them. Waiting for Jack and Gareshk to do whatever Ishek had tasked them with, his attention focused on evading the remaining pair of Nightmares while sticking close to the Specter's hull. "They're firing missiles at us!"

Caleb glanced at the stern feed just long enough to see the small objects streaking away from the enemy ships. He banked hard over, rolling Kitana on its side before pulling sharply back on the stick. The maneuver sent him directly into the path of one of the Nightmare's energy beams, but he took the indirect hit to avoid the missile. It streaked past Kitana and detonated against the Specter's shields. Shrapnel ricocheted off and hit their energy barrier, the smaller chunks disintegrating on contact.

Now would be nice, Caleb remarked to Ishek as he opened fire on one of the Nightmares. Energy pulses crackled through the ship's shields, digging into the armored fuselage without breaking through. *Or you could at least help me with these tangos.*

Any moment now.

Ishek's promise didn't offer Caleb much comfort. Neither did Stationmaster Klim's next report.

"Shields are at twenty percent. The lower wheel is lost. The primary reactor is down. We're on backup power. Please help us. If there's anything you can do."

Caleb's jaw clenched. There wasn't anything he could do. Not without help from a mutated Advocate he didn't trust. He had rarely felt so powerless, and he hated it.

We're running out of time, Ish, he pressed, his thoughts tense.

I do not know what is — there. Go for the hangar.

Caleb's attention darted to where he had seen the Nightmares exit. No doubt an invitation, he drew a bead on the opening hangar doors. Spinning Kitana sharply before firing the mains, he pegged the damaged Nightmare one more time, once more failing to disable the ship, as Kitana shot toward the lighted opening. With Dragonfire Station in the background, he noticed right away that the Specter's guns had ceased firing on the beleaguered station.

Gareshk did that? he asked excitedly.

And more. Stay focused.

The Nightmares, confused by the activity from the Specter, turned on Kitana, streams of fire blasting the ship. The shields absorbed the hits, protecting them until he could jerk the stick and hit the vectoring thrusters to push Kitana up through the hangar doors, the Nightmares blurring past beneath the Specter's hull. The doors immediately reversed course, sliding closed before the Nightmares could join them inside.

Caleb cut the thrusters and touched down behind the closing doors, landing roughly on the deck. He didn't waste any time getting out of his seat and heading for the back to grab his weapons. Elena joined him at the hatch.

Elena frowned. "This is your plan? For the two of us to take control of this thing?"

"No, it's Ishek's plan," Caleb replied, strapping his blaster to his hip. "I should have brought a bigger gun."

"Captain," Klim said over Kitana's comms. "The station's shields are at five percent, but we're no longer under fire. What just happened?"

Elena returned to the flight deck to answer. "We're on board the enemy Specter. One of our associates disabled the ship's guns. I don't really know how."

Neither did Caleb.

Gareshk overpowered the Advocate Captain. He deactivated the fire control system before attacking the bridge crew, who are all dead.

He can do that?

With Jack's help.

Can we do that?

Not against another Advocate. Not yet. Perhaps one day. The other khoron will try to stop him, we need to prevent that from happening.

"Elena, the guns are inactive for now, but they won't stay that way if we don't move."

"Klim, this isn't over yet," she said into the comms. "We'll be in contact when it is. If we don't die. Kitana out."

She hurried back to the hatch as Caleb opened it and jumped out onto the deck. The hangar housed an additional four Nightmares within its relatively small confines, plus a pair of dropships. Blast doors on either end of the bulkheads allowed access to the rest of the warship. There were no enemies in the hangar at the moment, but it certainly wouldn't stay that way for long.

Which way? he asked Ishek.

The forward exit.

Caleb sprinted toward the door facing the bow, Elena following close behind, her blaster drawn while Caleb left his holstered. The door slid open ahead of them, revealing a passageway similar to those on Gorgon. When they surprised a pair of unarmored Legionnaires, the men turned their way, raising their rifles before Caleb could react. He lunged at them as energy bolts crackled past his head and chest. Tackling one of them, he knocked him into the other one, taking both of them down. Momentum carried him over the soldiers, leaving him with enough time to roll back to his feet, turn and draw his sidearm on the Legionnaire he'd tackled. Already getting up and swinging his rifle around, Caleb shot him twice, once in the neck to kill his khoron and once between the man's eyes, just in case he'd missed the khoron.

Elena fired at nearly the same time, her blaster bolt striking the second guard in the neck, burning through it and into his brainstem. With both soldiers lying lifeless to the deck, she looked at Caleb. "Nice move."

"Thanks," Caleb replied, holstering his weapon.

They continued down the passageway, Ishek directing them left at the next junction. A second pair of Legionnaires waited just around the corner, rifles at the ready. Only one of them opened fire, squeezing off two quick rounds that missed both Caleb and Elena before her return fire cut him down. Without taking a a blast from either of them, the other one crumpled to the deck.

One for me.

Elena has two.

Are we letting her win?

No.

Caleb sensed Ishek's amusement as they moved past the fallen guards toward an elevator. It was already waiting with its doors open when they reached it. He entered first. Elena followed."Where to?" she asked, her hand paused over the control panel.

The bridge.

"Ishek says the bridge."

She tapped on the control panel, and the lift began to ascend.

There are Legionnaires approaching the elevator. They know we're coming.

How?

I told them.

Are you serious?

There are only four, and they are not wearing alloy armor. They are no match for us.

"Elena, get ready. There will be Legionnaires waiting outside the elevator when we arrive. I'll take point." He pulled the sword from his opposite hip, setting himself just behind the doors.

Oops. One just died. Two for me.

That's cheating. I can't even fight them yet.

Since when do Relyeh fight fair?

Caleb didn't have time to respond. The lift came to a stop, and the door slid open, revealing the four guards arranged across the front of the passageway, one already dead on the deck. Caleb charged the remaining Legionnaires as they fired at him. He ducked beneath the energy bolts, slashing out with his blade. The sharp edge cut through one guard's rifle before slicing deep into his chest. A second slash took off the second guard's head, killing both host and symbiote instantly.

Elena fired past him, her blaster taking down the last Legionnaire.

Three for Elena, three for me, Caleb mentioned. *You're in last place.*

I could change that quickly if I chose. Cheating is effective, but not as much fun.

How many more are between us and the bridge?

About a dozen. This ship is not heavily crewed. Obviously, it is only intended for space combat.

Obviously, Caleb repeated.

There is a group of Legionnaires advancing up ahead. They would like to be cautious, but they've realized Gareshk and I can take them out on the Collective if given enough time.

This hardly seems fair for them.

Isn't it a refreshing change? It would also please you to know that Gareshk has turned the Specter's guns against the Nightmares.

It definitely pleases me. And you were worried about me letting Jack out of his cell.

In this case, I am proven incorrect.

"Elena, we have incoming," Caleb said.

"Copy," she replied.

Here they come.

The first two Legionnaires rounded the corner at full speed, firing wildly in their direction as they barreled toward them. Elena shot one while Caleb ducked beneath the energy bolts before lunging forward and cutting down the other with his sword. The pair continued to move forward, reaching a second junction. They turned just as more Legionnaires reached the intersection ahead of them, forcing them into cover as the soldiers unleashed heavy firepower against them.

Elena leaned out around the corner, blasting away until she had to duck back to avoid their fire. "There's too many of them."

"I know," Caleb agreed. He looked up at the pipes on the ceiling, visually following them toward the Legionnaire's position. Stretching on tiptoes, he reached up, finding one pipe that was insulated but still warm to the touch. *Ish, take over.*

Really? Ishek replied with surprise.

You'll still be able to see them when Elena and I won't.

Keep them from locating us.

Caleb surrendered control to the Advocate, along for the

ride as Ishek pivoted out from cover just long enough to blast the pipe at the end of the passageway. Steam immediately flooded the area, obscuring the physical view. With Ishek still able to sense the khorons through the cloud, Caleb worked to push aside the enemies' efforts to sense Ish.

Rushing down the corridor, Ishek dove into the midst of the blinded Legionnaires, cutting one down before they realized he was even there. Too late, a second enemy maneuvered to shoot. Ishek stabbed him in the neck, killing the khoron and severing the bond. The third Legionnaire fired off two rounds that hit Caleb's coat, burning through the material but not penetrating his shirt or underlay. Ishek grabbed the soldier by the throat, slamming him up against a bulkhead hard enough to knock him out. Throwing him to the ground, he put six energy blasts into the khoron. Two more Legionnaires remained, but Ishek quickly dispatched them as well.

Ishek didn't wait for Caleb to request control, relinquishing it without argument.

Thank you.

Nice work, Ish. "Elena, it's safe to come forward."

"I think I'm starting to like this," she said after ducking around the steam from the pipe. "It feels good to fight back."

"You have no idea how much I understand that feeling," Caleb replied.

The pair raced down another passageway until it ended at a sealed blast door. A quick check of the controls showed it was locked tight.

The corridor leading to the bridge is on the other side of this door. There is one last group of guards trying to force their way onto the bridge to kill their captain.

How do we get past this door? Caleb asked.

The door opened before Ishek could offer an answer,

revealing the remaining Legionnaires behind it. They were at the far end of the passageway, facing the opposite direction, all of their attention on the hatch leading onto the bridge. They fired into it over and over, their energy blasts leaving a deep pit in the metal. Caleb knew the door couldn't absorb much more of their combined onslaught.

It was too easy. Caleb and Elena blasted the backs of the soldiers' necks from behind, killing them instantly.

You have no appreciation for subtlety or finesse.

Caleb laughed at Ishek's comment as he approached the hatch leading to the bridge. *I'm all for finesse. But this is war. Sometimes you need to be direct about things.*

In any case, I win.

What? A least half of the points you get when you're controlling my body go to me.

That isn't how it works.

As he approached it, the damaged hatch tried to open but stuck halfway. It still left more than enough space for Caleb and Elena to slip through. The ship's captain, a young woman with short hair and a sharp face, offered him a quick nod when he entered.

"Card," Gareshk spat before his expression softened. "I must admit, I enjoyed this much more than I expected. Perhaps you humans aren't complete trash after all." He grinned maliciously. "The ship is yours, Captain."

CHAPTER 11

Caleb stood on the Specter's bridge, looking out at Dragonfire Station. While the battle had ended, and they had come out of it victorious, he didn't feel exuberant by any means. All he felt was relief. The station had taken a beating, over half of it destroyed by this very warship before Jack and Gareshk had helped him gain control of it.

The station shields were down, much of the lower wheel was gone, and portions of both the upper wheel and central column were visibly open to space, debris floating away from the gaping holes. Thankfully, he saw nothing that looked like human bodies floating among the wreckage.

"I will release the ship's captain to you now, Card," Gareshk said. "She is decently strong, but you and Ishek should be able to handle her."

Caleb turned to the woman, putting his left hand on her shoulder and his blaster against her chest. "Go ahead. And thanks to both you and Jack."

"As if I had a choice," Gareshk complained.

Caleb knew the moment he had relinquished control of the captain by the look in her eyes. They still didn't gain the lively soul of a human gaze. Instead, they became more angry. The Advocate initially tried to back away, but he held the woman in place, pressing the muzzle of his blaster against her. "I wouldn't struggle if I were you."

She stopped moving, settling for an icy stare. "What did you do?" she hissed.

"For one, I'm commandeering your ship," Caleb replied. "But that's just the start. I want to speak to the woman whose body you're controlling."

"That will never happen."

"Won't it?" Caleb replied. *Ish, can you take care of him? Because he is weakened, yes.*

Ishek's presence faded. The captain's entire body stiffened, remaining that way for a few seconds. Now, the soul returned to her eyes, frightened and weak.

"Wh...what's going on? Am...am I free?" she asked, staring at Caleb.

"Not yet," he replied. "But you felt it, didn't you? When Gareshk seized control of the khoron inside you."

"Bachis," she said. "Its name is Bachis."

"Who are you?"

"Lieutenant Commander Amali Vestra," she answered. "Her Majesty's Royal Navy. Who are you?"

"My name is Caleb. So you really are a starship commander? Even better."

"I...I'm very confused."

"I understand, because I've been there myself. My Advocate's name is Ishek. He's keeping Bachis occupied at the moment so we can talk. Gareshk is my friend Jack's Advocate."

"Your advocate?" Amali questioned. "Do you mean, you control it?"

"I wouldn't use the word control. More like, we're partners. But I have final say."

"That...that's impossible."

"Jack said the same thing. But we're proof it isn't. Right

now, you think that you're a prisoner in your own body. That you've lost your control. And that's true. But it doesn't need to be a permanent loss. The khoron can be overcome, and forced into submission."

She seemed excited by the prospect. Unlike Gareshk, her Advocate wasn't strong enough to continue manipulating her while Ishek distracted him. Unlike Jack, she was military, and had fought for the Empress before the Legion had taken her. "How do you fight them?"

Caleb held up his blaster. "You have to do something every instinct in you tells you that you shouldn't, but deep inside, you know it's the only way. Or I can do it for you, but it's more risky."

She eyed the blaster. He didn't need to explain any more than that. He could tell by her expression that she understood. "I'll do it," she said firmly, putting out her hand.

Caleb passed her the blaster. Elena stood nearby, her weapon aimed at the woman, in case her reaction was a ruse. It didn't worry Caleb. He could tell it wasn't a trick. "The heart is the best location."

The captain nodded, turning the blaster on herself and pressing it to her chest.

Ish, let Bachis go.

Ishek did as Caleb asked. Immediately, Amali's eyes changed again, the soul slipping away. The gun moved from the captain's chest, turning toward Caleb. It paused halfway. He could see the struggle in Amali's eyes, fighting back against her khoron. She had learned quickly that she didn't need to be a victim.

The gun shifted again, snapping back against her chest. It went off, the energy blast burning through her uniform and deep into her chest. She dropped to the deck on her side, still and lifeless.

"This is crazy," Elena said in response.

"Captain," Damian said. "Do you copy?" Though Caleb

couldn't see Gorgon, that the transmission reached his comms patch meant they were close. The calm in his voice suggested Jack had already told them the outcome of their fight against the Specter.

"I hear you," Caleb replied. "Where are you?"

"Ten klicks to starboard," Damian replied. "The stars were kind to our field variability. I feel like my eyes are playing tricks on me to see a Specter just sitting there instead of attacking us on sight."

"Right now the easiest way to defeat the armor on a Specter is from the inside out." Caleb approached the ship's command station. The entire bridge resembled Gorgon's setup, but it appeared they had replaced the controls so only a khoron could use them, similar to the Nightmares. "Establish communications with Station-master Klim and see what he needs. Send Haverblaad onto the station with the boarding crews and offer whatever help we can.

"Aye, Captain. Will you be joining us?"

"Soon," Caleb replied, turning to Elena. "I want you to return to Gorgon and help Damian organize aid. Can you fly Kitana?"

"Aye, Captain. Well enough to go from point A to point B. What about you?"

"There's a good chance Iagorth knows from Sang where to find the Guardians. Since we lost Sang, our best hope to find them is to locate the information in the Spector's datastore, but the ship's controls are only operable by a khoron. So Ish and I have to stay."

"What if that information isn't on the datastore?"

Caleb shook his head. "Then we'll need another source, asap."

"I can try to ping my contacts again."

"No. Iagorth knew about Sang. He's infiltrated at least part of the resistance. We can't trust anything that comes from a third-party. We need to locate Ham and the others on our own."

"Aye, Captain. In that case, good hunting. I hope you find something."

"So do I. Contact me when you have Kitana ready for departure. I'll open the hangar doors for you."

Elena nodded and left the bridge.

Caleb glanced over at Amali's still form. "Ish, is she still alive?"

Yes. Bachis is struggling to heal her. It is a good sign.

Caleb knew from experience how much the process hurt. It would be worth it for her in the end. And for him. "Can we access the datastore?"

It is available and unsecured. Bachis did not expect his defeat.

"Neither did I," Caleb said. "I owe Jack his own quarters for this."

On Gorgon, or on this vessel?

That was a good question. Looking out at the condition of Dragonfire Station left him tempted to hand the Specter over to them so they could use it for protection. Except they needed at least one khoron to control the primary systems, which would mean leaving either Jack or Amali here. Assuming she survived her healing. There was the question too that if Crux or Iagorth were that determined to destroy the station, a single Specter wouldn't save them, anyway.

"I'll figure out where to assign Jack later. Can you hail Gorgon for me?"

The other ship had left its position near the Specter, visible through the forward viewscreen, approaching the station. Too far away now for personal comms to reach.

"Captain, is that you?" Damian said, his voice echoing across the empty bridge.

"Yes. I want you to speak to Klim about the possibility of relocating Dragonfire station. They aren't safe here anymore."

"Aye, Cap. I'll see to it."

"Card out." *Disconnect the comms*, he said to Ishek.

Disconnected. I'm scanning the datastore. It will take some time. Perhaps Lieutenant Commander Vestra has the intel we require.

"I'll ask her as soon as she revives," Caleb said. "In the meantime, keep searching."

I must admit, this is an interesting approach you have chosen, attempting to free more humans from khoron control. I always believed we were a special case, but apparently that is not so.

"Does that bother you?"

I'm not sure what I think about it, except that I believe there is great potential in such an idea. There is also great risk. Like all Relyeh, khoron are unsustainable without fear and the drive to feed is greater even than the desire to survive. If the host is too weak, they will be once more overcome. The consequences could be catastrophic.

"I'll keep that in mind, but right now it's a winning hand."

As if to emphasize his statement, Amali convulsed suddenly, signaling her return to life. She rolled onto her back, remaining there as her eyes shifted, looking all around the bridge until she saw him.

"Captain Card?" she said weakly.

"Lieutenant Commander Vestra," he replied. "How do you feel?"

A long pause prefaced her answer, a small smile slowly spreading across her face. "I feel...free."

CHAPTER 12

Amali eased the Specter toward Spoke Three on Dragonfire Station's top wheel. The small cargo hauler already occupied Spoke One, and Gorgon had linked on Spoke Six. Along with the devastation of the lower wheel, the ships made the station look more like a military base than a school for orphaned children.

"Umbilical is connected, Captain," she said, glancing at Caleb, who stood beside the command station. The primary benefit to the Specter's systems was that it only required a single person to fly the starship with relatively fine control. The support crew was mainly for redundancy and to spread the load to prevent quick fatigue.

"Thank you, Lieutenant Commander," Caleb replied. "Nice work."

"That wasn't me. Bachis brought us in."

"Under your command."

She beamed in response. "Yes. Under my command." She paused before speaking again. "It's strange though. All the things he made me do. The months I spent watching my life go by as if it were a movie. I'm not angry with Bachis. In fact, in a lot of ways I feel sorry for him."

"I know the bond between human and khoron brings them closer together and merges their personalities over time, but he enslaved you."

"Did he?" Amali questioned. "One Legionnaire held me down. Another opened a container and let Bachis out. He entered me and seized control of my mind, it's true. But..." She paused again, thoughtfully. "It's his nature. The way the stars made him. He didn't ask to be a parasite. He doesn't deserve to be my slave any more than I deserved to be his. Maybe less so."

"Except we can't extract him from you," Caleb said. "You'll both die if you're separated. You don't need to co-exist together as master and slave, but you do need to co-exist. I think you'll find the balance in time."

"Like you did?"

Caleb gave her a small smile. "Ishek and I are still working that out. But I do try to share the freedom more often. And we have come to terms with a lot of our internal conflict. Not all, but a lot."

Speak for yourself, meat sack. Ishek amused himself with the comment, his tone more jovial than it might have been in the past.

"Lock down the controls and let's go," he said.

"Aye, Captain."

Amali shut down the control stations on the bridge, leaving the reactor running and the thrusters warm but not pushing matter. The ship had no crew save for her; the rest killed by Caleb and his team. He felt a tinge of remorse for the violence after what she had just said about her Advocate. The khoron acted out of self-preservation, and the infected—mostly engineers and support crew rather than trained fighters—had had no choice but to fight the boarding. That left the Specter's bridge crew still together and functioning.

Amali led Caleb through the passageways to the amidships airlock, where they crossed over the umbilical and into the station.

"Captain Card," Liam said, waiting for his arrival. He surprised Caleb by throwing his arms around him in a warm embrace. "You saved us, Captain. You and your crew. Thank you so much."

Caleb squeezed Liam's shoulder before the boy backed up, turning to Amali. "I don't believe we've met, ma'am."

"Liam, this is Amali."

Amali smiled before her expression broke and tears rolled down her cheeks. "I'm sorry," she said. "I didn't want to do it."

Liam looked at Caleb, confused by the reaction. "Amali was under Relyeh control. She's the commander of the Specter. Her khoron used her to fire on the base, but she has control of Bachis now."

The boy didn't react with anger. Instead, he seemed stricken by her guilt. "Ma'am, please don't cry. We know about the Relyeh and what they do to people. This wasn't your fault."

"It was my mind that sent the orders. That activated the fire control systems and targeted your home."

"But it wasn't you," Liam said gently. "None of us blame you."

Amali wiped her eyes with her sleeve as she nodded. "You're too kind, Liam. Thank you."

"You're here with Captain Card now. And it's obvious how much you care. You have great capacity to do good from here on out."

"You're also too wise for someone so young," she added. "I'll definitely do my best."

"How many injuries do you have?" Caleb asked. "Any casualties?"

Liam nodded. "Sixteen adults and four children were

exposed to space before they could reach the hardened core. Nearly a hundred are hurt, but most of the injuries are minor. Your ship's doctor is working with our nurses to patch them up. I believe the greatest damage is psychological. The youngest don't really understand what happened well enough to be afraid. But the middlings are still frightened."

"Not you, though," Caleb said, smiling with approval at the boy. Ishek would have let him know if he was in the midst of a feeding frenzy, high on Liam's fear.

"I'm focused on helping however I can. It keeps my mind off the bad things. I can't promise I won't break down later."

"Definitely wise beyond your years," Caleb agreed.

"Stationmaster Klim is waiting with your people in the faculty conference room. I'll guide you there."

Liam led them from Spoke Three to the meeting room located off the last passageway ringing Dragonfire's central column. The walk brought them through the hardened zone, where most of the children were berthed, including past the mess hall, which had been converted into an impromptu medical center. The children there were quiet, sitting meekly while Doc Haverblaad and the station's doctor and nurses gently tended their wounds. A few kids looked up at Caleb as he paused to observe them, many of them smiling at Liam when they saw him.

They rounded part of the station, stopping at a door only a short distance from a closed blast door that had sealed off a breached part of the station. Liam knocked once before opening it and leading them inside. Klim waited there with Damian, Elena, Tae, Naya, and Johan. It was no accident that Gorgon's top engineers had come.

"Captain Card," Klim said, embracing him warmly. "I can never repay you for what you did for us today."

Caleb stiffened at the outpouring of affection. "I can't

accept your thanks," he replied. "If I hadn't come here, the Legion wouldn't have come here either."

"You didn't know, Captain," Klim replied. "It was as much a surprise to you as it was to us. You can't be faulted for that."

"I should have been more careful. I will be more careful in the future; I promise you that."

"Master Klim," Liam said. "This is Amali. The khoron that infected her is the one that attacked us. She feels very sad for her part in it."

Klim gained the same compassionate expression Liam had, and he made a point to embrace her as well. "Welcome to Dragonfire Station, Amali. Do not be ashamed. Evil is in the intent, and the intent wasn't your own."

"Thank you, Master Klim," she replied.

Caleb turned to Damian and the others. "I assume you've been discussing how to move the station?"

"Aye, Captain," Damian replied. "There's only one problem with that."

"Captain, I appreciate your concern," Klim said. "But we aren't going anywhere. We just need a short tow back into upper orbit, and we'll be fine."

"Klim, you won't be fine," Caleb argued. "It isn't like a Relyeh to leave loose ends or unfinished business. The Legion will be back, probably sooner rather than later. We can move you somewhere else. Somewhere they can't find you."

"And that would be somewhere no one else can find us," Klim countered. "This location is known across the Spiral. We sustain ourselves by harvesting Lanium from the red giant and we raise the little ones no one remembers or cares about. It's an imperative task for myself and all the faculty here. It's a task we all refuse to run and hide from. Thank you for your concern, but we'll take our chances here."

"I know the Relyeh. I've fought them most of my life. You'll all die if you stay here."

"If that is the fate the stars have written for us, then that is the fate we must endure," Klim answered.

"Why sacrifice the kids you're already responsible to protect for an obscure number that may or may not come your way in the future?"

"Nevertheless, Captain, that is my decision, not yours."

Caleb opened his mouth to further blast the man's idiotic decision before Ishek interrupted.

Do not waste your breath. Nothing you say will change his mind.

Four thousand children will die because of him.

Yes. But the decision is his, and he has made it.

Infuriated, Caleb looked over at Liam. "Are you okay with this?" he asked, his jaw clenching in anger.

"I trust in Master Klim's decision," Liam replied. "If we die for what this place stands for, then we will die."

Caleb shook his head. He would never understand this kind of thinking, but Ishek was right. He pushed his anger down. "If that's how you want it, then I suppose there's nothing more we can do for you here. We don't have any spare supplies or surplus materials to aid in your repairs."

"Nor are we asking for it. The lower wheel is destroyed. We'll salvage what we can from the wreckage and use it to repair the other damages. The station will never be the same as it was before, but at least we will still be here for the children who come to us."

Caleb wanted to ask, *but for how long*? Instead, he responded with a shrug. "Sarge..." He looked over at his crew. "...I'll need a skeleton crew to join me on the Specter. Johan, you're part of that crew."

"Aye, Captain," Johan said.

"Thirty crew," Caleb continued. "Half of engineering, plus Bones, Orin, and Jack to start."

"Then we're keeping the Specter?" Damian asked.

"I told you we would recover Crux's alloy for the resistance," Caleb answered.

Damian laughed. "You outdid yourself there, Captain."

Caleb turned back to Klim. "There's no reason for us to linger here any longer. Our presence only puts you in greater danger. Thank you for your hospitality. We'll be out of your hair as soon as we complete the crew transfer."

"Of course, Captain," Klim said. "Before you go, just because I need nothing from you, doesn't mean I have nothing for you."

"What do you mean?" Caleb asked.

"You came here looking for Sang because he's connected to the resistance, did you not?"

"We told you," Elena said. "Sang was an old friend."

"Yes, he was an acquaintance of yours during your years together in the Navy, Elena Shirin. But hardly the close friend you tried to pass him off as."

"Yes," Caleb admitted. "We're looking for General Haas and the Guardians. My friend Ham is with them. Do you know where they are?"

"The thing about children, Captain. No one takes them seriously enough to remain guarded around them. Easily underestimated, despite their abilities to learn a range of proficiencies, given the right teachers." The way he said it made it clear to Caleb that Dragonfire Station was more than it seemed.

"Where did they go?" he asked.

"Rakusha," Klim replied. "In the Draconian territories. Duke Draco is hiding them there. If Crux finds out..." He shook his head. "...it will be more than the rebels who pay. All of Draco's subjects will fall beneath the Legion's terror."

"How do we know we can trust you?" Elena asked. "Captain, do you remember what you said about third-party intel?"

"I do," Caleb replied, glaring into Klim's eyes.

"Doctor Haverblaad already administered a blood test on me," Klim said. "Whatever she was looking for, she said I was clean. Trust me or not, Captain, I know you will go to Rakusha. You can't risk not checking it out. Use caution approaching the planet. The Legion already has a presence in the quadrant."

"We'll be careful." Thank you again. We'll do our best to keep Crux too busy to send any more Specters out this way."

"I hope you succeed in that," Klim replied. "If they come, then so be it."

Caleb turned back to Damian and the others. "It's time to go."

"Aye, Captain," Damian replied, as they all got to their feet. Caleb led them back through the passageways back toward the upper wheel.

"Well, that was a waste of time," Tae commented along the way.

"Not entirely," Caleb said. "At least we know where Ham is now."

"If we can trust Klim," Damian said. "Before, I wouldn't have doubted him. Now?" He shook his head. "He's clean, but who knows if the person he received his intel from was clean. Or even trustworthy. Who's to say the original person with the intel was clean. With Iagorth, there's just no way to know."

"Which is why, like Klim suggested, we need to be careful," Caleb replied. "Controlling a Specter will help with that. Let's get the crew transfers done asap."

"Are you sure you want Jack on the Specter?" Damian asked. "What if—"

Caleb cut him off. "He and Gareshk just saved this station, not to mention Elena and me. And you still think he's a risk?"

"I'm being cautious, Captain. With running a skeleton crew on the Specter, it'll be impossible to keep a close eye on him. And you know as well as anyone how the Relyeh operate."

"And the situation with Iagorth here hasn't helped," Caleb agreed. "But we can't afford to second-guess every decision we make because it might lead us into another trap. We have to follow our instincts and handle the consequences as best we can. We won today. We can win again tomorrow."

Not to spoil the moment, but Damian's comments just reminded me about the boy who killed Sang. We've—

"Damn." Ishek's comment froze Caleb in his tracks. "In all the chaos, we lost track of him."

"Lost track of who?" Elena asked.

"The boy who attacked me. I never dealt with the moiety possessing him."

"Do you remember where you fought him?" Damian asked.

Caleb shook his head. "No. This place is like a maze to me. Ish?"

If we return to Sang's quarters, I may be able to retrace our steps.

"Sarge, take care of the transfer. I need to go back to Sang's quarters. Ish will lead me to the scene of the fight from there."

"Aye, Captain," Damian said. "I'll have it all wrapped up by the time you return." He nodded and continued toward Spoke Three with the others. Caleb turned around, intending to return to the meeting room. He hadn't gone far when he spotted Liam coming toward him.

"Captain Card," Liam said. "Is something wrong?"

"Yes," Caleb replied. "The boy who killed Sang. I lost track of him during the attack. I need to find him."

"Do you know where you saw him last?"

"Not exactly." Ishek's memory of the chase flowed into Caleb's mind, allowing him to describe the route to Liam.

"That's near the outer lifts, back that way," Liam said, pointing toward the sealed emergency doors. "That entire section was destroyed with the lower wheel. If he was there when that happened, he's dead now. Can you tell me what he looked like?"

"Eleven or twelve, thin, dark hair, a mischievous smile," Caleb said, doing his best not to show Liam how relieved he was that the boy was likely dead.. If indeed he was, the destruction would have jettisoned the moiety into space.

"We have a few like that, but I saw Devlin in the mess, and Paul is helping Professor Nori. It may have been Thomas. I'll check with Master Klim and the nurses to confirm if he's missing."

"I'm sorry, Liam. I didn't intend to leave him behind. We were separated when the fighting started." He hated to lie, but he preferred it to explaining Iagorth to the kid.

"It's not your fault. You hurried to help the rest of us. I'm sure you would have saved him if you could've."

"Good luck with everything. Maybe our paths will cross again one day."

"I hope they do, Captain," Liam replied. "Goodbye."

Caleb reversed course, heading for Spoke Three, knowing that Dragonfire Station was safe for now.

He couldn't say the same for Ham and the rebels.

CHAPTER 13

The transfer went quickly and smoothly, with Doctor Haverblaad the last Vulture to leave Dragonfire Station. The organized departure allowed both Gorgon and the Specter to depart within an hour of Caleb's brief meeting with Stationmaster Klim. Amali occupied the Specter's command terminal, Bachis following her commands and easing the captured starship away from the space station. Caleb stood to the side of the control station with Jack, whose grin hadn't diminished at all since he'd arrived from Gorgon with the others.

Besides the engineers, Damian had also sent him Penn, Orin, and Fitz, presumably to monitor Jack despite Caleb's decision to trust the pirate king's son. Damian's reluctance to trust Caleb's instincts had nearly led to him sending the trio back to Gorgon. Second thoughts had led him to realize he didn't want to get into a public feud with his second in command, especially since their presence didn't seem to bother Jack at all.

He would take up Damian's overstep with him later, in private, though Caleb could guess what he would say. He could hear Sarge's voice in his head right now. *It is better to be safe than sorry, and though I'm sorry, I find it more efficient to act first and apologize later.* Caleb couldn't claim he'd never done the same in his career as a Marine.

Elena and the Edgers rounded out the crew on the bridge. The engineers had all gone down to check on the reactors and the primary thrusters, and to set about modifying the ship's controls so they could be returned to manual human operation. It was on Johan to determine what level of work that would entail and how long it might take. Rakusha was seven days from Dragonfire Station and required an expansion and redirection to go around a huge asteroid field that sat directly between the station and the planet. That field would cost them almost an entire day to circumvent, which would have bothered Caleb except it would cost the Legion more than that if they had launched from the nearest known base of operations.

Already days behind the Legion, they needed every second they could get to catch up in time to save Ham and the others with General Haas.

"We're clear of Dragonfire Station, Captain," Amali said.

"Move to the rendezvous point," Caleb replied. "Slow ahead by half."

"Aye, Captain."

The Specter slowly changed vectors, moving diagonally away from both the station and the red giant. The slowest moving debris from the fighting regularly collided with their shields, burning up or bouncing off. Getting a glimpse of one of the station's coverall-clad adults as the body pushed further out into space sent a chill down Caleb's spine. At the same time, he remained thankful he had yet to see one of the child casualties. For as well as they had done in capturing the Specter, he would have gladly traded their successes to undo his failures.

The large sensor projection near the center of the bridge showed Gorgon making a similar move away from Dragonfire, staggered slightly from their course. The two ships would enter hyperspace simultaneously, along nearly identical headings.

"Specter, we're in position," Damian announced. "Coordinates are set. We're ready when you are."

"Copy," Amali replied. "Specter's coordinates are set as well." She glanced at Caleb.

"Initiate field expansion on my mark," he said to both her and Damian. Sparing a quick glance at Jack, who stood with a big grin on his face, enjoying every minute of the experience, and his newly earned freedom. "Sarge, I'll be in touch when we reach the first waypoint."

"Aye, Captain," Damian replied. "We'll see you there."

"Expansion initiated," both Damian and Amali said, nearly in unison.

Caleb watched the telltale signs of the hyperspace field spreading around the Specter while the sensor projection painted an expanding translucent bubble around Gorgon. Dragonfire Station remained on the projection as well, but only for a moment. The grid went blank as spacetime compressed around them, sending the Specter hurtling forward at multiple times the speed of light.

"Hyperspace compression complete," Amali announced, relaxing in her seat. The ship's computer would handle everything until they arrived at the first waypoint, where they would come out of hyperspace to update their vector before re-entering the compression field.

"I dislike the name of this ship," Orin commented from his place at one of the forward stations. He spun the seat to face Caleb. "Specter is not a name. It is a classification. It is true."

"It's also what the Legion calls the ships," Elena agreed. "I don't think we want to continue using their terms."

"No," Caleb said. "You're right. I have the perfect name."

"You do? That was fast."

Penn laughed. "Are you thinking what I'm thinking, Cap?"

"Could be. What are you thinking?" Caleb asked.

"Lo'ane."

Caleb nodded. "Great minds think alike. I believe the Empress would approve. I'll pass word of the christening along to Sarge when I speak to him later. In the meantime, I wouldn't mind a shower, a meal, and a nap. Amali, can you point us to berthing and the galley?"

"I can show you the way, Captain," Elena said. "I didn't realize when we first boarded through the hangar, probably because of the exterior and the fact that we were in the middle of a fight, but except for the controls, this ship is a Hiro class Navy destroyer on the inside. I could practically walk it with my eyes closed."

"I'd like to see that," Fitz commented.

"Maybe later," Caleb replied. "Lead the way."

Elena got up from her seat and crossed toward the exit. Penn joined them as they followed him through the damaged blast doors and into the passageway beyond. The dead Legionnaires were gone, moved to the hangar by the Edgers when they first came aboard. Now that they were in hyperspace they could jettison the bodies into the void.

Caleb noted their path as Elena guided them through the ship, certain that Ishek also did the same. Rather than lead them to general berthing where the engineers were billeted, she brought them to the officer's berthing, showing him to his quarters first. As a military vessel, the captain's quarters were small and basic, and unlike Gorgon, lacked a private shower. Caleb didn't mind that at all. The simple utility instantly felt more comfortable than his suite on Gorgon ever had.

He was also pleased to find his clothes were already in the closet, no doubt courtesy of Bones and his team.

"I assume I get my own berth?" Jack ventured hopefully on seeing the quarters.

"Absolutely," Caleb agreed. "You've earned it."

"And then some," Elena added. "You saved a lot of lives today, Jack. You should be proud of yourself."

"Thank you," Jack said, flushing in response to the compliments, "but Gareshk and I couldn't have done it without you, Cap. We appreciate your faith in us more than you'll ever know."

"I'm glad I could help, but don't give me too much credit. You two had to do the hard part yourselves."

"Aye, Captain."

"I didn't know where to billet any of the rest of you," Elena said to the others. "I already moved into the adjacent berth, but the rest of the officer's quarters are free, so stake your claim and let Bones know where you are so he can deliver your things."

"Just don't get too comfortable," Caleb warned. "We won't be staying on board for long."

"We won't?" Penn asked, confused.

"No. I intend to turn Lo'ane over to Haas and the Guardians once we locate them. Their ship barely made it out of orbit on its last flight. I doubt it'll succeed the next time. Besides, with the Nightmares in the hold, the resistance scientists can start trying to defeat the armor and level the playing field."

"Understood."

"At least that saves me the trouble of needing to unpack," Fitz said. "I never cared much for Naval destroyers, anyway. Gorgon feels so much less like a prison sentence."

Caleb noticed Jack's expression shift into dismay. "Don't worry, Jack, you'll still have your own space on Gorgon once we hand over the ship, even if that means I have to move to the lower decks."

"I wouldn't want you to do that, sir, but I appreciate the offer."

The others spread out through the area, quickly claiming all the compartments surrounding the captain's quarters. Afterward, Elena guided them to the officer's mess. Since the khoron's hosts were human, they still needed to eat. Unfortunately, the khoron didn't care that much about what their hosts ate, and had filled the galley with a single flavor of expired MREs. They all tasted like chalky dog food, but nobody complained. They all knew things could be a lot worse.

"Captain Card," Johan said, his voice coming through Caleb's comms patch. "Do you have a minute?"

"Go ahead, Johan," Caleb replied. He and his group had finished eating, and he'd been about to ask Elena to show him where to find the head and showers. The conversations among the others died out quickly when he responded to the engineer, providing a quieter environment.

"I just finished my initial assessment of the control systems as you requested. It appears they refactored some of the software to route operations away from physical terminals and network them into a single interface. There has to be a hardware component somewhere in the server compartment that's managing that interface, converting Relyeh to machine language."

"That reminds me of the Q-net," Caleb explained. "Which stands for Quantum Network. The Axon, an incredibly advanced, space faring race invented the system. In my part of the universe, they're the Relyeh's primary opposition. The only intelligent species who held back the enemy's hordes. The Quantum Network is their answer to the Collective, and it has a translation layer like you described. But I've seen no evidence that the Axon have ever set foot in this part of the universe."

"I've never heard of the Axon," Penn said.

"Me, neither," Fitz agreed.

"The Jiba-ki will never fall to the Relyeh," Orin growled. "I will see to that."

"Maybe someone else created the translation layer," Johan suggested. "An Advocate, like Ishek maybe."

"It wouldn't be easy," Caleb said. "But given the time that's passed since humans arrived here, it may be possible. In any case, we need to reverse the changes. Are you up to the task, Johan?"

"Aye, Captain," Johan replied. "It won't be simple, and there is some risk involved. We'll need to locate the translation hardware and disconnect it before we can complete the changeover. Which means there will be a period where we'll have no control over the ship. If anything goes wrong during the disconnect, we might not be able to restore the current setup because of its alien nature."

"I see. How risky are you thinking?"

"On a scale from one to ten, probably a four."

It was more than Caleb had hoped, but less than he feared. "Understood. How long do you estimate it will take to prepare the needed changes?"

"Five or six days, give or take."

"Pretty much the entire trip to Draconian space," Penn commented.

"Start the preparations immediately," Caleb said. "Let me know if your risk assessment changes at any point, and we'll make a final decision on how to proceed once we have all the information."

"Aye, Captain. I appreciate the balanced approach. I'll update you again as soon as I have something more to report."

"Thank you, Johan. Card out."

"I have to be honest, Captain," Penn said. "I was hopeful before, but now I'm starting to truly believe we can beat Crux and the Legion, and restore safety and stability to the

Spiral. I never in a million years thought I'd be choking down MREs inside a Specter outside of the brig."

"I'd drink to that, if I had a drink," Fitz said.

Orin pounded his fist on the table. "We will be victorious!"

Caleb smiled outwardly, in appreciation of the high morale, and his crew's currently positive outlook. Inwardly, he didn't feel as confident. It would take them seven days to reach Rakusha, and there was no way to know what they would find when they arrived.

Would the rebels be safely in hiding, or on a planet under siege?

CHAPTER 14

The next seven days went by relatively uneventfully for Caleb and most of his crew. While Elena had said the Specter was a standard Naval destroyer on the inside, the composition of the former crew had left them bereft of most of the comforts a human crew would normally rely on. There was no gym where they could work out. No video or book library on the ship's datastore and of course no access to the hypernet while inside the hyperspace field. While Amali made herself useful by helping Johan reverse-engineer the Relyeh to machine translator and the engineers stayed busy rewriting code and rewiring the terminals on the bridge to operate the ship's systems, the others were left to their own creativity to stave off boredom.

Caleb took the initiative by organizing workouts, spending hours every day sparring with Elena, Orin, Penn, and even Bones and his team as a way of keeping his skills sharp while also getting to know each of them better. The only one who refused to join him in the exercise was Jack, which wasn't too surprising. For as helpful as he tried to be, the kid just didn't have any interest or aptitude in direct combat. Jack preferred to watch from the sidelines and focus his energy on improving his bond with Gareshk. Caleb didn't push against his aloofness, instead spending some time talking with Jack every day to maintain their rapport. Jack had already proven his value once. He was both an asset Caleb intended to leverage again in the future, and in some ways the kid was growing into the son he'd never had.

"Jump complete," Amali announced on the seventh day of transit. "Welcome to the Draconian territories, Captain Card."

Caleb stood behind her station, watching the sensor grid as Gorgon appeared a few seconds later, nearly half an AU distant. The expansion variability had dropped them further away than intended. Not that it mattered. They had intentionally come out of hyperspace over a day's burn from Rakusha, hoping to balance the need to reach the planet with Klim's warning that there were Legion forces nearby. Right now, they needed to assess the situation. After all, the last thing he wanted to do was lead the enemy directly to Rakusha and Haas.

Caleb's gaze remained fixed to the grid as Ishek directly accessed the tactical controls to extend the range of the projection. Sensor data continued flowing into the grid as the space around Lo'ane increased, both the symbol representing the starship in the middle of the three-dimensional display and Gorgon's red mark shrinking in response.

"Captain, Gorgon is hailing us," Amali said.

"Open a channel," Caleb replied.

"Channel open, Captain."

"Gorgon, this is Lo'ane," Caleb said.

"Lo'ane?" Damian replied, pausing momentarily while he worked out the meaning of the greeting. "A fine name for a fine ship. I like it."

"I'm glad you approve. What's your sitrep?"

"Smooth sailing all the way, Cap. Maybe a little too smooth. I'm getting antsy for some excitement."

"Don't get too antsy. I'd prefer less excitement to more right now."

"Aye, Captain. Our sensors are clear so far, but they haven't stretched out to Rakusha yet."

"Neither have ours," Caleb agreed. "We're nearly in range, though. Let's hope if there are any other Specters nearby, they're not looking out—"

"Captain, are you seeing what—?" Damian asked.

"Yes," Caleb interrupted as the grid started painting the region of space closer to the planet. At first, only a single green mark appeared. Then a second joined it. A third. The sight of only three ships friendly to Lo'ane's sensors, which were still keyed to Legion signatures, sent an immediate shiver through him. "Damn it."

His sense of trepidation intensified when red marks appeared on the grid along with two more greens, suggesting a field of nearly twenty enemy ships were bunched around Rakusha. The planet appeared on the grid as a blue ball a short distance from the starship grouping.

"Amali, set coordinates for a jump to Rakusha. Sarge, have Rufus do the same."

I'm sure I don't need to tell you that this sector is crawling with khoron.

Not now, you don't. Why didn't you say something sooner? We've only been here for thirty seconds.

"We can't, Captain," Damian said. "Both ships need at least five minutes for their hyperdrives to recover."

"Damn it, I forgot about that," Caleb growled in frustration. "Amali, point us toward the fighting and open the mains, full ahead."

"Sir, even at maximum burn, it'll take us nearly twenty hours to reach Rakusha. The battle will be over by then."

"One, you don't know that. Two, even if it is, there's still a chance we can help Ham and the others, but not if we're sitting here. Besides, do you want to jump into that mess at such a low velocity? Update our vector and hit the mains, Lieutenant Commander. That's an order."

"Aye, Captain," she replied. Immediately, Lo'ane adjusted course, redirecting toward the fight. A red mark vanished from the grid, reinforcing her view that the battle would be over well before they could arrive, especially since everything on the grid had happened over a minute ago.

"Captain, there are five Specters out there," Damian said. "Even with Lo'ane, we can't possibly defeat them all."

"So what do you want us to do, Sarge?" Caleb snapped. "Let them all die? We don't have to fight those ships alone. There's an entire fleet out there."

"I told you what would happen if Crux found out Draco had taken in the Empress' retinue. Draco's fighting because he knows it's over for him, not because he thinks he has a chance."

"But maybe he has a chance if we can get there in time."

"Captain," Damian said. "Cal…" His voice softened as he spoke intimately to Caleb for the first time in front of the crew. "We chose these coordinates out of caution in response to Klim's warning. We can't just go rushing reck-lessly into the middle of a battle we can't win."

"Who says we can't win?" Caleb barked. "I thought you wanted excitement, Damian? You asked for it, and here it is. My friend is on Rakusha, along with Lo'ane's most loyal fighters. I am not leaving them to certain death!" He shouted the last part so loud it hurt his throat. "Amali, stay on course." He looked to Gorgon on the grid, noticing the ship hadn't joined him in the sub-light advance. "Sarge, get Gorgon moving."

"No," Damian replied.

Caleb flinched at his second's response. "What?"

"I said no, Captain. I know it's mutiny, but I refuse to send this crew to certain death. I owe them better than that. So do you. I know you want your friend back, but at the expense of all our lives, does that really make sense to you?"

"I made it very clear what everyone on my crew was getting into from the moment I took over from Graystone," Caleb said. "These are the moments that make heroes out of men. The moments we can least afford to back down. I understand if you're afraid. It's natural. But we came here to help the Guardians. We can't turn our backs on them in their greatest moment of need."

Silence filled Lo'ane's bridge while Caleb waited for Damian's response. The silence remained when the comms disconnected from Gorgon's end.

Caleb stared at Gorgon on the grid, numb except for a heart deep ache over his friend and second so readily abandoning him. And then Gorgon's vector shifted, anger hitting Caleb like a sledgehammer as the ship's opening burn carried it away from Rakusha.

"That son of a bitch!" Caleb clenched his fist until his knuckles turned white.

I wish we were back on Gorgon. He is wasting all that fear.

"Captain?" Elena prodded. "I can't believe he just—"

"Forget Gorgon," Caleb growled, sweeping the entire episode with Damian aside. "We have more important things to worry about. Jack, can Gareshk do anything to slow those Specters? Ish, what about you?"

I will try.

"Gareshk is searching for them on the Collective, Captain," Jack said from his seat at the non-functional comms station. "I can help him."

"Do it," Caleb said. "Shut off their shields, disable their guns. Do anything you can." He sensed Ishek fade from his consciousness, the symbiote's attention turning to the

Collective. Watching the grid, he wouldn't be able to see the outcome of their meddling until they considerably closed the gap between Lo'ane and the battle.

Another red mark disappeared from the grid. Another human ship battered to dust by the Legion's onslaught. Caleb could practically feel each second ticking away, passing ever so slowly in the heat of the moment. His eyes drifted slightly, to where Gorgon sat behind Lo'ane, burning ever further away. He shook his head, still unable to believe Damian had turned tail and run.

The man had claimed undying loyalty to the Empress and the Empire. He'd likewise vowed to follow Caleb into battle, wherever it took them. How could he abandon them all now, especially after overcoming such a difficult situation at Dragonfire Station? How could he show such little faith in their ability to win against the odds? It made no sense. If Haverblaad hadn't already tested his blood, Caleb might believe a moiety had seized control of him.

He had told the others to forget about Gorgon. He knew he needed to do the same.

He returned his attention to the grid. Six more red marks vanished, and he had to remind himself everything he saw was stale by the time it reached him. Those ships had gone down before Ishek and Gareshk had gone on the offensive.

While Caleb couldn't see the outcome on the grid, he could feel it in his body when Ishek came under attack. Sweat formed across his brow, his chest tightened as he sensed Ish vacillating between offense and defense, trying to play both roles to help hold the Specters at bay. Caleb would have joined to help him, but he needed to be present on the bridge commanding the overall battle.

"Amali, how long until we can get there?"

"Two minutes, Captain," she replied.

Ishek returned to his senses, a wave of fatigue passing between them.

It's too much. I stopped one from firing for nearly thirty seconds, but the other Legionnaires on the crew organized and attacked me, cutting me off. They're learning to counter our tricks.

What about Gareshk?

He is stronger, but even disabling one ship, there are still four more. I'm afraid Damian was right. We cannot win this fight.

We have to.

Cal, do not allow yourself to be blinded by your loyalty to Ham, or we will all perish. We can still retreat. It isn't too late.

Give me another option that isn't running away and leaving Ham and the others to the Relyeh. I never let that happen to anyone on Earth, I'm not about to do it here.

He glared at the sensor grid. Four more of the red marks had vanished from the screen, the Duke's armada cut in half in less than a minute. Was Ish right? Had Damian made the smart decision? As terrible as the pain was that gripped his heart at the thought of doing the same, was he leading this crew to their deaths?

He glanced around the bridge. Orin sat at the helm, while Penn occupied the tactical station and Jack remained at the comms. Despite Damian's refusal to follow him, they all trusted him so implicitly they hadn't questioned his decision to attack. Pride be damned, he had as much of a responsibility to them as he did to Ham. The best leaders knew when to set aside their pride because they knew they were beaten.

But how could he give up when they had yet to even arrive? Ishek and Gareshk weren't completely ineffective; they were just outnumbered. His gaze flipped to Amali, who didn't notice him looking.

You've had terrible plans before. This one is the worst.

You said that last time.

It isn't my fault you keep upping the ante.

"Johan," Caleb said, contacting him through his comms patch.

"Aye, Captain?" Johan replied from Engineering.

"The switch over is ready, correct?"

"Aye, Captain. I thought the plan was to wait until we boarded the Guardians' ship?"

"Change of plans," Caleb replied. "How quickly can you prep the switch?"

"A couple of minutes. You want to do it now?"

"I don't want to do it now; I need to do it now."

"There's a chance the whole thing will crash, leaving us without control over the ship."

"I know. It's a chance we have to take if the rebels are going to have a shot at survival. I need Amali and Bachis helping Ish and Gareshk, and they can't do that and fly the ship simultaneously."

"Aye, Captain. I'll start prepping immediately and let you know when I'm done."

"Do it quickly. Card out."

If the changeover doesn't work, we'll be sitting ducks. We'll be slaughtered.

If we don't stem the tide, the Specters will slaughter both Ham and the Guardians. We're the only chance they have.

"Orin, Penn, prepare to switch over to manual control," he said to the two Edgers. "Amali, once Johan flips the switch, I need you and Bachis to help Gareshk and Ishek."

"Aye, Captain. We're one minute to hyperdrive reset. Coordinates are already locked and loaded."

"Copy that." He looked at the grid again. A few more of Draco's ships had gone dark, leaving less than a dozen against five Specters. Damian had been right about that, too. Draco had to know they couldn't win, and yet he continued fighting. Bravery instead of cowardice. His position was a far cry from Gorgon's, the pirate ship still visible in the backdrop of the sensor grid. Alone and in retreat. Pitiful. He would rather die among the courageous than live in fear while murdering his soul.

"Captain, ten seconds," Amali announced. Looking out through the forward viewscreen, Caleb saw the hyperspace field expanding around them, spacetime compressing at its edge. At this distance, the jump would be more like a blink.

He counted down the seconds in his mind, jaw clenching when two more Draconian ships vanished from the grid.

"Just hang in there," he whispered. "The cavalry's coming."

One instant, a flicker of white light.

The next, the cavalry had arrived.

CHAPTER 15

Rufus had once explained to Caleb how risky a quick hyperspace jump could be. The variability principle of the algorithm that powered the hyperdrive and created the hyperspace field came from the system's dependency on chaos theory. Entering a hyperspace field within the range of the variability meant that the jump could, in theory, fail completely, leaving the exit only a short distance from the entrance. In even wilder cases, it could cause the hyperdrive in question to move backward. That part had tripped him up, too. The hyperdrive created the field and moved through compressed spacetime. The rest of the ship just happened to be tethered to it.

Then there was the complication of the number of ships occupying space within their variability range. The algorithms that guided a ship moving faster than light accounted for known obstacles, but they couldn't course correct for anything unexpected at the far end. That meant the chance that Lo'ane would collide with another ship was, while low, still greater than zero. On the opposite end, the possibility also existed that they would overshoot the target and wind up an hour away on the far side of Rakusha. An hour would have settled Caleb and Damian's argument with finality. The Draconian forces wouldn't last another ten minutes without help.

The stars had other plans, however. When Lo'ane came out of hyperspace, it did so less than ten thousand kilometers from its programmed destination, the hyperspace field expanding to oblivion directly between three of the five Specter warships and the remains of Draco's fleet. A quick glance at the sensor grid confirmed what he already knew. They were too late to save all but a handful of Draco's vessels. But maybe they weren't too late to make a difference in how many Specters survived the battle.

"Amali, keep us between the Specters and the Draconians," Caleb snapped.

"Aye, Captain," she replied.

Their sudden appearance seemed to confuse both the Legion and the Draconian ships. The Legion probably hadn't received reports of reinforcements and had yet to figure out the source of the attacks by Gareshk and Ishek. The Draconians obviously saw Lo'ane as another, more immediate enemy and changed targets. They now had Lo'ane in their sights.

"Amali, open the comms, wide band, all channels."

"Aye, Captain. Comms open."

Caleb drew in a powerful breath as the Draconian ships and Specters both opened fire on them. The shields absorbed the first assault without effort.

"We should have named the ship Lightning Rod," Fitz deadpanned.

"Draconian vessels," Caleb announced. "My name is Captain Caleb Card of the Specter-class starship Lo'ane. A week ago, my ship was in the hands of the Legion, who were using it to attack Dragonfire Station. If you aren't familiar with the place, there are five thousand people living there. Eighty percent of them are children. My crew and I defeated the Legion, and confiscated this ship. The Specters aren't unbeatable. The Legion isn't unstoppable. We're visual proof of that. Forget about your fear. Forget about your failures. Today is the day we make our first stand, but hardly the last. Today is the day we no longer fear the Legion. Today is the day the Legion begins to fear us."

"Captain," Jack said. "Gareshk has lowered the shields on the Specter closest to the bow."

A feral grin spread across Caleb's face. "Commander, target the lead Specter and fire all batteries!"

Amali didn't need to reply verbally. Caleb watched the scene play out through the viewscreen. All of Lo'ane's batteries opened up on the Specter, sending multiple energy beams pouring into the ship. A dozen beams struck the Legion ship, followed by a dozen more. The last group hit the rear of the ship, slicing cleanly into the alloy skin and piercing the ship's reactor. The vessel went dark, the huge gash in the hull venting atmosphere and bodies.

The Draconian ships stopped firing on Lo'ane, updating their vectors to resume firing on the enemy Specters. They recovered quickly, lashing into Lo'ane and the Draconians. Within seconds, the Legion overcame the shock and awe of Lo'ane's arrival, continuing their onslaught. Only now, Lo'ane was caught in the middle of it.

"Shields are diminishing quickly, Captain," Amali said. "Eighty percent."

Caleb hadn't expected them to win just by showing up. "Johan, are you ready?" he asked.

"Aye, Captain," he replied. "On your order."

"Amali, find a clear lane for us. If we lose control momentarily, I don't want the Draconians to think we're running."

"Aye, Captain," she answered fiercely, guiding the ship toward the nearest Specter.

"Orin, Penn, get ready. Johan...now!"

Caleb only knew Johan had flipped the switch because the sensor grid and forward viewscreen went offline, along with all the terminals and lights on the bridge, and likely across the entire ship. Rather than coming back up right away, the power failure persisted.

"This is not good," Orin said. "It is true."

"Shields are going to be down, too," Elena added.

"Johan, what happened?" Caleb asked. "You never said anything about a power failure."

"Someone rigged the Relyeh device," Johan replied in a panic. "It knocked out the power management module. The computer sent a signal that the reactor was overheating, and it went into cool down mode."

Lo'ane shuddered, the firepower of the Specters blasting into their shields. Caleb already knew how many hits it would take to penetrate. They had thirty seconds at best.

"Can you fix it?"

"Captain, I can't even see."

Things had gone from bad to impossible in an instant. Caleb refused to panic. "Amali, Jack, you need to do everything you can to keep those Specters from shooting at us. Grab a bridge crewman and attack the captain if you have to; just slow them down." Ish, you need to help them.

I can't defend myself very—

It doesn't matter. We're dead anyway if they keep shooting.

Ishek didn't like it, but he obeyed, fading from Caleb's notice as he returned to the Collective.

"Johan, I need a solution," Caleb said calmly. "Now."

"I...I don't know. There's no power. Which means there's no—"

Lo'ane shook violently. The force of what Caleb could only assume was a collision knocked him off his feet and sent him sliding across the bridge. He rolled onto his back and positioned his boots to hit the bulkhead first. The instant he slammed into it, he bent his knees to absorb the impact and maglocked himself in place. The others were equally affected, though they were all seated and restrained in place.

"Johan, are you okay? Johan?"

"I...I'm here, Captain. I have an idea."

"Make it quick! We're getting our asses kicked."

"I'm going to reset the system. I'm at the core, and all the backups are down. All I have to do is pull the plug." Caleb heard Johan straining through the comms. "Got it!" he cried. "Resetting." He heard a loud click. "Done!"

The bridge lights came back on first, followed by the forward viewscreen. Right away, Caleb saw the Specter that had hit them, still huge as it crossed their spinning bow. "Nice work, Chief!" Caleb cried out, getting back to his feet, his boots clamping securely to the deck. The sensor grid came back online, as did the individual stations. "Orin, evasive maneuvers!"

"Aye," Orin growled, extending his claws slightly to tap on the helm's control surface with better, faster precision. Immediately, Lo'ane started leveling out, dipping and turning through space.

"Penn, damage report."

"Still collecting sensor data," she replied.

The grid showed that only a half dozen Draconian ships remained, and they had all moved into hiding behind Lo'ane. The Specter had rammed the ship to make using it as cover more difficult, and their return to action had inadvertently left a few of the ships exposed. Fortunately, Bachis and Gareshk had silenced two of the Specters, their guns currently at rest. The fourth continued shooting at them, Lo'ane's shields still offline.

Ish, what are you doing? Caleb asked. The symbiote's activities had created a constant pressure in his head leaving him coated in a sheen of sweat.

Drawing attention from Gareshk and Bachis. Do not disturb me.

"Captain," Penn said. "We have some minor hull damage on decks three through six and a breach on decks twelve through sixteen closed off by emergency bulkheads. Three gun batteries are offline, and there's a problem with the shields. Fortunately, there are no casualties."

"There will be soon if we don't get those shields up," Caleb growled. "Johan, are you on it?"

"Aye, Captain," Johan replied. "I believe the restart blew out a few conduits that were already overloaded. We're replacing them now. Give us two minutes."

"I don't know if we have two minutes. Penn, keep the pressure on them. Don't stop shooting. Orin, roll us over so they're hitting our good side." He clenched his hand into a fist. Lo'ane was supposed to be a symbol of hope for the resistance. Right now, it didn't look like the ship would survive its first fight.

Target the third ship. Gareshk has disabled the entire bridge crew.

"Penn, target the third Specter, all batteries. Its shields are down."

"Aye, Captain."

"Elena, I need comms to the Draconian ships."

"Aye, sir," she replied, running across the bridge to the comms station. She leaned over Jack to use the terminal while the other man helped Gareshk in the Collective. "Comms open."

"Draconian ships, fire on my target!"

Energy beams lashed out from Lo'ane, digging into the incapacitated ship. The Draconians immediately moved out from cover, adding their punch. It would take the firepower of every gun combined to breach the Specter's hull, all while Lo'ane continued taking damage.

"Johan, where are my shields?" Caleb asked again.

"Almost there, Captain," he replied.

Caleb looked to the sensor projection. The Specter that had rammed them was coming about for another broadside hit to the most heavily damaged part of their hull.

"Amali, I need that Specter offline!"

"I'm sorry," she replied. "Bachis isn't strong enough to overpower that captain."

And he couldn't enlist Gareshk without returning control of his current target to the enemy, opening up the Draconian ships to that Specter's guns. Damned either way.

His eyes caught on the sensor grid, his mouth open to issue his next order just as a hyperspace bubble formed on the far side of the battlefield, closer to Rakusha. His order stuck in his throat as a familiar ship emerged from it. Another bubble appeared, then another, quickly followed by more than he could count.

The tactical system marked them all in red.

"Captain Card!" Sasha's voice pealed over the comms. "Did you miss us? We brought friends."

A powerful voice followed. "Fire on that Specter. Everything you've got!"

CHAPTER 16

Upon Damian's order, energy beams and pulses spewed from the newly arrived fleet, along with dozens of projectiles, the combined firepower lancing into the Specter that had been moments away from ending Lo'ane. The enemy ship didn't try to evade the barrage. It diverted half its batteries, directing their fire toward the newly arrived fleet, taking lifesaving pressure off Lo'ane.

Had Damian reconsidered, or had his apparent defection been a ruse to throw off any potential traitors onboard Gorgon? He would find out later. For now, Caleb was vastly relieved that the Specter's dwindling attack on Lo'ane was failing to breach her armor. Moments later, enemy fire ceased slamming into the ship entirely.

"Shields are back online, Captain!" Johan shouted excitedly through his comms patch.

The targeted Specter finally succumbed to the hundreds of hits it had taken. A quick detonation at the rear blew such a gaping hole in its armor that its atmosphere vented ship wide, setting it adrift.

"Jack, we need that other Specter disabled!" Caleb shouted.

"That commander is strong," Jack replied. "He killed his crew and locked the bridge down before we could get to him. Gareshk thinks he's Sanctified."

It's more than that. I believe a moiety infected this one. He is this fleet's commander.

That makes sense, Caleb told Ishek. "We'll take care of that one last. Jack, Amali, keep the other two disabled as best you can. Orin, give us a better angle of attack on those other two Specters. Penn, target the closest one. All ships follow our lead. Elena, you have the bridge."

"Aye, Captain," she replied, a series of voices responding to his orders as he hurried to the system's terminal, securing himself in the empty seat.

What are you doing?

You mean, what are we doing? Caleb replied. We're going after that Advocate.

If Gareshk cannot beat him, what makes you think we can?

It's like you said, Ish. Gareshk is strong, but he doesn't have experience against a moiety-infected Advocate. We do.

Yes. Ishek's malicious sense of hope flowed into Caleb. *Let us prove who is the strongest.*

Caleb closed his eyes, shifting his consciousness through Ishek and onto the Collective. He shuddered at first, unaccustomed to the number of contacts so close to his position. The remaining Specters had at least a few hundred khoron on board, a good deal more than had been on Lo'ane when they captured the ship. No doubt Crux had planned to drop forces onto Rakusha to once again go after Glory's Guardians.

Not if he could help it.

The enemy flagship's commander stood out from the crowd, his signature subtly different from any of the rest. With his bridge crew dead at his own hand, he had managed all the Specter's controls alone. That left him weakened and distracted on the Collective, which Caleb hoped to exploit.

Ish, manage the defenses. I'm going in.

Ishek didn't reply, but Caleb sensed him blocking the probes from both the nearby Legionnaires and more distant Relyeh seeking to disrupt them. He left Ishek to that job, casting himself out at the flagship commander.

At first, the commander's defenses brought him to a halt as if he had run into a brick wall. His efforts to penetrate the Advocate's core failed completely. Increasing his focus and intensity, he pressed into the enemy, sending dark tendrils against the commander's light, lashing out from multiple angles and varying degrees of pressure.

Still, the commander resisted, but that resistance quickly weakened. Caleb ratcheted up the intensity of his attack, mentally pushing against the Advocate, searching for a vulnerable pathway in., Each one of his psychic tendrils sank deeper into the enemy, stretching closer to the commander's core. Caleb pressed harder still, all of his focus and determination pouring into the assault. Resilience and fortitude were his primary strengths, and they translated well to the Collective.

For as hard as the commander tried to stop him, in the end he had no chance to succeed. Caleb's tendrils pierced the light, drowning it out, finally overtaking the enemy. He expected to find himself in the Advocate's consciousness, controlling the host's body, seeing through human eyes while also gaining control of the Specter. Instead, he found himself in a dark place of primordial material, where the entire universe shifted and undulated around him.

Tendrils reached out, reshaping into a crowd of dark doppelgangers sucked from his memories. John Washington, his old friend from the original Vultures. Riley Valentine, an old enemy. Sheriff Duke. General Haeri. Jii, Ham, and more. "Caleb Card," the Sheriff said, the only copy to move from its position. Slightly taller than Caleb, lean and strong, with a hardened face and soft but commanding voice. "We meet again."

"We didn't really meet last time, did we?" Caleb replied. "Why are you here?"

"Do you mean, why do I exist? I am here to fulfill a need which will allow me to continue my purpose. Just like you are here to prevent me from doing so."

"Destroying all intelligent life in the universe isn't a purpose. It's madness."

"To you. Destroying all life in the universe is the reason the Relyeh exist. Have you ever considered that we are the challenge presented by whatever force of nature made all that is? Only the strongest can stand against the Hunger. Only the smartest will survive. I don't blame you for your inability to see this basic truth. Even my brother cannot understand."

"Fine. Let's say I believe you. Why are you here in the Manticore Spiral? You've created an army of khoron, but you're not using it to destroy the intelligent life here. Only to seize control."

"If that is all you see, then perhaps that is all there is. Or perhaps not."

"Were you already in the Spiral, or did you stowaway on Pathfinder?"

"Does either circumstance change the equation? I've granted you an audience, and you're asking the wrong questions."

"Granted me an audience? I fought my way here. I overcame the Advocate you've infected."

"And where did that get you but inside his consciousness, where I already dwell? I could crush you like an ant in here if I desired."

"Why isn't it your desire? You've already tried to kill me

twice. You almost succeeded on Dragonfire Station. I think you're bluffing."

Iagorth smirked. The rest of the doppelgangers came to life, all of them lunging at Caleb. He punched Washington in the face, slipped away from Valentine, and kicked Jii away before grabbing Haeri and throwing him at the Sheriff. By then, Washington had recovered, grabbing him and wrapping him in an unbreakable bear hug. Valentine reached out, wrapping her hand around his throat and squeezing.

"I do not bluff, Caleb Card," Iagorth said. "An entire universe exists in every moiety, and every universe belongs to me. It is by my will alone that you live. And I can change that outcome with a mere..."

Caleb sensed Ishek's sudden presence, adding his strength. With it, he head-butted Washington with enough force to break his grip before grabbing Valentine's arm and breaking it. Before the others could grab him again, he pushed off from the dark, oozing floor and launched himself upward toward an overhead light that hadn't been there before Ishek's arrival. Tendrils snapped up from beneath him, stretching toward his legs, trying to grab and stop him.

They were too late.

His eyes snapped open, and it took him a second to regain his bearings. Still seated on Lo'ane's bridge, sweat soaking his entire body, he shivered from a freezing chill. A glance at the sensor projection revealed only one Specter remained in the fight. Iagorth's.

Ish, I owe you one.

You owe me more than one. It was difficult to get you out of there.

Let's make a note not to overpower any more moiety-infected Advocates.

Agreed.

"All ships, concentrate fire on the aft," Elena ordered. "Orin, don't let that one slip away."

"I will hunt them to the end of the universe, if need be," he replied.

From the number of red marks on the grid, the Draconian forces had taken no losses since Gorgon and the reinforcements arrived. And from the volume of fire hitting the last Specter, he didn't think they would suffer any more.

"Elena," he said, snaring her attention.

"Captain," she replied, maintaining her stoic expression until the outcome of the battle was decided. "You're finally back."

"How long was I gone?"

"Nearly fifteen minutes."

"It felt like less than five to me. It looks like we're winning."

"Unless that last Specter has a trick up its sleeve. I'm already assuming it does."

The concentrated assault continued. The Specter didn't try to run. Instead, even though it meant taking even more fire, it turned into the attack, moving in closer toward the Draconian ships. Shields across it failed soon after, the special alloy still only able to absorb so much. Even so, the Specter gained velocity, adjusting course to stay in close range of Draco's ships.

"Elena, I don't know what that Specter is doing, but I don't like it," Penn said.

"Me, neither," Caleb agreed. "Iagorth is controlling that ship. He can't be up to any good. Orin, put more distance between us and the Specter."

"Aye, Captain," he replied.

"Cap," Penn said. "The Specter's heat signature is expanding rapidly."

"Draconian ships, fall back," he shouted. "Now! Orin, get us away from it!"

"I am doing it, Captain," Orin replied.

The Draconian ships, also picking up the heat expansion on their sensors, started taking evasive maneuvers. Some flipped and tried to reverse course. Others increased their burn, hoping to pass over the Specter.

"He's overloading the reactor core," Elena said. "The debris alone will rip those Draconian ships to pieces."

"Sarge, get out of there!" Caleb shouted.

"Heat expansion is critical," Penn said. "The reactor's about to blow."

Caleb leaned forward in his seat, watching the aft feed on the viewscreen. The Specter was already falling apart from the massive heat buildup before the reactor detonated. The massive release of energy blew the hull into thousands of pieces, all of them shooting outward in a cloud of debris that punched through the ships that had tried crossing over the Specter. The blast knocked the least damaged offline and tore several completely apart before the cloud vanished almost as quickly as it had appeared.

Other ships that had been slow to come about or unfortunate enough to be at a bad angle to evade the blast took hits too, though few of those were destroyed. Gorgon was among them, the shards battering the shields and breaking through on the port side, ripping a gash along the side of the vessel. Lo'ane had gained enough distance to take only a minor hit, easily absorbed by the shields.

Looking at the sensor grid, Caleb lamented seeing that eight of the Draconian ships had been destroyed in the suicide attack. At the same time, he couldn't ignore the sense of elation because there were no additional Legion forces on the battlefield.

They had won!

"Arrrrooooooooooo!" Orin cried out in victory from his station. Penn joined him, doing her best to mimic his howling yell. Within seconds, the rest of the people on the bridge, save Caleb, did the same.

"Captain?" Elena asked, noticing his lack of a reaction to the win. "Is everything okay? The battle's over. We won."

He glanced over at her and nodded, a grin spreading across his face.

Did you see what I saw?

Ishek sounded pleased as well, for a reason beyond winning the day. A reason Caleb understood.

I think so. Iagorth thought he had us where he wanted us, but he just made a huge mistake.

Ishek's laughter rippled through Caleb's mind, expanding his grin even more.

"Captain, we're receiving a hail from Rakusha's surface," Jack said from the comms station.

"Put it on," Caleb replied.

"A crazy gambit against impossible odds results in five dead Specters," Ham said. "That can only be the work of Centurion Space Force Captain Caleb Card."

Caleb's grin exploded in a joyful laugh. "Ham! It's so good to hear your voice, man. I take it, you're well?"

"Good to hear yours too, sir. And believe me, I've been much better since you started attacking Crux's transports." He bellowed out a laugh. "That work finally convinced Haas that we really are on their side. Anyway, I can tell you my sad story later. I'm sure you have a lot of post-battle captaining to do. Seeing as how you just saved our bacon, General Haas thought it best to invite you to the surface as soon as you can get here. It seems safe to assume that we have a lot to talk about."

"We sure do."

"I'm sending the coordinates now. I'll see you soon, sir."

"I can't wait, my friend. Card out."

CHAPTER 17

After going through the damage reports with Johan and Elena, Caleb had Atrice transfer Tae and another handful of engineers to Medusa. He then boarded the shuttle himself for the return flight to Gorgon.

Stepping back on board Gorgon, he realized how much he had missed the pirate ship. Maybe it was because he'd always known he wouldn't be keeping the Specter. Or maybe it was because Gorgon had become his home.

Caleb had decided not to speak to Damian in private, mainly because the bridge crew needed to hear what he had to say. He hadn't told Damian he was coming back with Atrice, surprising him when he stepped onto the bridge while his second was in the middle of a conversation with someone over the comms. They had streamed video for the conversation, placing the worn, serious face of an older man with thinning white hair and a short beard front and center on the viewscreen.

"Captain," Sasha said softly, standing as he stepped onto the bridge. She nodded to him and smiled before returning to the comms station.

The man on the other end of the feed looked his way,

which drew Damian's attention in the same direction. Seeing him, he stood at attention. "Captain Card," he said. "I'm sorry, sir. I didn't know you were coming."

"That's because I didn't tell you I was coming," Caleb replied, quickly glancing at Naya. Her eyes were already on him, with no hint of upset at his unannounced appearance. He still had a hard time thinking she might be Crux's spy, but Ishek seemed so sure he couldn't help being suspicious. "As you were."

Damian relaxed and raised his hand to the viewscreen. "Captain Caleb Card, permit me to introduce Duke Winston Draco, the ruling noble of the Draconian Territories."

"I *was* the ruling noble of the Draconian Territories," Draco corrected. "Then I helped General Haas find a new place to hide. All of my efforts at secrecy were apparently for nothing. They've only been here six weeks, and somehow Crux found them. He sent five Specters here to Rakusha, twenty to Caprum. We had no choice but to turn over our capital planet to his administrator and run. They would have bombarded the cities otherwise. That's how Lord Crux forces the people to their knees."

"How did you arrive here so fast? Were you already on the way? "

"We took a position out of sight of the Specters, ready to swoop in and support Glory when the Guardians made their attempt to break through Crux's planetary barricade. Part of my fleet had already committed to the attack on his Specters when Glory tried to lift off. One of her main thrusters suffered a catastrophic failure, leaving them stranded on the ground. I have more warships than most, but pitting any less than five hundred standard warships against five Specters would mean their certain death."

"So you left your people already in the fight here to die?"

"They knew the risk going in. We all did. And none of

my people who died here today would have wanted me to sacrifice their comrades in a futile attempt to save them."

"Except it wasn't futile."

"Having an upstart pirate captain arrive in a commandeered Specter isn't something one could have foreseen," Draco countered. "Fortunately for both of us, Damian sent out an encrypted signal my comms officer decoded, and we learned of your arrival and that the stars might have shifted in our favor. We came as quickly as we could."

"And what about you, Sarge?" Caleb asked, his features set as if carved from stone. "You convinced me you had run off with your tail between your legs."

"I'm sorry, Cap," Damian replied. "I didn't know who I could trust, so I kept the entire plan to myself. I played a hunch that Duke Draco's fleet would be nearby and sent the encrypted signal personally from the command station. To Sasha's credit, she tried to convince me to turn back."

Caleb glanced at Sasha. "Thank you."

She blushed as she nodded. "Of course, sir."

"What if your hunch had been wrong? Would you still be heading in the opposite direction?"

"I wasn't wrong about what I said, if that's what you're asking. You have a reckless streak in you, Captain."

That's my influence.

For better or for worse, Caleb agreed.

Do you want to take bets that Glory's failed thruster was no accident?

It seems we're both having problems with rodents.

Moles aren't rodents.

Yes, they are.

No. They aren't.

How would you even know that? "I have confidence in my crew," he replied to Damian. "I had confidence in you, until you ran. I should've known you had a plan and why you didn't fill me in. I'm sorry I lost faith in you."

"You don't need to apologize, Captain. I understand. And I'm prepared for any punishment you deem appropriate for my desertion."

"We'll deal with punishment later," Caleb said. "Your actions saved us. And we won the day. All of us. Together. But you still disobeyed my orders."

"Aye, Captain."

"Duke Draco," Caleb said, returning his attention to the viewscreen. "How long would it take for a fleet of Specters to get here from Caprum?"

"Six days," Draco replied. "Rakusha is at the far edge of the Draconian Territories, bordering the Sartonian Kingdom."

"I'm confused. Why are you a Duke, but the Sartonians have a king?"

"Where are you from, Captain, that you don't understand the nature of territorial divisions in the Spiral?"

"A long way—and a long time—from here, I'm afraid."

"A story I would like to hear when time permits."

"One I'd be happy to tell. But right now, I need you to enlighten me about kingdom politics in relation to the ruling family."

"The kingdoms have only ever been tenuously loyal to the ruling family, and were more than willing to bend the knee to maintain their positions within Crux's new galaxy order. Though I played enough politics to prevent him from seizing my worlds before now, I have secretly remained steadfastly loyal to the Empire throughout his campaign of terror. I became an insider at the behest of the Emperor, and I stayed there for as long as I could for the sake of the rebellion. But Crux penetrated my deepest security. I still don't know how."

"I do," Caleb said. "Iagorth penetrated Dragonfire Station as well."

"Who is Iagorth?" Draco asked.

"The Empire's true enemy. A powerful Relyeh. He made Crux what he is today to serve his needs, not the other way around. His methods are much more subtle than Crux's."

"You seem to know a lot about what we're up against, for a pirate."

"I'm not much of a pirate, to be honest," Caleb replied. "I know because I've been fighting the Relyeh for a long time."

"Every word you speak leaves me more intrigued, Captain. I feel as though the stars have sent you to save us."

"Don't put me on any pedestals, Duke Draco. I'm just one man. We won today, but only barely. And we paid a heavy price in losses. We can't stand up to another attack like this one, nevermind facing twenty Specters."

"Of course, Captain. I'm glad you're on our side. I assume you will travel to the surface to meet with General Haas?"

"And to retrieve my pilot, Abraham," Caleb replied. "We were separated a few months back."

"Then I'll see you there. It will be an honor to meet you in person, Captain. And Damian, well done." The duke nodded slightly and the comms disconnected, the forward screen returning to a view of the ships arranged in orbit around Rakusha, including Lo'ane.

"Are we okay, Captain?" Damian asked immediately. "You know I consider you a friend, and the last thing I want is—"

"I wasn't happy when you betrayed me," Caleb replied, his voice no less hard than the unwavering look on his face. "It was the last thing I expected from you, but I see it now for what it was, and I respect your quick thinking and that you had the courage to play out your hunch. I assume it wasn't easy for you to turn tail and run."

"No, sir, it wasn't. In my estimation, it had to be done. If not for our potential spy, I could have openly told you my plan and received your approval."

Caleb nodded. "I'm getting sick and tired of all the leaks and the sabotage." He paused, glancing at Naya over Damian's shoulder.

If there are only a few suspects, there is one foolproof way to stop the spy.

And if I'm wrong about her? Then what? What if she's innocent?

Who cares? All wars have casualties. We have to stop the treachery, or we can keep fighting with one hand tied behind our back.

You don't have hands.

It is the only way to be certain, and the delay could have cost us more than it already has. I guarantee it will cost us major setbacks in the future if we don't act now.

Caleb exhaled sharply. He knew Ish was right. They couldn't keep guessing forever. Not when the stakes continued to rise. They had to uncover both the traitors among Gorgon's crew and the Guardians before they left Rakusha or their whereabouts wouldn't stay secret for long.

"Sarge," he said, making up his mind. "Escort Naya to the brig."

"What?" Naya cried, her face glazed with shock.

"Captain?" Damian asked, gawking at Caleb in disbelief before his features settled into a mask of agitation.

He ignored Damian's obvious disapproval and looked directly at Naya. "I'm placing you under detainment as a suspected enemy sympathizer. You'll be confined to the brig for the foreseeable future."

"Captain, you can't do this to me," she complained. "I did nothing wrong. I'm innocent."

"That may be true," Caleb replied. "But all the evidence so far points to either you or Tae. We can't risk any more random failures or running into another trap."

"So you're going to arrest Tae, too?"

"When the work he's doing to help repair Lo'ane is completed, yes."

"He could be sabotaging that entire ship right now."

"He's shadowing Johan. He's not allowed out of the man's sight."

Damian had overcome his initial shock, walking over to her. "Naya, please come quietly."

"This is complete crap!" she screamed at Damian, turning her vitriol on Caleb. "It's because I didn't crack Graystone's accounts, isn't it? You think I'm hiding the money from you, don't you?"

"This has nothing to do with that," Caleb replied.

"Naya," Damian requested again, reaching for her shoulder.

"Don't touch me!" she shouted, pulling away. "Captain, I'm a loyal member of your crew. I'm happy on Gorgon. Happier than I've ever been in my life." She deflated in an instant, shoulders slumping. "The truth is, I blew it. I'm locked out of Graystone's accounts. All of them. I never even got to see the balances. I didn't want to tell you because I didn't want you to think I'm incompetent and remove me from my position."

"If you had been honest up front, I would have believed you, and we could have moved on from it. How long did you think you could keep that from me?"

"I don't know. I wanted to come clean, but I've been so afraid this would all end." Tears rolled down her cheeks. "And now it has."

"I'm not detaining you because of the accounts. I'm detaining you because you and Tae are the only two people on this ship with the skills to both sabotage the ship and send untraceable messages. I need you where I can see you at all times, and where you don't have access to anything. Tae will join you soon enough. Sarge, take her away."

"Aye, Captain," Damian said.

"Please, Captain," Naya pleaded. "I'm innocent."

"As much as it sucks," Caleb replied. "It doesn't matter."

He watched Damian lead a defeated Naya off the bridge.

You did the right thing. The smart thing.

Don't talk to me right now, Ish.

He turned to Sasha. "You have the bridge."

"Aye, Captain. I have the bridge."

He agreed locking Naya up was a necessary evil. But he hated how it made him feel.

"If you need me, I'll be in my quarters. Showering off the filth."

CHAPTER 18

Caleb boarded Medusa a few hours later. He'd showered, shaved, and dressed in what Ish referred to as swash-buckler chic. A white shirt open at the top of the chest. A long, red coat made of animal hide lined with a flexible, protective material. Dark pants, polished knee-high magboots, a blaster on one hip and Hiro's sword in a black scabbard on the other rounded out the look.. All he needed now was a tri-corner hat with a jolly roger embroidered on the front and maybe a feather from some exotic bird sticking out of it.

"You look devilishly handsome, Captain," Penn commented as he entered the cabin. Damian and Orin sat in the seats behind her, leaving him in the front row.

"The last time General Haas saw me, I had the Empress Lo'ane by the throat," he replied. "I'd like to make a better impression this time, while still making it known that I'm not a lost, desperate soldier anymore. I'd like us to work together against Crux, but I don't need him anymore."

"He needs you and should beg you for aid," Orin agreed. "You are the only one holding all the cards. It is true." The Jiba-ki howled in laughter at his pun, which fell flat to everyone but Caleb. It certainly wasn't the first time he had heard that one.

"He doesn't even have a starship anymore," Damian said.

"I plan on rectifying that. Is Haverblaad on her way?" Caleb asked.

"She's already on the flight deck with Atrice," Penn answered, "and I stowed her gear."

He already suspected someone in the Guardian ranks had delivered both the rebel's position on Galatin and sabotaged the ship when they had tried to run from Rakusha. He hoped Haas had heeded his warnings about a traitor in their midst and taken appropriate precautions to prevent the same person from also revealing their new hiding place. But there was no proof Iagorth had gathered that intel from Sang's head, or from another loyalist connected to the former Royal Navy officer. At this point, there was no definitive proof Haas wasn't the traitor himself.

Even though they had all tested clean, the lack of a moiety didn't mean a lack of guilt. Whether or not he had wrongly imprisoned Naya, every sign pointed to someone on his crew working to help Crux and hinder him. Testing all of Empress Lo'ane's remaining retinue would at least confirm if they had the worst kind of traitor among them, or if someone wasn't who or what they appeared to be. Regardless of all that, he had no intention of allowing anyone on board Lo'ane without medically clearing them ahead of time.

He had to shift his scabbard to take his seat beside Penn, pushing it aside and bringing the restraints down over his head. "Cookie," he said, tapping on his comms patch. "We're set for launch."

"Aye, Captain," Atrice replied. "We'll be on our way shortly."

Caleb settled back in his seat. Medusa vibrated gently as

the thrusters came online, and he felt the slight change in inertia when the ship lifted off the deck. The sensation increased gradually as the ship launched into space and accelerated toward Rakusha's atmosphere.

"I'm sorry, Captain," Damian said behind him.

"You already apologized for the ruse," Caleb replied. "You don't need to say you're sorry again."

"Not for that. For sending Penn and the other Edgers across to Lo'ane to monitor Jack. I know I went above your orders to do it, but I thought it best to act in what I believed were your best interests and beg forgiveness later."

Caleb looked back at him over his shoulder. "I already had this conversation with you in my head. I'd decided not to bring it up, since Jack didn't mind the babysitters. He likes all of them, Fitz especially."

"Which is kind of strange," Penn commented. "Fitz doesn't like anyone that much. If you look up aloof on the hypernet, his picture is next to the definition."

"He likes you," Orin said.

"No, he follows my commands. There's a difference. None of you ever heard me say that, but Fitz thinks pretty much everyone is beneath him. He's an arrogant narcissist at his root."

Is she describing Fitz or me?

You aren't that bad anymore, Caleb replied to Ishek. "You know why he deserted the military, don't you?" Caleb asked.

Penn nodded. "I promised I wouldn't tell anyone."

"Then I won't press it."

"Thank you, Cap. Jack's the last person I would expect him to befriend. The kid is well-mannered, helpful, and compassionate. If I didn't know it was true, I'd never believe he's Jack Leighton's son."

"Leighton didn't seem that bad to me."

"That's because you were always on his good side. He

killed plenty of innocent people during his pirating days. And plenty of less-innocent people under the Consortium's umbrella. He had no qualms about using violence to achieve his aims."

"Which isn't uncommon among pirates," Damian pointed out.

"Graystone wasn't exactly a saint either, but he stuck to threats and manipulation. He only murdered other pirates. Anyway, knowing Fitz the way I do, I feel pretty safe saying that he wants something from the kid. Maybe an inside track to what's left of the Consortium."

"What do you mean?" Caleb asked. "Leighton's dead. Doesn't that mean Jack's out?"

"No, it means he's the heir to his father's enterprise. Leighton left some of it behind on Aroon, but not all. It's up to Jack to claim it before someone else does."

"It's been four months. I would imagine that's happened already. Jack never mentioned an inheritance."

"He might not even know. Or he might not care. He'd have to leave us to settle those affairs, and I think that's the last thing he wants. You didn't just free him from Gareshk, you helped him become stronger than he ever thought he'd be. He told me that himself."

"By shooting him in the chest," Caleb said with a smile. "It's not a normal way to make friends."

"There's nothing normal about you, Captain," Penn replied, returning his grin. "I mean that in a good way."

Caleb faced forward again as Medusa entered Rakusha's atmosphere. The shuttle shook slightly from turbulence before leveling out and descending smoothly. Looking at the viewscreen on his side of the ship, he took in the sight of the desert planet below. At first, endless sand, a dark brownish-pink, spread as far as his eye could see. A dry ocean covered in swells that reached as high as fifty-meters, it was an inhospitable place save for this oxygen-rich atmosphere and comparatively temperate climate. Over a hundred degrees Fahrenheit while the planet's sun swung across the sky, he knew from the hypernet that the temperature often dropped below freezing at night, owing to the crystalline reflectiveness of the sand which stored very little heat.

A massive pit soon appeared, at first looking to Caleb as if the sands had the properties of water and were tumbling into a ravine like a waterfall. Drawing nearer, he noticed rounded structures rising out of the dunes, nearly invisible from more than a few hundred meters off the surface. From orbit, it hadn't appeared the Legion had ever reached the surface during their attack, but now that he could see it all up close, he noticed that wasn't entirely true. Enormous craters marked the spots where the Specters had bombarded the area, while the remains of both defensive gun batteries and missile launchers joined the burned out shells of downed Nightmares and Draconian starfighters.

The gash in the ground gained in size as they angled in for approach, its narrow opening a mirage created by the reflections of the sun and sand. Caleb would never have guessed from higher up that the canyon would be large enough to hide Glory in its shadowy depths, but dipping into it, he could see that it obviously could. The sides of the gash were rocky rather than sandy, lined with machinery and tunnels that turned the pit into the entrance of what reminded Caleb of a termite's nest or ant hill. The machines were so dusty they had clearly been out of use for long before the rebels' arrival.

They dropped nearly a hundred meters before the Guardian starship came into view another two hundred meters down at the very bottom of the canyon. Part of the ship's top had a layer of dirt and rock strewn across it, likely the result of a near miss from one of the Specter's surface attacks. The rear, near the thrusters showed obvious damage from the failed thruster, the armor plating scorched and rent with holes and tears from an explosion. The sight made it uncomfortably clear how close Ham had come to being killed.

Medusa touched down in front of Glory, settling gently on its landing pads. Immediately, a group of Guardians led by General Haas emerged from the tunnel on Caleb's right, striding stiffly toward the shuttle.

Caleb removed his restraints and stood, letting the others proceed before making his way to the hatch. Doctor Haverblaad was already there. "Captain." She nodded to him, smiling warmly.

"Doc," he replied, returning her smile. "I hope you're well rested. It's going to be a long couple of days for you."

"Better than giving succor to the enemy, sir."

"Agreed." Caleb reached for the door control, tapping it open. He hopped out of the low-slung shuttle to the ground, kicking up a cloud of sand when he landed. Haas stood a short distance away, flanked by Colonel Campbell on one side, Abraham on the other.

Ham's presence surprised Caleb. He looked different from the last time Caleb had seen him, so much so that he barely recognized the man despite spending months on board Spirit with him. He had shaved his trademark beard and lost at least thirty pounds, not to mention he wore a Royal Guardian uniform, a small medal pinned to his chest.

"Captain Card," Haas said, but Caleb didn't pay him any attention.

"Ham!" He grinned and laughed as he marched up to Ham, throwing his arms out. "Damn, it's good to see you!"

"Captain," Ham replied, returning the huge grin an instant before they threw their arms around each other in a brotherly embrace that ended with each of them pounding the other on the back. "It's damn good to see you. You look...different. In a good way." His booming laugh echoed off the canyon walls. "I can't believe you're a space pirate."

"Hell, I'm the best damn space pirate in the Spiral," Caleb replied, standing back and looking Ham over. "And I can't believe you're a Guardian."

"Well, it was that or spend the last four months in the brig. Besides, I'm the best starship pilot they've got."

Caleb backed away. "That makes sense. You were the best starship pilot I had, too." He tapped the medal on Ham's chest. "Looks like you're earning your keep."

"The Star of Caprum," Ham replied. "Duke Draco gave it to me for getting everyone off Galatin alive. I should probably give it to you. We wouldn't have made it without your help."

"You still got them out. Besides, it suits you. I miss the beard, though."

"Me, too. Regulations. You know the deal."

"Captain Card," Haas repeated, trying to get Caleb's attention.

He clapped Ham on the shoulder before turning to the General. "Haas. It's good to see you again, too, when you aren't trying to kill me, that is."

"I owe you an apology, Captain. One I'm happy to give. I was wrong about your intentions, and I'm sorry."

Caleb nodded. "It takes a strong man to admit when he's wrong and with such humility. Apology accepted, with no hard feelings. Let's forget about the past and focus on the future."

"Agreed." Haas put out his hand. Caleb shook it firmly before the general laughed. "Although, I should probably arrest you right now. You're a criminal, stealing from the Empire."

"To outfit the rebellion," Caleb said. "I have two haulers full of supplies for you. Plus a Specter to turn over to your command."

Haas flinched, obviously shocked. "What? You're giving me the Specter?"

"To replace Glory. I hear her best days are behind her."

"Captain, I don't know what to say."

"Just say thank you. Commander Shirin tells me Lo'ane can accommodate three thousand crew. That's more than enough space for your people. She got a little beat up getting here, but she's still a fine ship."

"Any ship is finer than Glory at this point. Thank you, Captain. Truly."

"You should also know, General. The Empress' assassin is dead."

"Even more good news."

"I wish it were all as good. General, let me introduce you to Doctor Haverblaad. She's here to test your people's blood."

"Test our blood?" Campbell said, finally speaking up. "What for?"

"I'll go into more details later, but the short version is that the enemy who created Crux is a Relyeh Ancient known as Iagorth. He has an ability to infinitely split his consciousness into what we call moieties. He can use these moieties to gain control over other life forms. The bad news is that they can be easily passed from one host to another through means as simple as breathing them in. The good news is that they're easily discovered by a simple blood test. If any of your people are infected, we'll know it."

Correction. Not infinitely, per se. The moieties can only subdivide so many times before they are ineffective, unless Iagorth's root is here. And I highly doubt that is the case.

Noted, Ish. But that's more detail than they need right now.

"And what if we refuse this test?" Campbell asked.

He looks uncomfortable.

And sounds it, Caleb replied. "If you refuse, you won't board Lo'ane."

"That's not for you to decide, Captain Card," Campbell insisted. "You just turned the Specter over to us."

Haas glanced at Campbell. "This shouldn't be a controversial decision, Colonel. Why are you making it one? You can't honestly believe Glory's thruster failure was an accident."

"I just find it discomforting that an upstart pirate comes to us asking to sample our blood. How do we know he isn't working for this Iagorth?"

"Are you mad?" Haas said. "He saved our lives and gifted us a ship. And you still think we can't trust him?"

"He killed the Empress."

"A Relyeh assassin killed the Empress through him," Haas snapped. "He's more than made amends for that."

"If you believe that story. Which I don't."

"You're free to return to your quarters to pack, Colonel," Haas growled. "Disrespecting our guest like this is an embarrassment."

"Your quick acceptance of his lies is the real embarrassment. Didn't you care for the Empress? He should be in shackles."

"Campbell, why don't you go stuff yourself," Ham barked, growing angry.

"You can't speak to me that way," Campbell growled back. "I'm your superior officer. And your superior in every way."

"Doctor Haverblaad," Caleb said. "Why don't we test his blood first?"

"You'll do no such thing," Campbell complained.

"What are you afraid of, Colonel?" Haas said. "Do you have something to hide?"

"What? No," he insisted. "I don't agree with this. At all."

"You'll just have to suck it up and bear it. You will have your blood tested, and you will go first. That's an order."

Campbell's jaw clenched, but he didn't complain otherwise. "Fine." He shrugged off his uniform jacket and began rolling up his sleeve. "I'll do it right now."

"I'm not ready to run the tests," Haverblaad said. "I need to set up my equipment first."

Campbell pushed his sleeve back down. "Then let me know when you're ready. In the meantime, General, I'd like to take you up on your offer to go pack."

"Dismissed, Colonel," Haas said.

Campbell stormed back into the tunnel, vanishing around a corner.

"That was strange," Orin said. "It is true."

"Very telling without actually telling us he's infected," Penn agreed. "General, you should have someone watch him."

"I doubt he's infected," Haas replied. "He can be a touch contrarian but he's done nothing to betray my trust since I began investigating your warnings about a traitor, Captain."

"But you still believe someone sabotaged Glory's thruster. Are you sure Campbell can't be a suspect?"

Haas considered the question before turning to a Guardian behind him. "Detach a pair of Guardians to monitor Colonel Campbell. Be discreet."

"Yes, sir," the Guardian replied, stepping away to fulfill the order.

Haas looked to Haverblaad. "If you don't mind, I'll send my medical team, led by Doctor Ling, to assist you with your duties."

"I'll take all the help you're willing to give, General," she replied.

"Excellent." He returned his attention to Caleb. "Captain Card, if you and your crew will follow me, we can finish our introductions inside while we await Duke Draco's arrival. The sun will be down soon, and the temperature will drop faster than you would expect."

"Of course, General," Caleb said. "Can you tell me what happened to Private Marley?"

Haas smiled. "I thought you might ask about her. She's currently training to be a starship helmsman."

"I'm taking good care of her, Cap," Ham said. "We're study buddies. I'm not officially a starship pilot yet, either."

"I'm glad to hear she's okay," Caleb said. "She went through a lot to help me."

A dim overhead light drew Caleb's attention before Haas could lead him and his crew any closer to the tunnel. Looking up, he watched a more traditional wedge-shaped shuttle descend into the depths of the canyon. A pair of thruster nacelles angled out from the squared off stern below a large tail section. What made the shuttle stand out was the gold star crest on the fuselage.

I expected a dragon.

Me too, Caleb replied, his thoughts turning to the dragon statue still taking up space in Gorgon's hold. Maybe he could gift it to the duke.

It made little sense to continue inside with Draco's arrival imminent. The entire contingent turned and followed the shuttle to the canyon floor, where it landed beside Medusa.

"If you'll excuse me," Haas said, making his way to the shuttle with Ham and his retinue of Guardians.

Caleb waited patiently for Draco to disembark from the craft. The shuttle's hatch opened, and the duke stepped into view, flanked by a woman young enough to be the man's daughter but of course that didn't mean she wasn't his wife. She was thin, with long, golden hair and a regal bearing, though she and the duke both wore simple flight suits. Their armored underlays went up to their chins to protect their necks from potential khoron entry. The woman held a precocious young girl in her arms, who wriggled and shifted, eager to be put down.

"Istari," Damian said, sidling up beside Caleb. "Draco's daughter. And Namaya, his granddaughter."

"What happened to his wife?" Caleb asked.

"Killed by pirates," he replied stiffly. "Nearly twenty years ago, now."

The weight of Caleb's coat seemed to double in an instant. "You could have told me that sooner."

"Aye. I should have. My apologies."

Haas greeted Draco and his progeny, introducing them to Ham before stepping aside to clear the duke's path to Caleb and his crew.

"Captain Card! It is so good to meet you in person." He took Caleb's hand, shaking firmly before pulling him into a quick hug. After what Damian had just told him, the man's exuberant greeting took him by surprise. Releasing Caleb, Draco motioned to his daughter. "This is my daughter Istari, and the little rascal is Namaya."

"Down!" Namaya ordered, still wriggling.

"Not yet, Nama," Istari said before looking at Caleb. Her face flushed as she held out her hand. Caleb took it gently and bent, kissing the back of it.

"A pleasure, my lady," he said, Ishek cackling through his senses in response. "Captain Caleb Card, at your service."

"Captain Card," she replied, her cheeks finding a deeper shade of red. "The Draconian Duchy is indebted to you for your bravery, my father and I especially so. Lord Crux has declared us outlawed within our own territories. There is no end to the depths of his evil."

"But you've delivered another blow he won't quickly forget," Draco said. "With your help, perhaps we can reverse the direction of this fight."

"That's my goal," Caleb answered. "I won't rest as long as the Relyeh are a threat to anyone, anywhere."

"Down!" Namaya cried again.

Draco laughed. "She wants down so badly because she knows there's sand here that she isn't allowed to play in at home." He looked back at Haas. "She would love nothing more than to get dirty and make mud pies."

"Anna is still on the shuttle," Istari said. "She'll be along shortly to entertain Nama. It was important to us to represent our territories as an entire family." She looked at Caleb. "My husband was killed defending our planets from Crux during his initial attacks, an all too common story these days for many of our people. So many have lost loved ones to his quest for power."

"I wish I could say that's all this is," Caleb said. "Power-hungry despots are one thing. But this is bigger than that. I don't want to alarm you, but you need to know what we're really up against." He swept his gaze from Istari to Draco to Haas. "You all do."

Istari's face lost its reddish hue, quickly blanching. Draco nodded, accepting his warning.

"If you'll all follow me," Haas said. "We can discuss this inside."

CHAPTER 19

After introducing Draco to Doctor Haverblaad, Istari and General Haas led the way down into an enormous cavern dug out beneath the surface. A connecting tunnel ultimately took them into a massive underground bunker complex that had once been used as part of the canyon's mining operations. As a result, the entire bunker was already furnished with barracks for the Guardians, a mess hall, hospital, and more. They were passing the hospital when Doctor Ling and her assistant Merrick stepped out into the corridor.

"General Haas," Ling said, bowing her head to him and stepping aside to let the entourage pass. She smiled when she saw Caleb in the group. "Caleb?"

"Qiao," Caleb replied, returning her smile. "It's good to see you again. You too, Merrick."

"Hey, Caleb," Merrick said. "I need to thank you for making me look smart."

"What do you mean?"

"If I hadn't helped you escape time in the brig, none of us would be here right now."

You can't really argue with that.

Nope. "I'm glad to see you're well and apparently didn't suffer any undue punishment for helping me."

"Dr. Ling put in a good word for me." He slid her a smile.

"I see. Qiao, I'll find you later. I need to speak with you about something."

"Whatever you need," she replied. "I imagine I'll be assisting your ship's doctor with blood tests in the foreseeable future."

"We'll talk again soon," Caleb promised.

Ling and Merrick headed in the opposite direction, crossing paths with a young woman running through the passageway toward them. A hover cart floated behind her, loaded with the assortment of gear that typically came with a toddler.

"Duchess Istari!" she cried, breathlessly. "I'm here."

Istari smiled, passing Caleb and holding Namaya out to the woman. "Thank you, Anna. I'll let you know when we're ready to leave."

"Of course, my lady," Anna said, taking the child, who didn't seem to mind being separated from her mother. Before, she wanted down to play in the sand. Now, she wanted down to run around the tunnels.

Anna put her down, immediately chasing after her as she bolted away, the hover cart following behind.

"She is fast for a cub," Orin commented. "She will make a fine warrior one day."

"I very much hope not," Istari replied. "If the stars hear me, this war against Crux will be the last the Spiral ever needs to suffer through."

Wishful thinking. Caleb silently agreed with Ish.

They continued down the corridor, passing several doors open to what had probably been storage rooms that had been converted into staff offices. They stopped at the door where two Guardians stood at attention near the end of the hall. General Haas led them into the room, all of them taking a seat at a large conference table. Haas took the seat at the head of the table, while Ham, Draco and Istari sat on one side. Caleb and his crew filled in the other side.

"I'd offer refreshments," Haas said to get the ball rolling. "But I'm sure whatever you have on your respective ships is better than anything we can provide down here. Unless you really like MREs and questionably potable water."

"Was there a problem with the filtration units I sent?" Draco asked.

"Dwyane hasn't had time to finish installing them, and at this point it seems senseless to try."

"Which brings us to our first order of business," Caleb said. "We need to organize the transportation of the people from here to Lo'ane. Specters aren't designed for atmospheric operation. We'll have to shuttle everyone, and Medusa seats only eight maximum."

"I can provide shuttles and dropships. Enough to seat nearly four hundred on a single trip," Draco said.

"That'll help a lot. You can move them faster than we can test them."

"I heard Doctor Ling mention blood tests," Istari said. "What is that all about?"

"Maybe that's the first order of business," Ham remarked.

Caleb spent the next thirty minutes explaining everything he already knew and had learned about Iagorth and the Relyeh. He detailed his experiences with Iagorth's moieties on both the stardock and Dragonfire Station and then talked about his most recent encounter with the Ancient inside the collux of the moiety-infected Advocate that previously commanded Lo'ane. He hadn't yet told anyone about his meeting with Iagorth, leaving his crew as shocked as everyone else present.

"You actually spoke with him," Istari said, her frayed

nerves audible in her quivering voice. "What do you think he wants from you?"

"I don't know. It may have been a bluff because he didn't have as much control over me as he expected. I don't think I was supposed to escape from there, but Ishek pulled me out."

"I'm more intrigued by Jack Leighton Jr., and Lieutenant Commander Amali," Haas said. "You turned their khoron against the Relyeh, and that helped you turn the tide against the ships attacking us. That seems like a powerful weapon."

"When it works out in our favor and depending on the bond, it is a useful weapon," Caleb agreed. "But it's never guaranteed to work, depending on the intelligence and courage of the host. Jack needed months to overcome and gain equilibrium with Gareshk, while Amali only needed hours with Bachis. Since all people and all khoron are unique, every situation is unique."

"Understood. But if they can disable entire Specters—"

"I don't expect that to continue as an effective strategy," Caleb interrupted. "The Relyeh have means to defend themselves inside the Collective, either together or as a group. They'll be more prepared for our attempts to subvert them in the future. It doesn't mean it can never work, but it will become harder. Trying to convert enough Legionnaires to continue escalation will become an arms race we aren't guaranteed to win."

"In that case, how do you propose we continue our momentum against the Legion?" Draco asked.

"We need ships," Caleb replied. "Lots of ships. Which means we need more allies."

"We can rely on Duke Clayborne," Draco said. "And there are others who will rally to our side once they catch wind of what happened here."

"And we'll do everything we can to spread that news," Damian said.

"If we're going to have a chance, we need to flip some of the errant Kingdoms back to our side," Haas said. "One victory won't do that. We have to continue winning."

"Even that might not be enough," Istari said. "Empress Lo'ane is dead. Her line is broken. If not Crux, then who? Yes, he's a tyrant, but too many people accept him as the rightful ruler. The people want an end to this war."

"They might think being ruled by a puppet for a Relyeh is safer and simpler," Caleb said. "I guarantee it isn't."

"But they don't know that. Neither did we, until a few minutes ago. We can't sell them on a threat they don't understand."

"What can we sell them on, Isti?" Draco asked his daughter.

"Actions speak louder than words," Haas said. "If we pick our fights and win them, confidence in our ability to overthrow Crux will grow. You say the people will accept a tyrant, but I don't believe it. They'll secretly want him gone, and when they can smell his defeat, they'll do what they can to accelerate it."

"We would need a much larger information network than we have to pick out specific targets like that," Penn said.

"We have that network already," Draco countered. "Dragonfire Station is on our side."

"I didn't know they were spies until after we saved them from the Legion," Damian said.

"Let's keep that to ourselves," Istari suggested.

"Of course."

"If you're planning to go after Specters, you'll need help," Caleb said. "I can only ask Jack if he'll stay on Lo'ane and provide support. I can't force him. I'm pretty sure Amali will stay on with you, though. She's Royal Navy."

"I'll take anyone you can spare, Captain," Haas said. He paused. "Won't you be joining us in the hunt?"

"I love to hunt," Orin said. "It is true."

"No," Caleb replied, glancing at Orin. "We have a hunt of our own. We're looking for Empress Lo'ane's daughter."

The comment drew gasps from Draco and Istari, and a look of confusion from Haas. "Captain," he said. "Empress Lo'ane didn't have any children."

"That's where you may be wrong, General. She mentioned her daughter to Doctor Ling before we went out to help with the defense on Galatin. I intend to ask Qiao what she knows. If a rightful heir exists and we can find her, the line will be unbroken. I doubt the people will stand for a usurper when there's another familial choice. If Iagorth had known about a successor, he wouldn't have assassinated Lo'ane."

"If she has a child," Istari said, a glimmer of hope in her eyes, "it could go a long way in bringing the other territories back under her flag. It's an important mission." She looked at Caleb. "How can we help you succeed in this effort?"

"That depends on what Qiao knows. If she can give us a name or location for the girl, we should be able to handle it ourselves."

"And if she can't?"

"We'll need to go to Atlas and infiltrate the Royal Archives."

Draco coughed uncomfortably. "That's... not a good idea."

What else is new? Ishek commented.

"Probably not, but it may be our only course of action."

"If Lo'ane has a daughter and you can locate her, it may be more prudent for us to hold off on anything more than skirmishes where we have a definitive upper hand," Haas said. "I can already imagine presenting her to the Spiral on the bridge of the Specter named in her mother's honor. That could sway a lot of hearts and minds in our direction."

"That's the goal," Caleb agreed.

"Captain," Istari said. "What is it that Iagorth wants? Why do all of this instead of just using the Specters to bombard planets and destroy everything?"

"Ishek and I have a theory that Iagorth intends to use the armies of khoron-controlled humans he builds here to wage war against his brother, Shub'Nigu, and all the Ancients who don't prescribe to his view of the Relyeh's purpose."

It sounds more chilling when you say it out loud, Ishek said.

Doesn't it? Caleb agreed. "There's one more thing I want to mention. When Iagorth detonated the last Specter in the battle, Ishek and I both noticed that the properties of the ship's armor changed. It became brittle and shattered into millions of shards. We both think there's something to that we can exploit."

"That sounds promising," Haas agreed.

"I've heard there are scientists working to crack the code of Crux's alloy. There are Nightmares on Lo'ane they can use to test the theory."

"We can also provide feed recordings of the moment of the explosion, if they want to watch it in search of clues," Damian said.

"I'll definitely have our people look into it. You truly are from the stars, aren't you, Captain?"

"Technically, I suppose I am."

"Well, Captain," Draco said. "I believe your next step is to speak with Doctor Ling, and for General Haas and I to organize the transfer of the Guardians to Lo'ane. I'll also reach out to Duke Clayborne to see where he stands, both before and after I send him footage from the battle." He grinned at the same time his eyes darkened. "We lost over a dozen ships and hundreds of good people today. I ask that you join me in a moment of silence as our thoughts send them to their infinite place among the stars."

Haas and Istari bowed their heads, so Caleb did the same. He remained in that position as his comms patch buzzed violently behind his ear, indicating an emergency transmission.

"Captain," Haverblaad said, her voice weak. Gunfire echoed in the background. "Help."

CHAPTER 20

Caleb's head snapped up, his heart racing. "The hospital is under attack," he announced, jumping out of his seat at the conference table and rushing from the room. The others followed him as he ran down the hallway toward the hospital.

"What's going on?" Ham asked, running at his side. He tapped on his patch again. "Qiao? Qiao!" There was no answer.

"I don't know," he replied. "But Colonel Campbell seemed hell-bent on avoiding the blood test. It doesn't sound like he's the only one."

The gunfire grew louder with each step Caleb and the others took to reach Ling's location. He drew his blaster, grateful he had made the right decision this time to keep his weapons on him. Of course, Penn had brought a blaster, and Orin had his claws if nothing else. Haas carried a pistol as well, but the others were all unarmed.

"Duke Draco, Istari, go back," Caleb said. "You too, General. You're too valuable to lose. Sarge can take your pistol."

Caleb thought Haas would argue, but he didn't, slowing to pass his weapon to Damian. "Stop them, Captain."

"I will," Caleb replied.

The gunfire had nearly stopped by the time the entrance to the hospital came into sight. A dead Guardian lay face down outside the door, her back riddled with holes from plasma bolts.

Caleb looked at Penn. She nodded and moved up beside him, reaching out and shoving open one door before shifting to the other side of the doorway. No return fire came their way, so she took another look inside. Then she glanced back at Caleb, a grim frown on her face as she shook her head.

"It doesn't look like there's anyone alive," she said. "There are bodies everywhere."

She pushed through the door, leading the group into the hospital's main room. It was large enough to accommodate ten beds, each separated by simple rolling partitions. A nurse with three plasma holes in her chest lay in front of the now demolished blood testing machine. The framed curtain behind her had been knocked over. Haverblaad lay face up on the bed, the sheets already soaked with her blood. She was still alive, but the light in her eyes was fading fast.

"Irina," Damian said, rushing to her side. "What happened?"

"Two squads...Guardians," she squeezed out. "Must be...infected."

"Colonel Campbell?" Caleb asked.

"Don't..." Her voice trailed off as she died.

"Damn it!" Caleb cursed. "Qiao? Qiao, where are you?" He hurried down the line of beds, pushing the partitions aside in search of her, but she wasn't in the room. Where had she gone?

Was she one of Iagorth's slaves now?

Muted gunfire picked up again, coming this time from

outside the hospital and further down the corridor as it passed the junction with the access tunnel.

"Let's go," Caleb said, leading them out into the hallway and turning left toward the source of the noise. They passed another pair of dead Guardians before reaching the intersection.

Caleb slowed there, pausing long enough to glance around the corner without being seen or shot. He spotted a pair of Guardians halfway down the hallway. One of them stood over a downed Guardian, firing point blank into his helmet while Caleb watched.

Additional gunfire sounded from an adjacent tunnel, along the path he had seen Anna chasing Namaya earlier.

Caleb quickly gestured to Damian and Penn to go down the alternate corridor while he and Orin chased after the first group of Guardians. They nodded and turned back while he and Orin broke cover and rushed the Guardians in the hall. Caleb raised his blaster and fired at one killer as they noticed him coming their way. The blasts hit him dead-center in the chest but didn't penetrate his armor, leaving only scorch marks behind.

The infected Guardian raised his weapon toward Caleb's head. A sharp crack echoed through the passageway as Orin leaped over Caleb's shoulder, landing on top of the soldier and driving all four claws into his neck, riding the stricken soldier to the floor.

Backpedaling away from Caleb and Orin, the other infected Guardian fired wildly at them. They ducked to either side of the tunnel while plasma bolts zipped down the center of the passageway, hitting the wall at the intersection. Caleb returned fire, distracting the shooter while Orin charged him on all fours, launching across the gap with the speed of a cheetah. He growled as he lunged at the Guardian, once more digging his claws in and bringing the man down.

Gunfire echoed further ahead, along with a woman's shout. It had to be Ling.

Caleb and Orin sprinted along the corridors into a tunnel, hoping they were still heading down the right passageway, since they hadn't heard any more screams or gunfire to give them a clue as to where the infected Guardians were going or why. The route took them outside the primary complex, beyond the inhabited areas of the old mining complex. Iagorth had already done more than kill Haverblaad and stop the blood tests. He had forced the rebels into a tough decision. Wait until they had the equipment to resume the testing, or let everyone board Lo'ane with no idea who might be on the enemy's side. Meanwhile, the Specters from Caprum would be here in days, further limiting their options.

They caught up to two more infected Guardians as they rounded another corner, the two women posted outside an open door. They were waiting for Caleb to arrive, peppering him with plasma rifle fire.He rolled sideways to avoid it as Orin charged. One woman tracked him with her rifle, a bolt catching him in the shoulder. Though his underlay reduced the impact, Caleb growled in pain before leaping away to escape her continuing fire.

He came up shooting at the other Guardian, placing a group of energy blasts center mass, the force of the hits sending her stumbling backward until she fell, not dead but stunned. While still on one knee, he took a plasma bolt off his coat from the other Guardian. Though the material absorbed the bolt, it melted the area around the contact point. Pivoting on his knee, he fired back at her just as Orin's front paws pressed against his back. He braced himself, taking Orin's weight as the Jiba-ki launched himself over Caleb. He crashed into the shooter, a quick slash of his claws across her throat ending her life. He came up, holding a hand to the second hit he'd taken, this one to his abdomen.

"Orin, are you okay?" Caleb asked as he stood, placing a hand on his shoulder.

"It burns," Orin said, drawing a deep breath, "but I have suffered worse."

Caleb patted his shoulder. "Let's go then."

They advanced through the open door into what appeared to be the facility's power plant. A pair of smaller reactors with thick conduits running from them occupied each wall. A simple control terminal was placed on the far side, nearly twenty meters away. Ling stood in front of the terminal, her back to him. A pair of Guardians, perhaps the room's original guards, were sprawled out, dead on the floor between Ling and Caleb, plasma rifle wounds to their torsos still smoldering.

"Qiao," Caleb called out.

She ignored him, tapping on the terminal controls. He couldn't see what she was doing, but Orin had not only better eyesight but a better line of sight.

"She's shutting down the power," he hissed softly. "Without it, there will be no heat. We will all freeze. It is true."

Forcing a quicker evacuation to Lo'ane. There are moieties still in hiding among the Guardians. Iagorth wants them on the ship.

Caleb tensed in response to Ishek's spot on insight. *Do you think they were infected the entire time?*

Perhaps only one, who spread moieties to the others.

Campbell?

It almost seems too obvious.

Haas?

There's no way to know. They could be in anyone. We need to test them.

There might not be enough time.

Then we need to leave whoever isn't tested behind. There's no other way to be sure.

Then we need to stop Ling from shutting down the power, but we need her alive. "Doctor Ling!" he shouted, again trying to get her attention. She opened a menu on the terminal and began typing.

Caleb knew the khoron couldn't have completely taken her over as. Not yet. "Fight it, Qiao! You're still stronger than your khoron."

She paused.

"Orin, what if we shoot the terminal?" Caleb asked.

"Emergency protocols may also deactivate the reactors. Terminals deep in mines are not intended to be shot."

"Qiao, listen to me," he continued in a loud voice. "I know they put a moiety in you, but I also know you're strong enough not to let it win. You can fight it. You can stop it."

She cannot. Get the information you need and then kill her.

If I ask about Lo'ane's daughter, Iagorth will know about her, too.

He might already know.

He might not.

Then kill her and be done with it.

She resumed typing. An emergency shutdown button appeared on the screen.

"Qiao, you're a doctor," Caleb pleaded. "You took an oath to do no harm. If you shut down the reactor, you may kill us all!"

She paused again. This time, she turned around, clarity in her eyes as her gaze met his. Tears already rolled down her cheeks, one side mixing with blood where a plasma bolt had grazed the side of her head. "Caleb," she said, the strain obvious in the muscles on her forehead, and in her trembling arm, which seemed desperate to reach for the button. "Kill me. Now. Please."

He almost hesitated for too long. She spun suddenly, her arm stretching toward the terminal screen. He didn't even realize he had pulled the trigger until she slumped to her knees, out of reach of the shutdown switch. She glanced back at him, her eyes dark and angry.

"This galaxy is mine. It is inevitable."

She collapsed and didn't move again.

Don't forget to destroy the moiety.

How?

Plasma should do it.

Caleb recovered a plasma rifle from one of the dead guards and approached Ling. Reaching over her, he canceled the manual shutdown completely.

"Captain," Damian said over his comms patch. "The infected Guardians are neutralized."

"Not yet," he replied. "Check them all. Find the moieties and burn them with plasma."

"Aye, Captain."

"What about Campbell?"

"Dead, sir, but not by our hand. Killed by the infected."

No longer useful to Iagorth, Ishek surmised.

We should have detained him when he refused the blood test.

It was already too late.

"We're secure here, too," Caleb said to Damian. "Iagorth got to Ling. He used her to attempt to turn off the power to the complex. Orin and I stopped her, but I lost my chance to talk to her about Lo'ane's daughter."

"Captain," Penn said. "We found her assistant, Merrick. He's injured but still alive. He might know something."

"If we can help him. We don't have a doctor anymore. I'll be there as soon as I can."

"Aye, Captain."

Caleb waited nearly another minute before the moiety appeared, the blob oozing out of Ling's mouth. He didn't want to defile her body by shooting it there, and it seemed intelligent enough to recognize that. It sat mockingly on her lips, daring him to shoot it.

"Have it your way," Caleb said, changing the plasma rifle's setting from bolt to stream. "This galaxy will never be yours. No human inhabited galaxy will ever be yours."

He looked away as he squeezed the trigger, refusing to watch the hot gas melt the moiety and Ling's flesh around it.

He walked away, angrier and more determined than ever.

CHAPTER 21

After the bloodbath that had resulted in the deaths of both their doctors, the rebels weren't about to make the same mistake twice.

Iagorth had played his hand, exposing some of his moieties and revealing the likelihood that more secret copies of himself remained among the Guardians. With that in mind, Caleb had worked with General Haas and Duke Draco to gather every member of the resistance into a single, enormous cavern within the mining complex and had put them under guard by members of Caleb's crew. Even Sasha stood along the cavern's perimeter, hefting a plasma rifle while Draco's personal physician, Doctor Ambrose Burne, helped a trio of the Draconian flagship's medical personnel administer blood tests.

It had taken almost two entire days to repair the damaged testing machine and get the entire process back underway. Caleb had barely had a moment to close his eyes during that time, his hours jam packed with needed organizational tasks. Losing two days on Rakusha meant making up time somewhere else, but it was necessary to ensure that the handoff of Lo'ane to Haas went as smoothly as possible.

If everything went well, he would never step foot on the Specter again, instead returning to Gorgon to begin his quest to find Lo'ane's successor.

Ham had decided to stay with the rebels for the time being, since they needed him more than Caleb did. Jack wouldn't be coming with him, either. As Caleb had hoped, when given the choice, the kid had remained on board the Specter to lend his khoron-infused abilities to the rebels. Already, Haas had picked up potential targets from Klim's network of child spies, who had gathered the intel in brothels, bars, and on the streets across the Draconian territories. They'd also confirmed fifteen Specters of the twenty that were at Caprum were on the way to Rakusha and that they had three days to clear out before the enemy arrived.

The only wrinkle was that the rebels had nowhere safe to go. Draco's continued loyalty to the Empire and their success on Rakusha hadn't only made the duke a pariah, Crux sent ships to Duke Clayborne's territories as well, preemptively removing him from power before he too could turn against the Legion. From what Caleb had heard, the duke had barely escaped with his life, half his fleet destroyed in the effort. The only silver lining was that it was practically a given that Clayborne would join the resistance now. He hadn't refused to bend a knee to Crux just to drift aimlessly across the Spiral until he died.

Haas had ultimately decided to take Lo'ane to the sector of space where Caleb had stashed the two cargo haulers.There they would unload the members of their retinue who weren't combat qualified, while uploading the military supplies and equipment Caleb had left for them. From there, they would attack Crux's assets, similar to how Caleb had used Gorgon to harass and steal. The Guardians needed to be daring enough to gain notice from the general population of the Spiral, while cautious enough not to get themselves killed.

Caleb knew they had the easy job.

As he entered the hospital, his eyes drifted to the bed where Haverblaad had died. Someone had changed the sheets, of course, but he could still see the hint of dark stain beneath them, the mattress irreplaceable. He swallowed hard, pangs of guilt sweeping across his innards as he nodded to one of Draco's nurses, who hurried out the door toward the testing area. Continuing halfway, he paused at one partition, leaning his head around and knocking on the outside.

Merrick's eyes fluttered open, and he looked up at Caleb, a pain-ridden smile easing across his face. "Caleb," he said. "I was wondering when you would show up to pay your respects."

"Are you dying then?" Caleb asked.

"Sure feels like it. Gut shot ruined a good part of my left lung, and I came within a couple pints of bleeding out. I almost died. For real, not like that trick you pulled back on Galatin."

"Are you still mad at me for that?"

"A little." He tried to laugh, his face screwing up in pain.

"You heard about Qiao?" Caleb asked.

Merrick nodded. "I feel responsible."

"*You* feel responsible? I'm the one who screwed this up. I thought there was one mole. Maybe one moiety. Not an entire unit. I should have known better. Ishek always tells me not to underestimate his kind, and I still manage to make monumental mistakes."

"Qiao was such a good friend to me, and when she needed my protection the most, I couldn't give it to her," Merrick said. "I tried."

"That's all anyone can do. If you want to beat someone up, take it out on me."

"Nah," Merrick said. "You saved all of us here. The stars always seem to claim their share, no matter what you do."

He stared up at Caleb, eyebrows arching. "You didn't only come to see how I was feeling, did you?"

"That was the most important reason, but no."

"I don't know how I can help you like this, but if there's anything I can do..."

"What do you know about Empress Lo'ane having a child?" Caleb asked.

Merrick tried to smile again, but the pain won out and his face tightened. "Nothing like getting right to the point." He closed his eyes. "I remember when the Empress told Qiao to forget about her daughter. I asked her later about that comment." His eyes opened again. "She didn't want to tell me at first, but she needed to confide in someone and she trusted me."

"What did she say?"

"I promised her I wouldn't tell anyone."

"I respect that, and normally I wouldn't push, but it's important that the Empress has a successor."

"I suppose since she's one with the stars now, the need for the promise died with her. At least under the circumstances. Apparently, the empress had an illegitimate child with a Royal Marine cadet she met following a tour of the Imperium. She never expected to become pregnant, and she did everything she could to keep her father from finding out. Of course, she confided in Qiao. They were best friends. It was Qiao who suggested she find an excuse to go off-world for a while, to have the child in secret and put it up for adoption."

"Do you know where she went to deliver?" Caleb asked.

Merrick shook his head. "No. All I know is that Empress Lo'ane kept watch over her daughter for nearly twenty years. Watching her grow from afar, she decided she didn't like the type of person her daughter had become. She swore to Qiao that her offspring would never have even the smallest piece of the Empire."

Why do I get the feeling I would like Lo'ane's daughter very much?

"She must be something else for her own mother to revile her," Caleb said.

"Yeah, it seemed pretty bad."

"Qiao never mentioned anything about her to you? A name? A location? Even a hint of where she might be?"

"No. I'm sorry. I don't think she knew. The Empress never gave her a lot of detail."

"I had hoped to find a clue where to look for her that didn't include raiding the Royal Archives," Caleb said. "You're sure you have nothing that might help?"

"No. I'm sorry. That's it."

"During that same conversation, Lo'ane mentioned she had instructed who was to take the throne after her. Do you know anything about that?"

"That one I can answer, but you need to lean in close."

Caleb did as Merrick asked before pausing, wondering if it was a trick. He hated that he even needed to question it. "This is as close as I get. I can hear you."

Merrick nodded, keeping his voice low and glancing toward the door. "It was supposed to be Istari."

"Draco's daughter?"

"Yes. The Draco family has been loyal to the Empire for generations, and Istari has the same brave spirit that Lo'ane did. They're similar in a lot of ways."

"Why didn't anyone tell Istari about this?"

"From what I've heard, Duke Draco did. She refused."

Caleb could hardly believe it. "Why?"

"I don't know. That's just what I heard."

Caleb nodded, patting Merrick on the leg. "Thank you for the intel. I hope you heal up quickly."

"Thank you, Caleb. I hope what I gave you helps, even in some small way."

"I'm sure it will."

"Thanks for coming by."

They shook hands before Caleb left the hospital, returning to the cavern where the Guardians were being tested. He found Istari near the corner with Anna and Namaya. The toddler was having a great time riding on Orin's back as he galloped around, leaping and bucking like a horse. Caleb wasn't immediately sure which one of them was having more fun.

Are you going to ask her about her rejection of the title?

No, he'd decided. *I think I know why she turned it down. She's not a blood relative, which makes her claim only slightly stronger than Crux's. And like she mentioned during the meeting, that's not enough to dislodge the population's desire for peace, even if it means living under Relyeh rule.*

I suppose that means we're going to Atlas.

Yeah, I guess it does. Right into the middle of the hornet's nest.Can we kick it over while we're there?

Caleb smiled. *You never know.*

CHAPTER 22

None of the blood tests directly uncovered any of the additional infected. Instead, Iagorth's hosts were discovered by elimination, as they all refused to show up for the test. Eight in total, they'd apparently been selected for their unremarkable positions within the group. None of them were trained military, but rather support staff like Ki Huan, one of the Royal Palace's chefs, and the botanist Gertie Winthrop.

Since Iagorth hadn't been able to use them to create a second round of chaos, he had marched them off to succumb during the day to the extreme heat of the desert or to freeze to death at night. General Haas had sent out search parties of course, but with limited time before the Legion fleet arrived they could only hunt for the missing infected for so long. Caleb had hoped to find and subdue them, with an opportunity to find a way to remove the moieties without killing the host. But it never came to be. Only Gertie was ultimately located, at the bottom of a mine shaft. Whether or not she had fallen accidentally was undetermined. They left the other seven infected behind.

Already on board Gorgon, Caleb and Damian waited in

the hangar for Elena, Johan, Tae, Fitz, and Bones to arrive, along with most of the ship's crew who had been deployed to Lo'ane after her capture. As expected, both Jack and Amali had remained behind on the Specter, as had four of the engineering team from Tonneau. What had surprised Caleb was both Elena and Johan deciding not to remain on board Lo'ane. As former Royal Navy, they were perfect candidates to rejoin the Guardians, but it turned out that they both preferred being pirates. Or at least remaining under Caleb's command.

The shuttle eased through the hanger doors and across Gorgon's deck, rotating to face the bay doors before gently touching down between Medusa and Kitana. The rear of the craft dropped open, creating a ramp. Elena was first off the ship, a duffel slung over her shoulder. She smiled at Caleb and Damian as she approached, standing at attention in front of them.

"Captain," she said with a nod. "Lieutenant Commander Shirin reporting for duty."

Caleb returned the gesture. "Welcome back aboard Gorgon, Lieutenant Commander."

"Thank you, Captain." Her eyes shifted to Damian. "Sarge."

"Good to have you back, Ellie," he said. "I've been working way too hard."

She smiled and turned around as the others streamed out of the back of the shuttle with their duffels.

"If you'll excuse us," Caleb said as Tae descended the ramp behind Johan.

"Captain," Johan said on seeing him approach.

"Welcome back, Johan," Caleb replied without looking at him. "We'll catch up shortly. Tae."

The other engineer stopped walking, regarding Caleb suspiciously. "Aye, Captain? You have the look of a man who's about to swallow a mouthful of piss. And I'm the piss."

"I'm afraid so," Caleb agreed. "I'm placing you under detention. Sarge and I will escort you to the brig."

Tae froze in place, his eyes darting between the two men. For a long moment, Caleb thought the engineer might try to run, which considering the limited confines of the ship would have been a pointless idea. Logic won out, and he shrugged. "Okay." He put out his wrists. "Do you want to cuff me or anything?"

"I don't think that'll be necessary," Caleb said. "You seem a lot more accepting of this than Naya was."

"I don't love the idea, but I understand your point of view. Someone keeps screwing things up for us, and we're the most likely suspects. Therefore, you need to keep us contained."

"Exactly."

"And you'll let us out as soon as things go wrong again."

"If they go wrong again."

"They will, Captain. Naya and I are both loyal members of this crew. Neither of us is your traitor."

"How can you be sure it isn't Naya?" Caleb asked.

"She offered to sleep with me if I would help her with Graystone's accounts. She was terrified of failure. Now, I'm not against such offers at their root level, but she was such a sad case I couldn't bring myself to cash in. Anyway, the accounts were already locked out, and there was nothing I could do."

Either Naya's motive is honest, or they're working together.

Which we can't rule out, Caleb replied to Ishek. "I'll take that into consideration for her. But you realize you're incriminating yourself even more."

He shrugged again. "I have nothing to hide, Cap. You have my permission to search my quarters, my workshop, anything that makes you feel better. You can interrogate me, too. I won't lie." He looked around the hanger, where Elena and Johan had remained behind to wait. "You should probably take me in, I'm sure you have a lot to do."

"Sarge, I'll take Tae down," Caleb decided. "Sync up with Draco and Haas. They'll be departing soon. Bring Johan and Elena with you."

"Aye, Captain."

"Tae, let's go."

Caleb and Tae walked side-by-side, making their way toward the brig. Tae spoke up as soon as they had exited the hangar. "Captain, one concern is that I won't be able to work on the wormhole problem if I'm locked up without access to my research. I know the cells have pads inside, but I imagine you've already confiscated them, since Naya and I could both use them to access more sensitive systems, like the comms."

"We removed the pads," Caleb replied, though the comment still gave him pause. "Would that access be detectable?"

"You mean by Johan? Probably, but he'd have to know where and when to look."

"Could someone spoof the comms so that it looked like it came from the active terminal, even if it hadn't originally?"

"No need to spoof it. Just route the data to that terminal and erase the trail behind the access. Again, there would be breadcrumbs left behind but difficult to identify without specifically searching for them. You're worried someone bypassed your firewall, aren't you?"

"It crossed my mind. Should I be worried?"

"Yeah, probably. But Naya and I will be in the brig so it won't be a problem anymore."

He said it with no hint of malice or upset. It was simply a statement of fact that left Caleb with a growing certainty that he was barking up the wrong tree. Then again, with

Naya and Tae neutralized, the person responsible would need to be more careful if they didn't want to be caught.

"What about the wormhole problem?" Caleb asked. "We haven't checked in on that in a while."

"I have a theory about the algorithm, but I had to drop it once we transferred to Lo'ane. I won't have a chance to test it now, either."

"Can you verbalize it?"

"For one thing, I don't think the wormhole occurred naturally. I think it's an artifact."

"An artifact? You mean someone intentionally made it?"

"I'm not going that far. I think it may be residual pollution from some other attempt to twist spacetime. An unintended side effect. Which isn't really that important regarding traveling through it. I built a model from Benning's notes. Once I finish my theoretical work and plug it in, I can start tweaking it so that it matches your actual experience. That'll be our best step toward solving the equation."

"Based on what you have, do you think it's possible to go through the wormhole in the opposite direction?"

"Yes. I think it's possible. As you know, the wormhole has a spiraling funnel shape. Going back the other way means traversing into the narrow end, which is much more difficult for a human to navigate. And hitting the sides means being ejected from the spacetime dilution and into... I don't know where or what. Maybe vaporized."

"I'm sure you know, I don't really want to lock you up. It's a precaution, nothing more."

"I know. Limiting the variables is the smart move. At least I don't need to wear a shirt in the brig."

When they reached the brig, Naya stood as they entered, grinning when she saw Tae. "At least you're a man of your word, Captain."

"Good to see you too, Nye," Tae said. He opened the

door to the cell next to hers, stepped in, and pulled it closed behind him. "I hope you won't mind my snoring."

"As long as you keep your shirt on, we'll be fine," she answered.

Caleb couldn't stop himself from laughing as Tae frowned. "I don't want to cause any distress with my impeccable physique."

"I intend for this to be a temporary arrangement," Caleb said. "Tae gave me some tips to dig deeper into system operations that might help uncover the real threat."

"So you believe I'm not responsible now?" Naya asked.

"I'm leaning that way, but honestly I don't know what to believe. Which is why you're both here. Give me some time."

Naya didn't look happy, but she nodded. "Aye, Captain."

"Elena is back on board. Reach out to her or Bones if you need anything."

"Aye, Cap," Tae said, flopping down on the mattress. "At least I can catch up on my beauty sleep."

Caleb left the brig, heading to the bridge. Johan had taken Naya's position at the systems terminal. Everyone else was in their usual places. Damian stood in front of the command seat, on audio-only comms with Draco and Haas.

"Captain Card just arrived," he said.

"Captain," Draco said. "The fleet is ready for departure. I wanted to wish you the best of luck with your efforts. You have the gratitude of the Draconian territories and the Empire at large for your support."

"Thank you, Duke Draco," Caleb replied. "I'll report back as soon as I can. In the meantime, be careful. I promised Ham I would get him home to his family, and I still intend to keep that promise. Bring him back to me breathing, please."

"Lieutenant Abraham will be as safe as any of us on

Lo'ane," Haas said. "Thank you for the ship, Captain. Knowing its capabilities and the protection it offers has already raised morale among the Guardians. We needed it after what happened in the mines."

"Good hunting to both of you," Caleb said. "The plan is set. Now, it's up to each of us to execute it."

"For the Empire," Draco said.

"For the Empire," Haas repeated.

"For humankind," Caleb said. "Gorgon out."

Sasha closed the comms. A few seconds later, the sensor grid showed growing hyperspace fields around the assembled starships, thirty-two in total with Lo'ane at the center.

"Rufus, are we ready to jump?" Caleb asked.

"Aye, Captain. On your command."

"Initiate hyperspace field. Let's go find a princess."

CHAPTER 23

Of course, as fugitives wanted by the Royal Guard for piracy and treason, there was no way Caleb could bring Gorgon anywhere near Atlas without drawing a lot of the wrong attention and risking everyone's quick demise. And that was only the first complication. With the Royal Archives in the Imperium, they would still be anything but easy to access, even once the away team reached the surface of Atlas.

For Caleb, planning the ingress was the focus of every second he spent awake during the nine-day journey to the Spiral's center, and it took Ishek virtually what little time he slept to process all the options. Finally, multiple meetings with senior staff, including Damian, Elena, Orin, Penn, and Johan, pulled a tenuous plan together, but no matter how they sliced it, every approach remained over-saturated with risks and uncertainties.

Reaching the Imperium Royal Archives and extracting the data they needed would be one of the hardest things Caleb had ever done. Given a choice, he would have gone another round against Arluthu before picking this level of espionage. He was a Marine after all, not James Bond or Ethan Hunt.

That brought him back to the subject of reaching Atlas' surface, which found him entering the hangar bay where Penn, Fitz, and Johan waited. His away team, though the engineer was definitely a reluctant participant. He had begged to stay behind and run the technical part of the operation from orbit, or at the very least operate from Medusa's safer confines. But the archives weren't accessible on the hypernet, which meant he had to be present when they reached the single terminal in the Imperium with access to that datastore.

"Sarge, ETA to field expansion?" Caleb asked over his comms patch as he approached the shuttle.

"Seven minutes," Damian replied.

The first stage of the plan was the easiest. Gorgon would drop out of hyperspace behind Atlas' star and release Medusa before tucking in as close to the star as they dared. At that point, the ship would go dark, running only emergency life support systems that would hopefully keep it from attracting attention. The reduced output would no doubt cause the interior to heat, which meant they would need to leave within eighteen hours. If that meant stranding the away team on Atlas, then so be it.

Medusa would continue to Atlas under a false identifier. While the shuttle wasn't a common build, it had enough presence in the galaxy not to be instantly suspicious. As long as Atlas Orbital Control didn't look too closely or think too hard about their ID, they would be permitted to land, the first stage completed.

It seemed simple enough, but Caleb knew how many things could go wrong at the least opportune time. It had happened before.

And yet we're still alive, Ishek reminded him.

One day, that won't be true, Caleb replied.

Perhaps. But that day isn't today.

How do you know?

Because I said it. Do not make me a liar.

"Knuckle up people," Caleb said as he reached his team. "We're T-Minus seven minutes. Is all the gear stowed?"

"Aye, Captain," Penn replied. "Nice suit, by the way."

Caleb glanced down at his formal attire. They had decided to go in as white-collar business types, in full suits that easily hid their underlays. Fashion in the Spiral meant Penn wore pants too, though hers were high-waisted and hugged her curves. Caleb didn't mind the Spiral's version of formal attire as much as he had Earth's. He liked the lighter, more comfortable material it was made of, but the best thing about it...no tie. However, perusing himself in the mirror, he'd concluded that the rounded collars made him look like a priest. Otherwise he thought he looked pretty good. And the jacket did a great job hiding his blaster and a knife.

"You look pretty spiffy yourself," he replied, grinning at her.

Johan growled, tugging at the tighter fit of his suit collar versus his loose coveralls. "The only good thing about hauling cargo for Crux's Navy was that the Legion didn't enforce a dress code. "Are you sure you need me to tag along, Cap?"

"Sorry, Johan. I absolutely need you to tag along. And if you think that suit is bad, wait until later."

"If we get to later," he complained.

They boarded Medusa. While the others went directly to the main cabin, Caleb stepped onto the flight deck with Atrice, securing himself in the co-pilot seat.

"You know this whole thing is insane, don't you, Captain?" Atrice asked.

"What's more insane is that there's a part of me that's enjoying the hell out of it already," Caleb replied. "What happens here today could ultimately make the difference in the war's outcome."

"I'm excited to be your pilot for it, Cap. Though returning to Atlas is tough."

"I understand. Just stay focused, and let me do the talking."

"Aye, Captain. No problem there."

The seven minutes to expansion felt like seven years to Caleb, who waited impatiently to get the mission started. Despite the risky nature of the plan, he had confidence his team would put forth their best effort, and if they failed, it wouldn't be from fear or from lack of trying.

"You're cleared for launch as soon as the expansion is complete," Damian said. "T-Minus ten seconds and counting. Good hunting out there, Captain."

"Thank you," Caleb replied. "Remember, don't stick around if we aren't back in time. We'll meet at the secondary rendezvous point. You know what to do if we don't show up at all."

"Aye, Captain. But let's not entertain that morbid thought, shall we? At least not at this point. We have our fingers crossed. Hyperdrive is winding down, expansion has started."

Warning lights flashed beside the hangar doors. They started slowly opening, the hyperspace field visible between them, the universe curving around the distortion in spacetime. Atrice fired up the thrusters and lifted Medusa off the deck, drifting slowly forward using only vectoring nozzles.

"How close are we?" Caleb asked.

"Twenty minutes out from our optimal drop point," Damian replied. "Still close enough we shouldn't draw attention but we'll be running bright longer than we wanted. There's no reason for you to stick around while we maneuver."

An auspicious beginning. I hope our luck improves.

Luck always balances out. A bad turn in the beginning usually leads to a good one later on.

You keep telling yourself that.

"Should I launch, Captain?" Atrice asked.

"Confirmed. You're go for launch," he replied.

Atrice pushed the throttle forward, sending Medusa out through the hangar door and away from Gorgon. Atrice made a hard turn to starboard, bringing them over the top of Gorgon. The forward viewscreen worked overtime to filter the sudden blast of light from Atlas' life-giving star, which filled the entire flight deck. Caleb squinted against it despite the filter as Atrice punched the throttle to full.

His initial surge of excitement faded quickly, replaced by the monotony of sub-light travel. Their ingress position left them four hours away from Atlas' orbit, which he perceived as the next thing to a lifetime.

Things got a lot more exciting as they drew closer to the planet. While Aroon had had a steady stream of ships moving in and out of the surrounding orbit, Atlas was its own beast. Instead of dozens of ships, there were hundreds, if not thousands, arranged around the planet everywhere Caleb looked—arriving, departing, or simply loitering. The variety was unending. The assortment of sizes, shapes, and conditions reminded him of the parking lot of Petco Park after a baseball game, only it felt more crowded.

His breath caught a little when he spotted the Specters among the chaos, eyes quickly dancing from one to another as he counted them. He spotted eight right away, picking out two more on a recount and certain there were more he had yet to identify. While smaller than the fleet Crux had sent to Caprum, their numbers were still much more than enough to defend the planet from invasion.

"Atrice, open a channel to Atlas Orbital Control," Caleb said.

"Aye, Captain." He tapped on his control screen, nodding to Caleb to make contact.

"Atlas Orbital Control," he said. "This is the starship Boomerang, requesting permission to land at the Haydrun spaceport."

The response came back a few seconds later. "Boomerang, this is Atlas Orbital Control. We're tracking you and passing a loiter marker. Take up position there and await further instructions."

"Thank you, control. Do you have an estimated length for the wait?"

"Inspections are moving more slowly than usual. We're estimating six to eight hours."

Caleb's jaw clenched. They didn't have six hours to wait just to land.

What were you saying about our luck turning?

"I'm sure you hear this a lot, but we're in a bit of a hurry. We're meeting potential clients planetside to pitch them on our new business proposal."

"You'll have to wait like everyone else, Boomerang."

"I have a thousand coin that says we don't," Caleb remarked.

"Boomerang, are you aware that attempting to bribe an orbital control officer is a capital offense?"

"I don't know, am I attempting to bribe anyone?" Caleb glanced at Atrice, who looked back with a pained face. Caleb didn't know if it was because they were on the way to being arrested or because he was handling control like a two-bit mobster.

"It appears as if one ship in the cue failed to pay their landing fee," the officer said.

"That's a shame," Caleb replied. "How much is the fee?"

"Fifty-thousand coin."

"Transferring now. I don't want to be late with the payment and miss my place in line."

Control was silent for a minute. "This is strange. It looks like we've had a spate of cancellations and reschedules. You're sixth in line, Boomerang."

"That's great news!" Caleb exclaimed. "For us, anyway. We're nearing the loiter marker now."

They still ended up waiting nearly thirty minutes before control came back on the line. "Boomerang, you've been passed over for inspection based on the size of your transport. You're cleared for atmospheric entry. Follow the guide path into Haydrun spaceport."

"Copy that, Control. Have a wonderful day."

Caleb nodded to Atrice, who redirected Medusa toward Atlas, winding around the other waiting ships as they jumped the line. Finally clear of traffic, Caleb looked down on the planet with a sense of wonder, his eyes searching the landscape. Atlas appeared to be a slightly larger version of Earth with different shaped land masses. Otherwise, he could have been fooled by the identical cloud covering and colors, the gravity, the molecular composition of the atmosphere, and more. It almost made him homesick.

His gaze settled on the portion of the largest continent where Control's marker flashed. Haydrun Municipal Spaceport sat just outside the capital city of the same name, a massive landing field that appeared as speckled gray from their current distance. It nearly matched the size of a small city.

Not that Haydrun was small. It spread for kilometers in every direction, a sea of tall skyscrapers interlaced with a surprising amount of greenery. An incredible sight to behold, it stood for what New York, London, Tokyo, or any other large Earth city might have become if given another hundred years to prosper.

He found the Imperial Palace first. Near the center of Haydrun, it broke up the rows of tall buildings and modern construction with its throwback style. Likely modeled after

Buckingham Palace, it sat long and low, occupying nearly ten full city blocks, with large gardens surrounding the primary structure. He would have liked to see more of it, but knowing who it now belonged to left his hands clenched with anger.

"Captain, look to the port side and out toward the mountains," Penn said over the comms.

Caleb found the feed on the left side of the viewscreen. His heart immediately started racing, his eyes fixing on the hulk of metal somewhat hidden beneath a moss and vine shell.

Pathfinder.

He had left Proxima to find the ship, and there it was.

CHAPTER 24

A narrow road led away from Pathfinder toward the city, but there was no indication anyone still visited the craft. It had become little more than a fixture in the landscape, forgotten by the population who owed that ship and its original crew for their existence. Then again, the Relyeh had seen to it that most of the people in this universe didn't even know where Pathfinder had come from.

Caleb promised himself he would visit the ship the next time he came to Atlas, right after returning the Empire to its rightful heir.

"Captain," Atrice said. "We're coming up on final approach."

Caleb tore his eyes from Pathfinder, returning his attention to the center of the viewscreen. He didn't have time to locate the Imperium during the descent. The landing marker was near the front of the spaceport, tucked into a small zone between a pair of larger pleasure yachts.

"It looks like that fifty-thousand bought us the VIP treatment, sir," Atrice added.

"I guess so," Caleb replied with a grin. They wouldn't need to wait for a ground shuttle to swing past their landing zone. The spot was close enough to walk straight into the spaceport's primary arrival gate.

Atrice guided them smoothly through the atmosphere and down onto the tarmac. They landed gently, engines shutting off as Medusa shuddered slightly before settling on her skids. Caleb unstrapped himself and rose from his seat. "You know the deal, Cookie. We'll be back in ten hours or less."

"Aye, Captain. We'll be here."

Caleb left the flight deck behind, joining up with Penn, Fitz, and Johan beside the main hatch. Penn carried a large handbag, which she opened and reached into, separating the lining to reveal a hidden compartment inside. "Weapons, boys," she said with a smile.

Caleb removed his blaster from under his coat and dropped it into the bag, as did Fitz.

"I'm not carrying," Johan said.

"I gave you a blaster," Fitz said.

"I've never used one before. It felt like more of a liability than a benefit, so I left it behind."

Fitz sighed. "Being an engineer only is a choice."

"What's that supposed to mean?"

"I think you know perfectly well what it means."

"Focus, people," Caleb said. "We made it to the surface; now the hard part begins."

Penn closed the bag's hidden compartment before throwing an assortment of items from her coat pockets in on top of it. "Ready," she said, closing it back up.

They exited the shuttle, joining a handful of new arrivals on the way into the spaceport terminal. The inside wasn't that much different from an airport. High, arched ceilings made of colored glass cast light down onto long hallways lined with a variety of shops and eateries. The smell of food wafted through the air. There were no cows or chickens in the Spiral, so the meat came from other creatures that gave off a similar but subtly different scent. The spices were different too, more pungent and less appealing to his nose, but not so much that he detested the smell.

"Ooooh. They have karuti here," Fitz commented, drawing in the smells with a deep breath. "I haven't had karuti in ages."

"What is it?" Caleb asked.

"Marinated karu meat. It melts in your mouth. You have to try it, Cap."

"Maybe later."

Much like an airport on Earth before the war, Caleb and his crew found themselves waiting in a long line to get past security scanners before they could get through the terminal to catch a shuttle to Haydrun proper. The wait gave them time to observe the other travelers around them. Their clothing styles were all a little different than on Earth, but the proportion of business, casual, and in between remained the same.

Fortunately, there were no Royal Armed Forces members bolstering security in the spaceport. Instead, the checkpoints were occupied by orbital control guards dressed in plain brown uniforms. They carried nothing more than simple stunner wands and pistols. Caleb didn't expect any trouble here, but it was always better to be prepared.

They spent twenty minutes advancing to the front of the security line. Once there, a bored-looking guard requested identification and asked a few basic questions before dropping Penn's bag onto a belt that took it through his scanner. The bag went through with no problem, the hidden pouch protecting the guns from the microwaves. After handing over his fake identification and providing false information, Caleb followed the guard's directions to another scanner, passing through it without incident, as did the others. Penn collected her bag, and they were on their way.

"Are you sure we can't stop for karuti?" Fitz asked. "The smell is killing me."

"We're on the clock," Caleb replied. "I'd prefer to return to Gorgon sooner rather than later, and we still need to acquire uniforms and access credentials."

"Maybe I can get an order to go."

"Will you knock it off?" Penn snapped at Fitz.

He fell into a disgruntled silence as they made their way through the spaceport, joining an increasingly dense crowd headed for the shuttle to Haydrun. It all felt so familiar to Caleb. So normal. At the moment, it was as if he was back on Earth, with the trife never having existed. Like the war never happened.

The safe simplicity made him unexpectedly tense. His heart raced, a line of sweat breaking across his forehead. He suddenly couldn't breathe, his eyes taking in the crowds of people, his mind unable to process it all.

Cal, what is wrong?

Ishek's question only confused him more. Nothing looked wrong, but everything felt wrong.

"Cal?" Penn asked, noticing his distress when he slowed and fell back from the group. She hurried back to him, laying her hand on his shoulder. "Are you okay?"

"I don't know," Caleb replied. "I should be, but..."

"He's having a panic attack. PTSD maybe," Fitz said, joining them. "When's the last time you were around so many people?"

"Sixty years?" he guessed.

I can provide hormones that will help.

No. Save it for when I really need it. I-I'll...get through this.

Penn and Fitz looked at one another as the stories they'd heard Caleb tell about his experiences and the related time-line suddenly hit home. "Just breathe," Penn said to him, taking his hand. "Focus on the feel of my hand in yours."

He did as she said, letting her lead him through the

crowds. Fitz did his best to run interference, creating a path for him to move through, while Johan fell back a few steps, creating some space behind him. They made it onto the shuttle, an elongated pod similar to the ones on Aroon that traveled overland instead of beneath the sea. It crossed the ten kilometers into Haydrun in half a minute, which Caleb appreciated. He stayed close to Penn during the ride, her arm wrapped around his, her head on his shoulder. Her empathy and gentleness surprised him. Calmed him.

The shuttle stopped, letting them out in another crowded station. Thanks to the efforts of his crew, Caleb finally released a long shuddering breath, his breathing leveling out. "I'm okay now," he said. "It's passed."

Penn nodded, letting go of his arm. "First time?"

"Yeah. I've been through…things." Frowning, he faintly shook his head, trying to free himself from the memories assaulting his thoughts. The hordes of trife he'd fought his way through and survived while losing his first squad of Vultures. Men and women who'd been like brothers and sisters to him. Yet, he could barely remember their faces, something that left him with so damn much guilt.

"That's why. It's not the chaos of battle that gets to you. It's the lack of it that gives your mind too much time to remember the bad times and process it all. You have trouble with crowds. I have trouble with silence."

"Always?"

"Not always, but usually. It comes and goes. We've got your back, you know."

"I know you do. I'm sorry I lost it."

"Don't be. We've all been through it."

"Speak for yourself," Fitz said. "I haven't."

"You're so full of it." Penn scowled at him.

"Charisma and charm, I know. We can get a taxi over to the Hind quarter once we reach the rooftop." He pointed to a bank of lifts, each cab filling in tight with people before the doors closed. Half went up to transportation, the other half down to street level. They joined the line for a lift going up. A few minutes later they were inside a cab ascending to the roof.

They exited on the top level into another crowded terminal, this one more open than those below, thanks to large windows along three sides. Swooping in to pick up passengers before lifting off again, automated airborne taxis created a constant arc along the rooftop, a line of people winding back and forth in a roped off queue to board the cabs as quickly as possible. When one elderly couple boarded their ride too slowly, the taxi behind them was forced to bypass the roof, drawing shouts of ire from others in line until the well-oiled machine resumed its normally speedy function.

Caleb's team reached their turn within minutes, boarding an empty taxi, two rows of seats facing each other. Penn continued to stay close to Caleb, sitting beside him. Fitz and Johan settled into seats facing them on the other side.

"Where are you headed?" a warm male voice asked through speakers in the cab's roof as it lifted from the rooftop, climbing into the airborne traffic.

"Hind quarter," Fitz replied.

"Acknowledged. Your fare will be sixteen point four-six coin."

Penn reached into her bag, retrieving a personal access device. As she held it up, a laser scanned it, pulling the coin from her account. "I assume you'll reimburse me for all of my expenses, sir?" she asked Caleb.

"Of course," he replied as the taxi changed directions, rising and turning quickly to join a different traffic flow.

Penn had explained during their planning sessions that the Hind quarter had a double-meaning. One, as a play on words for the rear of an animal, and second as a derivative of the word hindrance, given to the area because it was known for being rough and tumble. A far cry from the Imperial Palace or any of the other wealthier neighborhoods most residents aspired toward. Still, compared to a lot of what Caleb had seen on Earth, the area still would have been considered upscale.

Approaching their destination, Caleb noticed the buildings were all at least three stories tall and constructed of stone, each one unique in its own way. There were fewer people on the streets here than in other areas, but most of them wore uniforms of one branch of the Royal Armed Forces or another.

Any Khoron? Caleb questioned Ishek.

None that I can detect, he replied. *But I am keeping a low profile to avoid notice.*

Good idea. I don't imagine khoron care at all about human vices.

Especially since neither they nor their host can get drunk. It is safe to assume these fighters are either clean or carrying moieties.

That's not a welcome epiphany.

Agreed. If Iagorth has moieties in this place, we have already lost.

The taxi landed smoothly, the door opening before the cab had finished slowing to a stop. "Thank you for riding with us," the warm voice said. "Please return soon."

"Thanks," Caleb replied, getting out first.

This time, making their way to the lifts, they descended to ground level with no waiting time. The Hind quarter looked more dilapidated up close than it had from above. The buildings were clearly older and in an advanced state of decay, the stone pock marked from weathering, the mortar cracked and chipping.

Even though business attire apparently wasn't common apparel in the area, the servicemen they passed didn't pay them any mind. Based on Caleb's observations, it seemed like some white collar types frequented the Hind quarter for the action to be found at one of the shadier watering holes.

They walked through the streets toward an open air market filled with tables displaying everything from food and clothing to electronics and toys. Business seemed to be booming, with buyers and sellers haggling over prices and completing deals.

"This way," Fitz said, leading them around the perimeter of the market and through a pair of large doors propped open by stone blocks. The interior of the building was dark compared to the brightness outside. It took time for Caleb's eyes to adjust, his ears immediately picking up loud music coming from somewhere deeper in the building. "It's been a long time since I visited the Mirage."

A popular hangout for the officers stationed at the Imperium, Penn had suggested the venue as the place to go to move their plan forward. It was one of the most exclusive places in the Hind, and the primary reason they had gone with suits over uniforms.

"When were you ever in the Mirage?" Johan asked, showing that he was as familiar with the place as Fitz.

"I used to know someone in the Imperium," he replied. "Her name was Linda."

"You don't mean Linda Aberjani?" Penn asked.

"Yeah."

"Vice. Admiral. Aberjani?"

"Yeah, so?"

"You never told me you knew her."

He shrugged. "I haven't told you a lot of things. Anyway, what does it matter? She died the night Crux seized the Empire, just like all the Imperium's senior officers."

"How can you be so blase about the death of someone

you apparently knew intimately?" Johan asked. "Where are your emotions?"

"We broke up years ago, when she was still a junior officer," Fitz answered, as if that absolved him of all compassion. "Anyway, she had an honorable death. No way I'll ever be able to say the same." He shrugged the whole thing off. "Better pucker up," he said, using his eyes to motion to the combat-armored bouncers guarding the closed double doors to the venue.

They approached the pair, who predictably moved into a more intimidating posture as they neared. Trying to convince the pair that they too worked at the Imperium might have worked, but posing as arms dealers looking to earn their company a leg up on the next supply contract seemed much more efficient.

"Good evening, gentlemen," Fitz said. "My name is—"

"I don't give a flying fig what your name is," the bouncer interrupted. "You here to do business?"

"That's right," Fitz answered, not the least bit phased by the abrupt reproach.

"Then let's do business. Which company do you represent?"

"Nelson Heavy Industries," Penn said. "We specialize in—"

"Why do you keep trying to talk so much? I've never heard of Nelson Heavy Industries. Have you Asali?"

The other guard shook her head. "No, but honestly there are so many arms dealers these days, I've lost track of them all."

"Where are you located?" the first bouncer asked.

"Draconian territories," Fitz said.

"What planet?" Asali asked in a tone that suggested it should have been part of the first answer.

"Capaldi. I have a business ca—"

"What we want to see is your pad, and a flash of your bank account," the first bouncer said.

"You'll get your bribe, but I'm not letting you see our account values first. That would be awful for business."

The bouncers laughed. "That depends on how badly you want to get through these doors."

Do we have to play these games? Ishek asked. *We should take them out and walk over their corpses.*

Caleb glanced around the room. There didn't appear to be any cameras watching them, or anyone else approaching the entrance to the bar. He could put them both down before they knew what hit them.

And you should.

"We don't need to play games," Fitz said. "We all know how this works. How much?"

"The rules have changed," Asali said. "Bad actors are looking to take advantage of our officers. The rebels want to bring down Lord Crux, and that makes the Imperium a target."

"The rebels?" Penn said. "I thought the Legion chased them all to parts unknown?"

"Even if they haven't, we have tech to sell," Fritz added. "New tech that's unlike anything you've ever seen before. It'll help the Legion finish the resistance and bring anyone in line who dares cross the rule of Lord Crux."

The bouncers laughed. "Every dealer who wants to get in says that."

"Maybe so, but I mean it."

"They say that too."

Fitz pulled his pad out of his pocket. Of course, they'd planned for this possibility. His screen showed a logo for the company, along with an identifier. "We're legit. See?"

"Yeah, it looks good," the first bouncer said, eying the logo. "Ten thousand gets you through these doors."

"Shouldn't we check their ID?" Asali asked.

"Yeah, run it." He pointed at Fitz. "You send the transfer."

"Before you check the ID?" Fitz asked, screwing up his face.

"Why? Are you worried it won't check out?"

Fitz smiled. "Pads?"

Asali had already taken hers out of a pocket to check their company identifier. Fitz pointed his pad at it, transferring the funds. Caleb glanced back at Johan, the engineer nodding almost imperceptibly. The funds had transferred successfully.

"Looks like it's legit," Asali said. "Nelson Heavy Industries on Capaldi. A small company, but making some waves recently." She looked up at them. "Thanks for the lunch money."

"Anytime," Fitz said as the bouncers opened the doors for them to enter the Mirage.

CHAPTER 25

Passing through the doors into the Mirage, Caleb and the others followed Fitz down a corridor toward the music playing somewhere ahead of them.

"What did I tell you?" Fitz said. "I knew our plan would work."

"You ass, you told me my plan would never work," Johan said. "We wouldn't have gotten in without it."

"I would have figured something out."

"You should probably turn the signal hijack off now," Caleb said. "Great work, both of you."

"I'm just getting warmed up," Fitz said.

The corridor ended at another pair of closed doors, which automatically opened into an expansive room filled with tables and chairs, all arranged around a stage where a live band played loud enough to shake the floor beneath Caleb's feet. The room was already crowded, but there was a table available near the bar. They made their way there, pulling out the chairs and sitting. Scanning the place, Caleb couldn't help but notice the number of people wearing Royal Armed Forces uniforms. It wasn't so much that there were members of the military here, it was that unless they were infected with Iagorth's moieties, none of these people were beholden to the Relyeh. They were loyal to Crux by choice, traitors to the Empire and to the oaths they had taken when they joined the service. They might not know about Crux's relation to the Hunger, but their sedition made him sick.

"I'm getting us drinks," Fitz said, standing up. "What do you want?"

"Doesn't matter, Ishek will counter the alcohol content anyway," Caleb replied. Penn shook her head while Johan asked for a glass of water.

"Are you serious?" Fitz asked, making a face at Johan.

"You shouldn't drink either," Penn said.

"We're here undercover. We won't stay that way if they see us tossing back nothing but H2O."

Fitz returned with three mugs on a tray, setting them down on the table before taking a long drink out of one. "That hits the spot."

Caleb took a sip of his and smiled. It didn't seem to matter how many light years separated them from Earth. Everywhere in the universe had beer. He drank more deeply, knowing he couldn't get the least bit drunk. Barely able to hear each other over the music, they mostly stayed quiet and watched the surrounding patrons. Caleb's eyes danced over the hardware on the chests of the officers, picking them out by rank. They needed someone with a decent pay grade who looked like they wanted some company. Except most of the patrons appeared to have come in groups or were already paired up.

"This is going to be harder than we thought," Penn said after some time had passed. "We might need to alter our plan."

Caleb was about to reply when he spotted a woman sitting alone at a table near the stage, nursing a drink and looking bored. Her uniform sported two silver bars on either side of a crown—a commodore in the Royal Navy. He tapped his finger against his mug, drawing attention from the others as he nodded subtly toward her. She wasn't bad-looking, but that wasn't why Caleb had picked her out. The way she presented herself made him think she would be more receptive to their offer if only because she looked lonely.

Fitz turned back around, following Caleb's eyes. He smiled when he saw the target. "Good eye, Cap," he said loudly enough for Penn and Johan to hear over the band.

"I don't know," Penn replied, also having to shout. "She looks pretty uptight."

"She is," Fitz replied. "That's Commodore Petra Burke."

"Don't tell me you had a fling with her, too."

He shrugged, an unashamed grin on his face. "We didn't part on the best terms, but that's a fire that never completely extinguished. I'll go talk to her." He moved to stand. Caleb grabbed his wrist before he could leave.

"Are you sure she won't rat us out? She knows you're not an arms dealer."

"Does she?" Fitz said. "How would she know that, Cap? Crystall ball? I disappeared from all this garbage over a year ago. I could be doing anything these days."

"Patch active," Caleb said before letting go of Fitz, who finished rising to his feet. He tapped on his comms patch to keep it turned on before walking over to Commodore Burke's table. Her head swiveled slightly as he approached, looking at him sidelong with a hint of interest that faded almost instantly when her gaze fell on his face. Her forming smile flattened into a pained grimace, which quickly transformed to an angry glare as Fitz reached her.

"Petey," he said, grinning widely, spreading his arms wide in greeting. "It's been a minute."

She stood up angrily, right hand curling into a fist. Caleb's ears burned when she shouted a few choice curses at him while jabbing a finger in his chest hard enough that it looked painful from Caleb's vantage point. Then she stormed away toward another set of doors near the back corner of the bar. Fitz returned to their table, shaking his head and grinning sheepishly.

"You must be a real dog, Fitz," Penn said sarcastically.

"Smooth," Johan added.

"She'll calm down," Fitz replied confidently, returning to his seat. "Give it time."

"She could be on the comms with the Royal Guard right now," Johan complained.

"Nah, she went to the ladies' room. She'll let off some steam, freshen up, probably ask herself what the hell she thinks she's doing thinking about getting involved with me again. She'll go back and forth a few times in the mirror, but at the end, she'll return to her seat and wait for me to approach her again."

"You're a pig," Penn said.

He laughed. "I'm just sitting here enjoying the moment."

"What makes you so great that women react to you that way?"

"Some people have it, some people don't. I do."

"You exploit women is what you do. You're disgusting."

"Hey, I'm a bad guy, Penny. You know how that is."

"Did I say disgusting? I meant deplorable."

Fitz laughed again. "That's why I respect and follow you. You're the one person who sees right through me."

They waited fifteen minutes. Caleb monitored the area where Burke had disappeared, not surprised when she emerged from the crowd, her makeup fresh, her uniform just so. She'd let her hair down, framing her face in auburn waves.

"Showtime," Fitz said, returning to his feet and patting Caleb on the shoulder on his way past.

Caleb monitored his comms patch and sipped his beer

as he watched Fitz from out of the corner of his eye. He pulled out the chair across from Burke and sat down. "You look great, Petey," he said, folding his hands on the table and leaning just slightly toward her. "I see you've been practicing the judo I taught you." He rubbed a thumb over the bruise she'd undoubtedly left on his chest. "That'll leave a mark, you know."

She glared at him again."I certainly hope so. You're a traitor, Fitz. I hate you. " Despite her verbal assault, Caleb could almost see the war raging inside her mind. She obviously knew Fitz was a self-centered, womanizing jerk, but he could see there was something intangible about him she liked and had missed.

"You still missed me. I can tell," Fitz said, shooting her a knowing look. "Found anyone to take my place on the mats yet? I bet you haven't."

"As a matter of fact," she replied, "I haven't found anyone to teach me some new moves since you left."

"Maybe we can rectify that problem," Fitz replied, with just a hint of a smile.

She hesitated. "You know, you're the last person I would have expected to see back at the Mirage."

"Yeah, I didn't exactly plan things this way, either. But business brought me here. You know how that goes."

"You're working for one of our suppliers now?"

"That's right. Nelson Heavy Industries."

"I've never heard of them."

"You will soon enough. I don't suppose you can get me in the door?"

"That depends on how the rest of my night goes."

Caleb raised his eyebrow as he glanced at Penn. She rolled her eyes but said nothing, waiting patiently while Fitz worked Burke. Caleb didn't know if she could help them or not, but Fitz seemed to think she could. He tuned out the conversation between Burke and Fitz through his comms patch within a few minutes, disinterested in their opening small talk and their continued flirting. It wasn't long before they both stood up, leaving together and heading for the exit, Fitz's hand at the small of her back.

Caleb, Penn and Johan looked at one another in silence until Johan spoke. "That's it? We're just going to wait here?"

"No," Caleb replied, sliding his chair back. "We're going to follow them."

CHAPTER 26

Caleb rose from his seat, leaving his beer behind as he headed toward the exit. Penn and Johan followed, catching up to him on the way through the double doors they'd entered through.

"Leaving so soon?" Asali asked, getting Caleb's attention as he approached her. "You paid a lot of coin for such a brief visit."

"You win some, you lose some," Caleb replied. He could hear Fitz chatting with Burke through his comms patch until the smooth-flowing conversation began to break up, leaving progressively more and more blank spots as they moved out of range. "We got a lead. That's all we came for. Have a good night."

He continued out of the building and back into the market. "Johan?" he asked, glancing at the engineer, who pulled out his pad.

"That way," Johan said, pointing. "Down that alley, turn left, two blocks, then take a right and we'll be where they are right now."

"Damn, they're moving fast," Penn said.

"Fitz knows we're on the clock," Caleb replied.

"I doubt that's why."

The streets were quieter now than they had been before, most of the vendors having packed up their goods or closed shop while others left with friends after long days working hard for meager pay.

They turned down a dark alley lined by tall apartment buildings, their reflective windows hiding any potential onlookers. Knowing they appeared to be easy pickings for thieves, Caleb expected them to be jumped at any moment.

We should be so lucky.

I don't want to be delayed, Caleb replied to Ishek's comment.

Penn apparently thought the same. Digging into her bag, she handed him his blaster before retrieving hers. They both stuck the weapons in the backs of their pants, hiding them under their coats. Reaching the end of the alley without a problem, they made the left turn and hurried the two blocks down before turning right. There was no sign of Fitz up ahead, but the comm signal had grown a little stronger. Fitz had lowered his voice, making it hard for Caleb to make out what he was saying, but Burke laughed loudly enough to give them an idea of what Fitz might have said.

"Johan, don't lose them," Caleb said.

"We can take a shortcut down that alley up ahead," he replied.

Caleb led them down it. Unlike the previous alley, unsightly stone walls lined this one on both sides. He imagined the apartment highrises on either side had view screens for windows, each one simulating an appealing outdoor scene of their choice.

They were halfway down the alley when doors at the base of both buildings opened both in front and behind them. A dozen young thugs carrying an array of knives and blunt instruments emerged, quickly surrounding them.

Jackpot!

Caleb fought to keep Ishek's burst of laughter off his face.

"Hand over your pads, and nobody gets hurt," the oldest and apparent leader blurted."

Can I please take over for this?

Not a chance. They're only kids.

You owe me for saving you from Iagorth. Do you remember when I pulled you out?

This isn't the best time.

There is no best time, and I hunger.

I can't believe I'm agreeing to this, but fine. Just don't kill them.

Caleb retreated to the back of his mind as Ishek took control. He didn't hold back his amusement, laughing in the leader's face.

"Are you seriously laughing?" Johan asked, squinting indignantly at Caleb.

"Yeah, man," the gang leader agreed. "Is there something wrong with you? If I don't get those pads in ten seconds, you'll all go to the hospital with multiple lacerations, maybe even concussions. Or maybe you don't make it there alive at all."

Ishek laughed even harder. "If you had any brain cells in your head, you would have turned and run as soon as I started laughing at you." Caleb's expression sobered dramatically. "You are in over your head, pathetic human child. I will only give you one more opportunity to flee before I delight in your terror."

"Ish?" Penn asked, glancing at Caleb.

"In the flesh," he replied.

"What the hell is going on?" Johan whined.

"Do you want to dance?" Ishek asked Penn.

She shrugged. "Why not?"

"Let's teach these assholes a lesson," the gang leader

growled. "Stick 'em." He pulled his own knife and lunged at Caleb, only to find Caleb's hand wrapped like a vice grip around his wrist. Ish squeezed the kid's hand so tight, the weapon dropped from his hand. His eyes widened with fear when Ishek grabbed the wrist of the freckle-faced redhead next to him and twisted it. The bone broke with an audible crack, the smaller kid screaming bloody murder before Ish landed Caleb's size twelve in the center of his chest. The force of it laid him out cold on the pavement, his head bouncing once before lolling to one side and going still.

"I am most delighted," Ishek hissed, baring Caleb's pearly whites and breathing in deeply before punching the gang leader in the temple. He toppled to the ground as well.

Meanwhile, Penn went on the offensive, rushing the nearest gang members. She quickly wrapped an arm around the throat of a black kid with bad acne while locking his foot in hers and pushing him over backwards. She stomped on his groin, using his body to somersault over him, leaving him curled into a fetal ball, wailing and clutching his bruised assets. Done with him, she ducked beneath the swing of a pipe and drove her palm up and into her attacker's nose. It cracked and spewed blood as the kid landed hard on his butt and burst into tears. He sat there, holding his broken nose, blood seeping through his fingers. A hefty girl ran past him screaming like a banshee and swinging a pipe.

Johan's eyes widened in numb horror as she came at him. Until that moment, he'd just been standing there, a virtual spectator. About to take the pipe in the side of his head, he was too slow in backpedaling away. Right before it collided with Johan's head, Caleb's hand caught the pipe as though it was barely moving. He pulled the weapon and Johan's attacker forward, ripping the pipe out of her hand.

She took one look at the crazed look on Caleb's face, punctuated by his insane laughter, and ran screaming down the alley as if the hounds of hell were on her heels.

Still laughing, Ishek turned to look for another target, only to find the gang retreating through the apartment doors, which closed behind them, leaving only one kid trapped outside. Still clutching himself in obvious pain, he stumbled to his feet, clearly terrified as Ishek walked toward him.

"I huunnnnggeeerrrr," Ishek growled.

A wet stain appeared on the kid's pant leg, and he sprinted down the alley, vanishing around the corner.

"Now, that is what I call amusement," Ishek said, brushing imaginary dirt off Caleb's hands as he turned back around. "You should participate next time, Johan."

"Uh, I'm good," Johan replied. "Really."

Ish, time's up.

Ishek didn't argue. Satisfied with his meal, he returned control to Caleb.

"Johan, which way now?"

"Captain?" Johan guessed. "Is that you?"

"Yeah, which way did Fitz and the Commodore go?"

"I need to get used to that slug of yours." He looked at his pad. "Uh. Well. Sorry, Cap. We lost them."

CHAPTER 27

"We need to find them again," Caleb said. "Do you have their last position?"

"Aye, Captain," Johan replied. "This way."

The trio moved more quickly now, practically running through the streets of Haydrun in pursuit of Fitz and the Commodore. Reaching a busier street, Caleb slowed them down when he spotted law enforcement drones passing over the area. He didn't want to do anything that made them look suspicious. As soon as the drones had moved on, he picked up the pace again, following Johan's directions.

"This is the edge of the Hind," Penn said as they reached Fitz's last known position.

"He's still out of range," Johan said.

"Can we guess where he's headed based on his route?"

"Oscar," Johan said. "Can you extrapolate a likely desti-nation for the mapped comms signal based on our origin and current position?"

Oscar? Ishek commented, amused by the name of Johan's personal access device.

A circle with a three-block radius appeared over the

map of Haydrun. "Based on my calculations, this area falls within the ninetieth percentile for accuracy."

"Good enough," Johan said. "That should get us close."

"Commodore Burke's done well for herself becoming a traitor to the Empire," Penn said. "That's the Glitz. One of the poshest sections of Haydrun. Even the Admiral of the Royal Navy doesn't live there."

"Maybe she married into money," Caleb suggested.

"And brought Fitz home with her?" Johan asked.

Caleb shrugged. "I'm not saying I agree with it, but it is what it is."

They continued through the streets of Haydrun toward the Glitz. The buildings grew taller and more opulent as they neared the area, the storefronts and shops scaling up in look and feel, as did their clientele. There were no RAF members on leave in this part of town. They couldn't afford any of the entertainment or shopping here. There were fewer people on the streets here and those who were present seemed intent on getting where they needed to be in a hurry and without incident. When a pair of peace officers passed them, their silver armor reflecting the bright gleam of the city's lights, Caleb eyed them warily. However, the officers ignored them completely as their higher-end apparel blended right in with everyone else's.

Reaching the edge of Oscar's circle didn't immediately put them in range of Fitz's comms. They spent nearly another hour walking the perimeter, with Caleb growing increasingly frustrated by the time being wasted. At first, taking in the sights and sounds of the modern city on a planet millions of light years from Earth was enough to keep his mind off the delay, but that only lasted so long.

"Johan, maybe you can get into a database somewhere and find out where Burke lives. This is getting us nowhere."

"If I had all my gear, I probably could," Johan replied.

"But with just a pad? I might be able to, but it'll take a while."

Caleb sighed heavily as he continued walking. "Get started then. We might need it."

"Aye, Captain." He looked around, spotting a cafe at the corner of one skyscraper. "I'll duck in there, grab a coffee and a seat. I can't look at my pad too long while in motion without getting nauseous."

"Okay," Caleb nodded. "Do it. Penn, we'll start expanding the perimeter. Take the north side. I'll go south. Stay in comms range with Johan as our anchor."

"Aye, Captain."

Caleb and Penn split apart, leaving Johan behind as they moved in opposite directions. Picking up his pace, Caleb wandered along the streets of Haydrun, memorizing his path—or rather, Ishek kept track of his path—so he could quickly double-back if needed.

I hope Burke doesn't turn out to be a dead end, Caleb mentioned silently to the symbiote.

Fitz seemed confident he could get something from her.

Yeah, but is he thinking about what we need, or what he wants?

With Fitz, it's hard to know for sure.

"Cap, I'm trying to get access to local tax records, looking for Burke's return and home address," Johan said softly through the comms. "Probably take an hour or two."

"Copy that," Caleb replied. "Do whatever you can to speed things up."

"Aye, sir. I'll do my best."

"Any word from Penn?"

"Not yet. I'll let you know as soon as I hear something."

"Copy."

Caleb crossed another couple of blocks, his comms silent. No news from Penn was bad news. Turning east, he continued along a relatively quiet street, tall apartments rising on either side and vanishing into light cloud cover. Air traffic lanes maneuvered well around the buildings, keeping the resident's views clear.

"... had no choice, Petey," Fitz said, his voice suddenly breaking into the comms. "Do you know what they were asking me to do?"

"The honest thing, for once in your life?" Burke guessed.

"You know it wasn't like that."

"Yes, it was. You were one of the best operatives the Star Guard ever had. You'd still be if you hadn't gone AWOL to play pirate. It's so beneath you, Fitz."

"Johan, cancel your hack," Caleb said. "I've got them."

"Aye, Captain. I'll pass the word to Penn."

"Have her meet you at the shop, then both of you meet me at my location."

"Aye, sir."

Caleb moved closer to the nearest building to wait while listening to Fitz's conversation with Burke. From the heated nature, it was obvious things had gone sour for him after initially going home with her.

"It's not for you to decide what's beneath me," Fitz said. "I worked my ass off for the Star Guard. Risked my life plenty of times. And for what? They didn't appreciate me or my skills. So when they tasked me to recover millions in untraceable coin, I figured they owed me some of it? What I still don't know is how they found out. They didn't know the value of the stash. Only that it was a lot. Anyway, that's ancient history."

"It was a year ago. That's hardly ancient."

Caleb had always assumed Fitz's desertion had a sordid backstory, but he'd never guessed the RAF already wanted the man before he fled. That Fitz was even talking about it made him wonder if he'd forgotten his comms were transmitting. He'd kept the reasons for going AWOL so secret, he couldn't imagine Fitz wanted him to learn about it this way.

"The entire Spiral has come under new management since then. That makes it ancient. And I'm not playing pirate. Not anymore. I'm playing on a team, and we're doing the right thing. You should talk about doing the honest thing. You bent your knee to a usurper and tyrant. A man who's subservient to the Relyeh. You spit on your promise to protect the Empire and the Empress. If that wasn't enough, you married one of his government cronies, who's just as much of an evil bastard as he is."

"You need to watch your mouth, Fitz. I might have invited you here, but that doesn't mean I'll stand here and let you badmouth him. I care about my husband."

"You mean, you care about what he's provided for you. And I guess I'm here for what he hasn't provided."

"You son of a bitch," Burke hissed. "You haven't changed at all."

"Why would you expect me to change?" Fitz replied. "Isn't that why I'm here?"

Caleb expected the fight to continue. Instead, Burke started laughing. "Yeah, I guess it is. I told myself I was crazy for inviting you back to my place. I'm still pretty sure I am, but since I've already committed to it, and have missed you like crazy..."

He wanted to turn the comms off when he heard them kiss. Fortunately, it didn't last long. Fitz could have wasted more time by having his fun. Instead, Caleb heard the soft thud of Burke being lowered to the floor, followed by Fitz's voice.

"Cap, you there?"

CHAPTER 28

"I'm here," Caleb replied. "Where are you?"

"Burke's place," Fitz replied. "Haven't you been listening? I just put her under."

"We lost track of you on the way. What's the address."

"Fourteen Emerald Way, apartment nine-thousand one. It's the penthouse. Ring, and I'll admit you to the penthouse elevator."

"I heard what you said about your desertion," Caleb said, looking up when he noticed Johan and Penn across the street. He waved them, and they hurried to his position.

"Yeah," Fitz answered, his change in tone making it clear he didn't want to talk about it. "I couldn't really avoid the topic. I'm not as proud of it as I originally thought I would be. I didn't want you to know because I didn't think you would trust me if you did. But things have changed."

"I heard that, too," Caleb agreed. "We're on our way to you now." He looked at Johan. "Fourteen Emerald Way."

"That's just one street east of here," Johan replied, showing him on the map.

Caleb led Johan and Penn toward Emerald Way and the

building on the corner. Like the other apartment buildings in the Glitz, the building with the number fourteen on it rose high into the night sky, the large red numbers brightly backlit. Unlike the others, its windows shimmered with embedded lights that constantly changed colors, creating massive overhead artwork mingled with advertisements. A pair of doormen in long red coats and white gloves watched them approach. "Good evening," one of them said before the other one added, "Whom are you here to see?"

"Commodore Burke," Caleb said.

"Ah, yes, she arrived with a friend a few minutes ago. Please, go on in," he said, opening the door and motioning them through with a wave of his hand. "Her elevator is number nine on your left. It will open directly into her penthouse once she approves your visit. Just ring the button on the speaker panel."

"Thank you."

"Of course, sir."

They filed into the building's lobby. Ostentatiously decorated in modern furniture and artwork, with two huge crystal chandeliers emitting multicolored lights, it was all too much for Caleb's taste, but Johan had a different opinion. "I hope to live in a place like this in my next life," he said, giving the large room an appreciative once over.

"What about this life?" Penn asked. "You aren't done living it yet."

"As either a wanted pirate or a Naval engineer? Not happening."

"You never know."

They crossed to the elevator, and Caleb pressed the button. Silent to his ears, he assumed it rang in the penthouse. Fitz didn't bother speaking to them to confirm their identities. The doors opened ahead of them, the cab already waiting. Spotless in silver with wood trim, it was as nice as anything Caleb had ever seen.

"Wow, I could get used to this treatment," Penn said as they stepped in, the doors closing behind them and the cab ascending briskly to the penthouse. Fitz was there waiting when the doors opened again.

"Captain," he said, nodding before thrusting a uniform out at Penn. "You'll need this."

Penn smiled as she accepted Burke's clothes. "Good thing we're about the same size."

"That's why Petra was a good choice," Fitz said. He reached into his pocket as they stepped off the elevator, holding a pad out to Johan. "And this is hers."

"I need more than that," Johan replied, taking Burke's personal device. "Where is she?"

"In the bedroom, sleeping like a baby. This way."

Fitz led them through the huge, posh apartment. Decorated with several styles of fancy furniture and the ugliest sculptures and paintings Caleb had ever seen, he thought the sum total of it all lacked a cohesive theme. He had never wrapped his head around Earth's modern art, and this was a hundred times worse.

Entering the bedroom, Caleb saw that Fitz had laid Commodore Burke out flat, still dressed in the same uniform she'd worn to the Mirage, her chest gently rising and falling. The syringe full of tranquilizer Fitz had poked her with would keep her out for at least four more hours.

"What about her husband?" he asked as Johan leaned over her with his pad. He used his free hand to hold open her eyelid while he scanned her eyeball, which thankfully hadn't rolled back yet.

"Off-world," Fitz replied. "Dealing with a situation on Caprum." He made a face like he was about to puke.

"So she's soon to be the new Queen of the Draconian territories?" Penn asked.

"It sure seems that way."

Johan finished with her eyes, moving down to her

hands. He pressed her fingertips against the screen of his pad, capturing her prints. "Biometrics are done, but we still need her passcode to get to the most secure sections of the Imperium."

"You said you could lift it from her pad," Caleb replied.

"I can. It'll take time."

"Better get started then."

Johan nodded and left the bedroom.

"Nice work, Fitz," Caleb said.

"Isn't it?" he replied. "Running into Burke at the Mirage was a stroke of serendipity. The stars are with us today."

"Let's hope our luck holds out. We'll wait here until Johan finishes cracking her access device. Then we move on to the Imperium."

"Aye, Captain," Fitz said. "I'll keep an eye on Petra, to make sure she doesn't wake up too soon."

"Ever again would be too soon," Penn growled. "She sold out the Empire for a nice apartment and a shot at the nobility."

"Power and prestige are potent lures," Caleb replied.

"That's no excuse. It's one thing to steal some coin," Penn asserted. "It's another to help a usurper destroy everything you swore to protect. Hundreds of thousands of people died because of people like her."

"I'm not trying to excuse it. I understand your anger, but let's not do anything we'll regret."

"I'm not sure I would regret it."

"Stand down, Penn," Fitz said. "I'll watch her. Why don't you go get some air?"

Penn glared at him before storming out of the bedroom. Caleb and Johan followed. Johan settled at a table while Caleb sought out Penn, who had moved to the balcony to fume over Fitz's comments.

She turned around as he approached. "What's eating at you, Penn? Fitz is Fitz; you should know that by now."

She shook her head. "He's making excuses for her. I'm not just pissed because she sold us out. I'm mad about how easily people like her can be bought and corrupted by promises of power. They're so desperate to be important they don't see it's all a lie. Even Crux is a damn lie. They're going to give the entire galaxy to Iagorth and thank him for the privilege." She looked back out over Haydrun and sighed heavily. "This place looks so clean from up here, but there's squalor and filth everywhere if you dig deep enough." She pointed out toward a nearby mountain, where several lights revealed the position of the Imperium. "Especially there."

"We'll get what we came for," Caleb said. "Then we'll do something about it."

She nodded. "I hope so."

They stood together in silence for a while, watching the city below them before returning inside to Johan. The engineer had already cracked Burke's pad and was working his way through her access credentials when they rejoined him at the table.

He glanced up at their approach. "It took longer than I expected to bypass her security protocols, but now that I'm in, I can see why Fitz thought she was such a good target. Her clearance is pretty damn impressive. Once I can hack her military passcodes, we should be able to get pretty much anywhere inside the Imperium that we need to go."

"That's great news," Caleb said. "How much longer do you need?"

"It's hard to say. It could be ten minutes. It could be two hours. I have Oscar working on it." He motioned to the two pads, which he had linked with what appeared to be a homegrown cable. A loupe, tweezer, and small soldering device rested beside the electronics.

"Where did you learn to do all this?" Caleb asked.

"I grew up in poverty," Johan replied. "My father was a

hard worker, but farmhands earn little pay, especially when there are machines that can do the work faster and better. We were on government support. Not much, but enough for food, shelter, clothing. The basics. I promised my parents that when I grew up, I would make sure they didn't die the way they lived. To me, the best way to keep that promise was to fix the machines that took my dad's job. So I started tinkering, and one thing led to another." He smiled at the memories. "I found out I was pretty good at it, and when I reached eighteen I joined the Navy, planning to do a five-year tour before moving into the private sector. I didn't expect to love the service as much as I did, and I stayed on. With such low expenses, I sent almost every coin I earned back home and made good on my promise. This was my third tour. It was a great career before Crux screwed it all up for me."

"I'm glad you're with us," Caleb said. "And that you kept Penn and me from being blown to bits on Tonneau."

Johan laughed. "I would have been blown to bits, too, so I'm also glad that didn't happen."

Caleb smiled, enjoying the rare moment of levity.

Of course, it didn't last.

The private elevator doors slid open, and Caleb and Penn both jumped to their feet, reaching for their blasters as an older man who had to be Burke's husband emerged from the elevator.

There was no question how to deal with the man's sudden appearance. The only question was who would get him first. Penn or him?

As Caleb took aim, Penn fired a trio of stun rounds that caught Burke's husband in the chest. He straightened and convulsed for a moment before toppling forward. With his body half in and half out of the elevator, the doors remained open.

"Beat you to the draw," Penn said, looking back at Caleb with a smile.

"This time," he replied. "I must be slowing down in my old age."

"I know a nice nursing home on Caprum you might like. It's right on the ocean. Great views."

"Do they have Jell-O?"

"What's Jell-O?"

"That'll take some time to explain."

Fitz came running out of the bedroom at the noise, gun in hand. "What the hell is..." He trailed off when he saw the gray-haired old man laid out on the floor. "He's supposed to be halfway across the galaxy."

"Maybe our efforts on Rakusha canceled his plans," Penn guessed. "Either way, he's here, not there, and now we have a complication."

"We have enough tranq to keep him out, too," Fitz assured her.

"Fitz, get over here and help me carry him to the bed," Caleb said. He paused, looking down at the briefcase the man had dropped. A suitcase hovered behind him in the elevator. "He's someone important, right?"

"Baron Arnot Riessling," Fitz groused, sneering down at him. "That depends on your definition of important."

Caleb put his hands under the baron's shoulders. Fitz took the man's feet. He and Caleb carried him to the bedroom, laying him down on the bed next to his wife. Fitz pressed the sides of the ring on his left ring finger, revealing a small needle underneath, glistening with the tranquilizer. He pressed it into the back of Riessling's hand. "That should do him for a while."

"Johan should be done soon, I hope," Caleb said.

"Aye, Captain."

Penn had already picked up and opened the briefcase by the time Caleb returned to the table, and was busy rifling through the pages inside. "I didn't think people still used briefcases," he said, sitting. "Or paper."

"The one good thing about paper, it's easy to destroy," she replied. "People still use it for sensitive information."

"By carrying it in a case without a lock?"

She glanced at him mischievously. "Who said it wasn't locked?" She turned it toward him, showing him the small screen to enter a six-digit code.

"How'd you know the code?"

"Burke's birthday. Got it on the first try."

"People never learn, do they? What are the papers?"

"I've only skimmed over them so far. The other thing about paper, it's traditional. These appear to be formal documents intended to transfer control of the Draconian Territories from Duke Draco to Baron Reissling." She continued flipping through the documents. Caleb could see now that they were handmade and inked with colorful flourishes. She held one out for Caleb to peruse. The calligraphy was hard to read, but it seemed to be a declaration changing the name of the Draconian Territories to the Kingdom of Riessling. "The thing about these docs, none of them are signed."

"Crux didn't sign them? What do you think happened?"

"My best guess? Crux planned to visit Caprum himself for a pompous ceremony to sign the papers. When he started losing Specters at Rakusha, he probably canceled the event."

"Well, that makes me feel all warm and fuzzy inside."

Penn smiled. "Me, too. We ruined this old fart's dreams of becoming a king. At least temporarily."

"Yeah. Seems we sent the bastard home with his tail between his legs," Johan said. "I love it."

Penn finished looking at the papers. Rather than dropping them back in the briefcase, she gathered them and stood up.

"What are you doing?" Caleb asked.

"Come see," she replied.

Both Caleb and Johan followed her out to the balcony. She slid open a pane of glass to expose the outside, allowing cool air to enter and swirl in the small space. "Blaster?" she asked.

Caleb raised an eyebrow curiously as he pulled his weapon. Penn held the group of papers outside the widow. "Give it your best shot, Captain."

Smiling, Caleb put a burning hole through the papers, lighting them all on fire. Penn released them, sending them flying away and scattering as they combusted. The trio watched them drift and burn until there was nothing left to see.

"That felt good," Penn said.

"Johan," Oscar called from the table. "Mission complete. I have extracted your requested data."

"That's it, Captain," Johan said. "The passcodes are mine. We're ready to roll."

CHAPTER 29

There was one benefit to Baron Riessling's early arrival. A quick review of his pad revealed access to a personal transport. After Penn changed into Burke's uniform, Caleb and the others rode the elevator up to a rooftop garage, where several flying vehicles were tucked into marked spaces. Johan found Riessling's by activating the vehicle and seeing which one's lights came on.

The transport in question, which Caleb couldn't help but think of as a flying car since it served the same general purpose, was sleek, dark, and luxurious. Obviously expensive, the interior outdid the finest Rolls-Royce, with thick, buttery leather and tomblike insulation. Both Fitz and Penn knew how to fly the car, but in this case it wasn't necessary. Riesling's ride was fully automated. All they had to do was pick a seat inside and direct the machine using the baron's pad.

Flight time from downtown Haydrun to the Imperium was less than twenty minutes, and the air traffic thinned considerably as they headed away from the city. Having reached the most critical point of their mission, the tension among the group had thickened, and they rode mostly in silence.

Not the full buffet I'd most enjoy. But a worthy appetizer. Though I am surprised, you are more nervous than Fitz.

There's a lot riding on this, Ish, Caleb replied.

There may not be. The Archives won't lead you directly to the supposed princess. Only point you to where she may have been born. What if the trail goes cold there?

Are you trying to make me more nervous? Draco and Haas both believe uncovering the princess will bolster the resistance. So do I. It's a chance we have to take.

I still think convincing Istari to rise to Lo'ane's dying request would have been the more pragmatic route.

I know, you've told me that multiple times. You need to let it go. We're here.

At least I got a good fight out of it. We should do that again sometime. I would have beat Penn to the shot on Riessling.

No, you wouldn't.

A bright green light illuminated the front of the car, drawing Caleb's attention. It vanished quickly, revealing the Imperium looming ahead of them. Heavy and imposing, the immense stone structure reminiscent of a medieval castle, sat embedded in the mountain's side. From here, Caleb could see the landing area at the top of the facility, where a handful of military transports and atmospheric defense ships were already parked, along with a handful of personal cars.

"What was that green light?" Caleb asked.

"They scanned the transport," Fitz replied. "They know it belongs to Riessling, and it hasn't been reported stolen or anything, so they let it pass instead of issuing a challenge or sending a command for the automated system to turn us away."

"I didn't realize it would be so easy to get in."

"That's only the first gate, Cap. The hard part will be to pass Penn off as a Commodore."

"What are you trying to say?" Penn asked.

"You should put your hair back," Fitz replied. "It's more professional looking."

She glowered at him. "I don't have any clips or hair pins to work with."

Fitz dug both out of his pocket. "I brought some for you."

Penn laughed, taking the clips. "You're a piece of work."

"I know."

She had her hair pulled back tight against her head and wrapped into a bun by the time the car landed on the Imperium's rooftop. The door opened and they climbed out. Caleb looked around as he exited the vehicle. There weren't any guards here, but he doubted it would stay that way for long.

Having been to the Imperium before, Penn guided the group forward, acting as though she were bringing them into the building for a tour. At least Caleb didn't need to pretend to be a curious tourist. He looked around the rooftop, gawking at the military vehicles parked nearby.

A short walk brought them to a broad stone tower rising from the face of the Imperium, which served as its entrance. A heavy blast door slid open ahead of them, revealing a pair of elevators and a stairwell behind a guarded checkpoint. Two Royal Guards stood on either side of the access point, both in full combat armor with rifles slung across their chests. One of them stepped forward when they approached while his partner remained silent, watching them closely.

"Commodore Burke," he said in greeting, his expression invisible behind his dark faceplate. He paused, and Caleb could imagine the look of confusion on his face. "I didn't realize there was more than one Commodore Burke in the Royal Navy."

Penn smiled confidently, advancing toward him without hesitation. Caleb knew she was nervous, but she didn't show it at all. She had been trained for this kind of thing. "That's okay, I don't know the names of all the Royal Guard colonels, either. I'm Commodore Celia Burke. No relation to Commodore Petra Burke."

The guard nodded, satisfied as necessary with the explanation. "Of course, Commodore." He turned back to his station and tapped on a control surface. "Of course, I'll need to confirm your access. If you'll look toward the red light there."

Caleb noticed Johan's movement, hand shifting in his pocket to activate his frequency hijack device as Penn looked at the LED. A scanner quickly captured her face, passing it into the RAF database. A full dossier appeared on the checkpoint terminal a split second later.

"Access confirmed," he said as Johan switched off the device. Both Guards stood at attention. "Sir."

"At ease," she replied. "These men are representatives from Nelson Heavy Industries. They've been hired as consultants to review the Imperium's security measures and make recommendations based on their observations."

"You handled your duties well, Corporal," Caleb said. "You as well, Private. Well done."

"Thank you, sir," the Guard replied.

"This way, gentlemen," Penn said, leading them into an elevator while the two guards returned to their parade rest behind them. As soon as the doors were closed, she let go of a heavy breath, shaking slightly from adrenaline-fueled nerves

He put his hand on her shoulder. "Nice job, Penn."

"I wasn't sure Johan's device would work on the Imperium's network," she replied.

"Me neither," Johan admitted.

"You're kidding, right?" Fitz asked.

"Uh. Yeah," Johan answered. "Kidding. Yup."

"What floor?" Caleb asked.

"One-oh-four," Penn replied. "The Archives are in the subterranean part of the Imperium."

Caleb tapped the controls, but the elevator didn't budge. A fingerprint scanner flashed, indicating the cab was secured. Johan sprang into action, removing his pad and activating a high-resolution hologram of Burke's print. He placed it just in front of the scanner, which accepted the digital copy as legit. The elevator began its descent.

"I'm impressed, " Caleb said to Johan.

Johan smiled proudly. "Thank you, Captain."

The elevator continued down for another minute before slowing to a stop at level one-oh-four. The doors slid open, revealing an empty corridor ahead of them. The walls were made of hewn stone, the floor gray tile. Simple pendant lights hung from wires at regular intervals, illuminating the long passageway. There were several doors on each side of the hallway as well, all of them closed.

"There it is," Penn said, pointing to a secured blast door.

They hurried through the passageway until they reached a heavy blast door blocking further access. A control panel rested on the wall beside it, and again Johan used Burke's fingerprint scan to open the door without incident. Another passageway angled toward what Caleb guessed was the side of the Imperium embedded in the mountain. They passed a Royal Marine major in utilities who nodded to Penn on the way past, ignoring the rest of the group. That was fine with Caleb. That he hadn't thought them out of the ordinary reassured him they were going to make it to their objective.

Penn finally pulled to a stop outside a door with a bronze placard over it that revealed it as the Royal

Archives. It was more protected than the elevator or the first door, requiring both a retina and fingerprint scan, as well as a passcode. It seemed strange to Caleb that historical records would be more protected than anything else, leaving him to wonder if the truth about Pathfinder's origins might be hidden somewhere inside, tucked away and forgotten.

Johan worked his magic, using holograms to fake the biometric scanners. His finger shivered as he typed in Burke's hacked passcode, clearly nervous that it wouldn't get them through the door. He heaved a relieved sigh when the electromagnetic lock clicked off and the door slid aside.

They stepped into the Archives. Caleb had expected a handful of terminals hooked into a mainframe hidden even deeper in the Imperium, or perhaps partitioned with the rest of the computer systems in the place. Instead, the Archives bore a greater resemblance to an old-fashioned library, except it sported new-fangled tech. Rows of shelves lined a wide corridor with an open space in front of each row for browsing and research. The shelves were full of data storage devices that reminded Caleb of BluRay discs, though these were half the size. He assumed they contained records from the Empire's history going back to Pathfinder's arrival. Maybe further. It seemed impossible to think about how much information was stored down here, especially considering there was no sign of anyone working at any of the terminals. Caleb figured that someone had to be responsible for organizing and maintaining the data drives.

"Where do we start?" he asked as the door closed behind them.

Penn pointed ahead of them. "We can use that terminal to pinpoint which data drive we need."

They walked over to the nearest terminal. Penn moved around it, tapping on its controls while Johan passed her Burke's pad.

She entered the Commodore's passcode, gaining access to the terminal and the Archives. She typed in some commands, bringing up a search screen. They already knew the dates that Lo'ane had been off-world, so she entered the query as a basic prompt, asking the terminal about the Empress' whereabouts.

SECTION 9, DRIVE 47.

"I'll get it," Johan said, darting away from the terminal and pacing along the rows of drives until he found the right one. He picked it off the shelf and returned it to Penn, who placed it into a reader. A waiting screen kept them in suspense.

"This is painful," Fitz commented.

"What do you expect?" Johan answered. "This tech is four hundred years old. They can't exactly upgrade it."

"Why not?"

"It would take too long for me to explain."

"Apparently, we have all day."

The wait screen finally cleared, the answer to the query printing out on the screen.

Princess Lo'ane embarked on a six-month journey through the Kallio Combine. Her itinerary included stops at eight of the worlds within the Combine, as well as visits to an asteroid mining facility, orphanages, and multiple hospitals where she met with her loyal subjects, providing aid and comfort to them in her father's name.

"The Kallio Combine?" Fitz said. "That's the edge of explored space, nearly three weeks out from here. It's a group of dinkus planets clustered around a dwarf star. The only thing notable about the Combine is that nobody cares about it."

"Obviously Empress Lo'ane cared," Penn said.

"Yeah, to use it to disappear while she cranked out a kid and gave it up for adoption. How much does that have to suck? Her daughter could have grown up as royalty.

Instead, she's probably a miner. No wonder she didn't want her to become the next Empress. Asteroid miners can't deal with regular gravity. Their bones are too brittle. And they aren't known for their social graces or learning, either."

"You're making a lot of assumptions."

"I'm guessing she delivered her child at one of those hospitals," Caleb said. "And maybe handed it over at one of the orphanages. Are any of the hospitals and orphanages on the same planet and in the same general vicinity?"

"Let's find out," Penn said, typing the query into the terminal. The list of results was shorter this time.

Princess Lo'ane visited Acala Primary Hospital in the city of Acala on the planet Callus. She also visited the Nexus Orphanage, located two hours from Acala on the banks of the Senai river, where she spent the afternoon playing with the children.

"What did she do at the hospital?" Caleb asked. Penn typed the question into the terminal.

I'm sorry. The details of her visit to the hospital are not part of the official record.

"Well, that's interesting," Penn said. She entered another prompt, asking if there were any other hospital and orphanage visits on the same day.

There is only one instance of this combination on her itinerary.

Penn looked back at Caleb. "I think we have our lead."

"Agreed."

"That means it's time to go, right?" Johan asked.

"Not yet," Caleb replied. "Ask about the origins of Pathfinder."

Penn did as he requested.

SECTION 77, DRIVE 100

Johan searched the shelves, stopping toward the back of the room. He pointed toward rows of data drives before ducking low, searching for number one hundred before straightening up. "Captain, the drives end at ninety-nine."

Why are we not surprised?

It's about time you chimed in, Caleb replied to Ishek. *Were you sleeping?*

You know I don't sleep. Much. I just had nothing to say. You should take that as a compliment. It means you were doing something right for a change.

Do you think Crux took the drive?

No. I think it's been missing for a long, long time. More likely destroyed.

At least it's not mission critical. "Forget it, Johan. We don't need it. We have what we came for. It's time to go."

Penn stood up, but before they could take a single step toward the door, it slid open.

Nearly two dozen Legionnaires streamed in, weapons ready. They quickly surrounded the group as their commander stepped into the Archives.

"Burke?" Penn hissed.

CHAPTER 30

"Well, well, well," Commodore Burke said. "What do we have here? A group of rebel rats caught in a trap."

Ish, why didn't you tell me there were khoron here? Caleb asked.

There are no khoron here.

They're Legionnaires.

They are all human. I'm certain of it.

They're Legion, Ish. They can't be human.

I'm telling you, Cal. They are.

"How the hell did you get here?" Penn growled. "You should be knocked out on your bed with your hubby."

Burke's gaze turned to Fitz, ignoring Penn. "I knew we could count on you."

"One Captain Caleb Card, locked down and delivered as promised," Fitz replied, backing away from the terminal and toward Burke.

"You?" Penn said, her voice echoing her disbelief. "You're the mole? You traitorous son of a bitch!"

"Are you really that surprised?" Fitz asked. "You know me, Penelope. I've never been a good guy."

"But this? What did she promise you? I can only imagine."

"Nothing like that, I can assure you," Burke said. "Lord Crux lavishes rewards on his most loyal subjects, and few have been as loyal as you, Fitz."

"You don't need to overdo it, Petey," he said, looking at Caleb. "It's not personal, Captain. But I had my eye on Gorgon's command before you came along, and you ruined it. I knew I couldn't get you out of the picture on my own. You're too damn good at what you do, so I reached out to an old friend, and we made a deal."

"That sounds pretty personal to me," Johan said.

Fitz shrugged. "Okay, maybe it is. Who cares?"

"You tampered with the ship on Aroon?" Caleb asked.

He nodded. "They taught me a lot of unique skills in the Star Guard."

"You nearly got us all killed. Including yourself."

"I was in the hangar during the fight, ready to bail if necessary. High reward comes with high risk."

"And you directed the Specters to Dragonfire station," Penn said. "Children died, Fitz. *Children!*"

"They weren't my children. The funnest part is that you've had Naya and Tae locked up for the last few weeks, and they had the best chance of figuring the whole thing out."

"So all of this was just to get to me," Caleb said. "Why?"

"Crux demands it," Burke said.

"On behalf of Iagorth, I'm sure," Caleb replied. "And I bet he wants me alive, too."

"You would be dead already, otherwise. Rebels in the Royal Archives. No one would question it. And since you brought it up, Crux demanded we rein you in. Your companions are expendable. Specters are on their way to your little hiding spot behind the star, and a contingent of Royal Guards will apprehend your pilot any minute now.

It's over, Captain Card. Come quietly, and I'll imprison these two instead of killing them."

Caleb glanced at Penn. She shook her head, urging him not to go quietly. She and Johan were as good as dead anyway, and she knew it. But there was no way they could take on two dozen Legionnaires, especially when his blaster was in Penn's bag. Burke was right.

It was over.

"I'll come quietly, but they come with me," he said.

"You aren't in a position to make demands."

"Then call it a request. As you said, I'm a rat caught in a trap. What's the harm?"

Burke considered before nodding. "Fine. Let's go."

Caleb rounded the terminal, Penn and Johan flanking him. The Legionnaires closed in. Caleb eyed them suspiciously. Ishek could insist all he wanted; he still didn't believe they were human. Burke could have brought Royal Guards down to capture them, but she had specifically come with them. Was Crux trying to show off that they had figured out how to make themselves invisible to Ish, the same way Ish had made himself invisible to them?

That's not possible.

How can you be so sure? Caleb replied.

Ishek remained silent. He couldn't.

Three Legionnaires moved away from the group. "Hold out your hands, like this," one of them said, putting his hands up, each pointed toward the other. Caleb did as he asked without question; so did Penn and Johan. The Legionnaires produced short, narrow tubes from their belts. Grabbing Caleb's hand, the Legionnaire slid one end of the tube on one index finger, the other end on the index finger of the opposite hand. When the device activated, the ends rotated outward until they clamped his fingers in an impossible to break hold. Penn and Johan were bound in the same fashion.

"Let's go," Burke said, turning to leave the room. Fitz moved to her side, the two of them leading the procession out of the Archives.

Ish, take over, Caleb said.

Now? What for? There's nothing I can do.

You don't only get to drive when things are going well. Take over.

You're thinking of going into the Collective on your own. That's a bad idea.

It has to be better than our current situation. You can't see the khoron, but I'm positive they're here. Maybe I can look in a way you can't.

You aren't a Relyeh. You do not know.

My point exactly.

I suppose we're dead either way.

As Caleb allowed his consciousness to retreat, Ishek took his place more reluctantly this time, freeing him to focus on his plan. Sending his attention through Ishek and out onto the Collective, the din of signals immediately overwhelmed him all around him. Even if Ish was right and the Legionnaires with them in the Imperium were human, he couldn't say the same for Atlas. The Legion had a large presence on and around the planet. More than anywhere else they had been.

He remained vaguely aware of his physical movements as Burke led them out of the Archives and through the corridors toward the elevator. Inside the Collective, he focused on separating the sounds, doing his best to isolate the individuals and dial in the proximity. He noticed quickly that none of the other Relyeh attempted to attack him, which he found suspicious. Would a Relyeh trying to enter his mind give him a clue as to how the Legionnaires remained hidden? Or did they just not see him as a threat?

Either way, he struggled to break apart the sounds and close in on his more immediate surroundings. The number of Hunger on Atlas was too plentiful, their voices too loud. He could try overpowering one of them, but the odds that it would be a Legionnaire in the group escorting him were slim. He realized suddenly that was the primary difference between this experience on the Collective and that of all his prior visits. He hadn't been anywhere else where the Legion had had such a large presence. He had never needed to fight through so much noise to pick up a signal before. Neither had Ishek. Not that the symbiote couldn't sense the Legionnaires, it was more like they were grains of sand on a beach, lost in the crowd.

He needed help to pinpoint them, and there was only one way he could think of.

Ish, he said, retreating from the Collective. *I think I figured it out.*

Do tell. And hurry. We're almost back to the surface. I expect Burke will separate us there, and take all of us to places we do not want to go.

You need to attack one of the Legionnaires.

You want me to do what? Under normal circumstances, I would respond with eagerness and enthusiasm. But these aren't normal circumstances.

You heard me. Hit a guard hard, kill them if you can. If I can sense the change in the Collective, I'll have a better chance of identifying the group surrounding us. To filter the one signal from all the other noise.

I believe this is crazy, but perhaps you're onto something. You should attack the guard, and I will hunt for the difference in signal.

You're offering to give back control?

We are a team, are we not?

I love you, too, Ish.

That is disgusting.

Ishek surrendered control, bringing Caleb back into his body. He was in the elevator, ascending toward the surface.

The cab wasn't big enough for everyone, so he was in the elevator with half a dozen Legionnaires, plus Fitz. Everyone else had to be in another cab.

It's going to be harder in such close quarters, he said.

Or easier. I am prepared.

I need one more thing first. Boost me.

Already ahead of you.

Caleb immediately tingled, hormones and adrenaline racing into his system. He glanced down at his hands, bound by the finger constraints. "How does this thing work?" he asked.

Fitz faced him. "Proximity sensor. Once it's active, as long as you're close to the transmitter, it'll stay locked."

"Interesting."

"I would have thought you'd spend the ride up telling me what an awful person I am, not thinking about the peculiarities of these cuffs."

"I already know you're awful. Person? I'm not so sure. I've never seen anything like these cuffs. They're interesting." They had nearly reached the surface. He was out of time to act. Shifting his head to his left, his focus landed on the faceplate of his chosen Legionnaire, the one who had cuffed him. *Here we go, Ish.* "Do you know what else I think, Fitz?"

Standing directly in front of him, Fitz turned his head to sneer at him. "What?"

Caleb threw his head forward, slamming his forehead into Fitz's nose, satisfied by the crunch and the quick flow of blood. Fitz stumbled sideways, his shoulder slamming against the cab door as the Legionnaires surrounding Caleb immediately moved to grab him, the tight confines making it hard for them to coordinate their movements. Caleb swung his arm out like a hammer, planting the back of his closed fist into his chosen Legionnaire faceplate. It cracked from the powerful blow. Although failing to kill him, it jolted his head back enough to send him stumbling into the Legionnaire behind him.

Got it!

"You son of a bitch," Fitz growled, lunging at Caleb. The Legionnaire next to Caleb stepped between them,shoving Fitz back against the cab doors before whirling around and opening fire on the other Legionnaires. Too slow to react, he shot three before they could shoot back. Caleb threw a boosted punch into the throat of another. As he fell, one hand clutching his crushed larynx, Caleb jerked the rifle out of his other hand and slammed the butt into the side of another Legionnaire's helmet, knocking him to his knees. Sweeping his leg around, he kicked the kneecap of the only Legionnaire left standing, breaking his knee despite his armor. He then slammed the gun butt down on the man's faceplate before shooting him through it.

Finally, at point blank range, Ishek prompted his Legionnaire to shoot the guard getting up off his knees, the blast melting the man's faceplate before killing him. Ish then had his Legionnaire open his own faceplate and turn the weapon on himself.

Caleb spun back toward Fitz. Still leaning against the cab doors, he looked stunned by the quick turnaround. "Want to see what I do to awful things?" Caleb asked, moving toward him, intending to rip his head from his shoulders.

The cab reached the surface just then; the doors sliding open and dropping Fitz out backwards, buying him a reprieve.

You could have shot the cuffs off me first, Caleb complained, following Fitz out of the elevator. The traitor crab walked backward out of his way as the other lift, which Burke, Penn, Johan, and five additional Legionnaires, arrived, the doors opening. Before they realized Caleb was free, one of the Legionnaires fired on him, the well-aimed plasma blast melting through the cuffs in the narrow gap between Caleb's index fingers.

Happy now? Ish asked.

Yes. Thank you.

Caleb left Fitz behind and charged across the gap between elevators, headed directly for Burke.

"Stop him!" she shouted.

Two of the Legionnaires moved into position to intercept him, while another took aim at him with her rifle. His senses enhanced by Ishek's chemical cocktail, he twisted aside and leaned back, the two bolts burning past his chest to slam into the stone wall of the entrance. At the same time, Penn threw herself at Burke, grabbing the woman by the throat and dragging her to the walkway.

As Ishek's new Legionnaire fired into the faceplate of the guard beside him, Caleb grabbed the first Legionnaire to get to him. Gripping her helmet in both hands, he twisted her head, snapping her neck. He let her go, and she dropped like a rock.

Another Legionnaire would have shot him in the back, but Johan pushed his gun aside, sending the plasma bolt wide. The Legionnaire backhanded him to send him sprawling, again taking aim at Caleb, only to stiffen when Ishek overpowered him. Instead of pulling the trigger, he let the rifle fall from his hands.

"Fitz." Caleb's eyes whipped around to where he had left him. Gone. His gaze shifted again to one of the elevators as its doors closed, likely with the bastard inside.

"Forget him," Penn said, climbing off an unconscious Commodore Burke. "We need to get out of here."

CHAPTER 31

"Johan, call Atrice," Caleb said, scanning the rooftop for a ride. They couldn't use Riessling's car, it would never fly fast enough to let them outrun the ships he knew would soon chase them. In fact, there were Royal Marines racing toward them already, having seen the altercation.

"It's kind of hard with this on my hands," Johan replied, holding up his cuffs. He had just finished the sentence when Ishek's Legionnaire melted them, setting his hands free. He did the same for Penn before trying to contact Atrice on his pad.

"I'll slow them down," Ishek said through his puppet khoron as he prompted its host into a dead sprint after the Royal Marines. When the Legionnaire opened fire on them, they all dove for whatever cover they could find.

Caleb motioned to a military transport a short distance away. "Penn, can you fly that one?"

"With my eyes closed," she replied, leading the sprint toward it.

"That's good, but let's keep them open for this one," Caleb quipped back.

"Captain, I can't get Atrice on the line," Johan said

through heavy breathing. Caleb had to slow to ensure he didn't leave the engineer behind.

"Burke said he was being arrested," Caleb replied. "Keep trying."

"Aye, Captain."

Glancing over his shoulder, Caleb watched as the Legionnaire under Ishek's control took fire from the Royal Marines. The Legionnaire's special armor absorbed an abundance of firepower, allowing Ish to keep the Marines pinned down.

An energy blast ahead drew Caleb's attention, just in time to watch Penn push the downed pilot out of the transport and onto the tarmac. Caleb jumped over him and into the craft, turning and holding out his hand. He helped Johan up and in.

Ish, we're clear.

The Legionnaire rushed a group of approaching Marines, taking plasma bolt after plasma bolt in the chest and shoulders before slamming into one car and pushing it toward the Marines. They dove away from the machine, scattering for cover.

Leave them, Caleb ordered. *They're human.*

They're enemy combatants, and they betrayed their oaths. That amuses me, but I believe it means something to you.

We're done here. Leave them.

He could sense Ishek's grousing, but he didn't continue the argument. Instead, the symbiote finished the khoron, which dropped the Legionnaire to the tarmac. Dead.

Caleb joined Penn in the transport's front, dropping into the passenger seat. Penn tapped a couple of buttons and grabbed the joystick and throttle. She pushed the throttle open, lifting the transport off the rooftop and away from the Imperium, plasma sizzling ineffectively against the vehicle's armored shell.

"Whoohoo!" Johan shouted. "We did it!"

"Let's not get ahead of ourselves," Caleb said, eying the transport's sensor grid. He doubted the three other vessels launching from the rooftop were friendly. "Get us back to the spaceport. Johan, switch your tracker to look for Atrice. We aren't leaving him behind if I can help it."

"Aye aye, Captain," Penn answered. She banked hard right, pushing the throttle open even further and sending them rocketing toward the spaceport at full speed. Caleb watched the three ships behind them speed up in pursuit.

"Those are combat aircraft," Penn said, watching them in the rearview display on the dashboard. "We can't outrun them, out-gun them, or outmaneuver them."

"So don't try," Caleb replied. "Spaceport, full throttle, and hope for the best."

She smiled, pushing the throttle all the way open.

"Transport HMT two-zero-zero-nine," a harsh voice spat over the comms. "Cut your velocity and reset your course for the Imperium immediately, or you will be fired upon. This is your only warning."

"Bite me," Penn answered, switching off the comms. "Hopefully, I can out-fly them." She dipped the transport's nose toward the city ahead, angling to cut between the skyscrapers.

A pair of flashes signaled one of the chasing combat craft releasing missiles. They streaked toward the transport, which had no countermeasures. Instead, Penn shoved the stick forward, pointing the transport toward the ground. They lost altitude in a hurry, diving at the houses on the outskirts of Haydrun proper, the missiles hot on their tail.

"I don't want to die," Johan whimpered, his face turning white as the G-forces increased.

Penn remained focused on their heading and velocity, jaw tensing as they neared the ground. A shrill tone warned them of an imminent collision, but still she stayed the course, the missiles getting that much closer.

Finally, she pulled back on the stick and cut the throttle, letting friction slow them as they came out of the dive. The missiles streaked past and smashed into the ground, throwing up enough earth to splatter the hull of the transport when they detonated.

Penn ripped across the landscape, passing only a few feet above peoples' heads and splitting between the homes speckling Haydrun's suburbs. Other traffic occupied the skies overhead, though it had yet to gain the density it would once they reached the city proper. Too concerned with hitting civilians by firing on them again, the combat ships shadowed them from above. The Royal Guards were fortunate their first volley had hit dirt instead of a house.

Knowing the military craft would resume their attack the moment they made a move toward the spaceport, Penn turned the transport in the other direction, shooting between the increasingly taller buildings leading into downtown. Bystanders on the ground reacted with surprise to see them flying so low, gawking at the ship as it flew past.

"Cap, I just picked up Atrice's comm signal," Johan said, following up a moment later. "Oh, hell, it's gone."

"Did you get the last location?"

"Aye." He held his pad between Caleb and Penn so they could see the map. "Looks like a Royal Guard station."

"We need to go back for him," Caleb said.

"Are you crazy?" Penn replied. "It'll be a gift from the stars for us to make it to Medusa alive as it is."

"We don't leave anyone behind. If Burke gets a hold of him, she'll feed him to the Legion."

"Damn. Okay."

"Just swing back and slow down. I'll get out. You get to the spaceport. Grab Medusa and come back this way. We'll meet you on the roof."

Penn pushed out an exasperated half-laugh. "You make it sound so simple."

"You wanted something to fight for, didn't you? Right now that's me and Cookie."

Penn navigated the transport around the buildings, cursing when one of the combat craft dipped low, vectoring in from their flank. "Crux's flunkies are getting impatient."

"Good," Caleb answered. "It'll make them reckless, and becoming reckless will make them dead." Caleb abandoned the passenger seat, Johan taking his seat as he moved to the back of the transport. Opening Penn's bag, he retrieved both his blaster and hers.

We haven't done this in a while.

I didn't forget how, Caleb replied, hitting the door control. Of course, the hatch complained about opening in flight. Caleb hit the override, wind blasting into him as the hatch moved aside. "Just say when!" he shouted up to the front of the transport.

He felt them slowing and looked out of the hatch. Spotting the combat ship approaching from the side, he opened fire with his blaster. The guards returned fire with their machine guns, peppering the transport's armor and the doorway. Caleb had no choice but to duck back inside.

"Bombs away!" Penn shouted.

The bad timing nearly cost Caleb his chance. He knuckled up, and with rounds still punishing the transport, he threw himself out through the open door.

CHAPTER 32

Luckily, there weren't many people on the street near the Royal Guard station. Even more fortuitous, the Royal Guards had transported Atrice in a ground vehicle. With a perfectly timed swan-dive, Caleb's landing dented in the car's roof, the give in the metal absorbing much of the impact to Caleb's body. His still-pumping adrenaline did the rest, and he rolled off, able to move with little to no pain.

The entry to the Royal Guard station was directly in front of him. He raced up six steps to it, aware of the pedestrians staring at him in disbelief. One guard moved to body block him at the door, Caleb merely stopped in front of him, pulled his blaster, and shot him in the chest. He shrugged and grinned at the man when it didn't penetrate his armor; the subterfuge working to distract the guard. Caleb dropped his blaster and snatched the man's stunner baton from his hip, jabbing the business end into the guard's neck. Paralyzed in place and wild-eyed with fear, the Guard quaked for several long seconds until Caleb pulled the baton back and yanked him past him, sending him tumbling down the steps.

Picking up his blaster and keeping the baton, he burst through the door, surprising two more guards, still unprepared for his brazen assault. He hit them both with his blaster to distract them before jabbing them with the baton. Reaching for their weapons, they dropped in their tracks.

The station lobby had four desks and a few doors leading out of it. No doubt, one of them led to the cell where they were holding Atrice. A pair of officers rushed toward him when he entered; both went down at the end of the stun baton.

Can I come out and play?

You had your fun already, Caleb replied. *It's my turn.* "Atrice!" he shouted, "Where are you?"

"Captain!" Atrice's muffled reply came from behind the closed door on Caleb's right. It opened as he raced toward it, a Royal Guard emerging, blaster in hand. He opened fire on Caleb as soon as he saw him, nearly burning off his ear as he dove behind a desk. Rather than use it as cover, he dropped and slid into the foot space under the desktop and rose to a squat.His enhanced strength allowed him to rise with it on his shoulders and throw it at the guard. He couldn't get out of the way fast enough. The desk bowled him over, pinning his legs but not his gun hand. The stunt still threw him off his game long enough for Caleb to stun him as he ran past.

Once through the open doorway, he spotted Atrice locked in a small holding cell. There was no one else in the room.

For now, anyway.

"Captain," Atrice said breathlessly, a wide smile stretching across his face as he leaped from the bench he was sitting on and wrapped his hands around two of the bars on the door. "I'm glad you came for me."

"I wouldn't leave you here to become a Legionnaire," Caleb replied, hitting the door control to open the cell door.

They quickly exited the holding room, returning to the lobby where Atrice picked up a stun baton and a blaster from one of the downed guards.

"Where are the others?" he asked as they paused at the open door to look out.

"Penn and Johan went to get Medusa. We need to meet them on the roof."

"How do you know they'll succeed? The Royal Guards have the spaceport on lockdown and Medusa blockaded."

"Penn's got a military transport and a lot of motivation. She'll get it done."

"What about Fitz?"

Caleb's face fell as he leveled a bitter look at Atrice. "He was the mole."

"Fitz? Damn. That's hard to believe."

"He's the reason they captured you. We were in their hands for a while, too."

"How did you escape?"

"I'll give you all the details later; right now, we need to move." He pointed to the front of the station, where a group of peace officers and Royal Marine vehicles had appeared.

"The guards brought me in the back way," Atrice said, pointing to the closed door at the rear of the room. "There's a stairwell back there leading up. I imagine it goes all the way to the roof."

They ran that way, throwing the door open and escaping down a hallway that led to the stairwell. Behind them, they heard the heavy pounding of boots racing up the front stairs and into the station lobby .

"It's a long way up," Atrice said.

"There's only one way out. By air," Caleb replied. "Start climbing."

Atrice took the lead, running up the steps as fast as he could. Caleb paced him easily, keeping one eye behind them. Fortunately, the twisting stairwell was enclosed, making it difficult, if not impossible, for the chasing defenders to get line-of-sight on them, nevermind firing openly on them.

That didn't prevent the Marines from landing additional units on the roof and coming down the opposite way.

It also didn't stop Atrice from getting tired. Even with the threat of death behind them, the pilot had slowed noticeably by the time they reached the fiftieth floor, which Caleb couldn't argue felt like the longest slog of his life. The only good news was that the Marines, while in better shape, were carrying more weight with their gear and had slowed by almost the same amount. Caleb could hear their boots on the stairs a few floors down, still hidden by the elevator shaft that went down the center of the stairwell.

"Cap, I can't...do this...anymore," Atrice heaved.

"You should have spent less time tasting your dishes and more time at the gym," Caleb replied. "Don't give up. We're halfway there."

"Halfway?" Atrice wheezed. For a moment, Caleb thought he would give up and sit down on the steps.

"Captain, do you copy?" Penn's voice was like a symphony behind Caleb's ear.

"I copy. What's your status?" he replied.

"We got Medusa off the ground. I'm afraid I might have accidentally shot down three Marine aircraft with great malice. We're headed your way. I assume since you still have your comms, you're on the roof?"

Caleb glanced at Atrice. "Not quite. Fifty-second floor."

"You're not even close, Cap."

"I think I've been eating too much of Cookie's stew."

"We can't afford to wait for you. They saw what Medusa had up her sleeves. They're sending in the big guns now."

"ETA to the tower?" Caleb asked.

"Less than a minute."

It was a good run. We gave it our best shot.

"It's not over yet," Caleb hissed in response to Ishek's fatalistic outburst. "We don't quit until we're dead." He moved up beside Atrice on the steps before passing him completely. At the next floor, he grabbed the door and pulled it open, waving the pilot through.

"We're done climbing?"

Caleb put a finger to his lips as he softly closed the door. It took only a few seconds before the Marines passed them, still under the impression we'd continued ascending. Turning away from the stairwell door, Caleb practically dragged Atrice along the hallway, searching for a window.

"ETA twenty seconds, Cap," Penn announced.

"We're on floor fifty-four, on our way to a window."

"What?"

"We'll only have one shot at this. You need to bring Medusa to the window with the hatch open. Get as close as you can, we'll need to jump the gap."

"Jump the gap?" Atrice asked softly.

"It's our only shot," Caleb replied.

"Aye, Captain," Penn said. "Better hurry."

Caleb ran along the hallway, flinching when he heard a door slam open behind them, followed by too-many footsteps. The Marines going up had encountered the Marines coming down, leading them to search this floor.

"The south side exterior should be through there," Caleb said, pointing to a door. He and Atrice sprinted to it, the Marines reaching the hallway at the same time. Caleb whirled and fired, exchanging a quick round of fire with them before pushing through the door. The office they entered occupied the entire corner of the building, in an open floor plan with desks scattered across tiled flooring. Men and women in business attire looked at them with wide-eyed fear.

Delicious.

"Penn, south-east corner," Caleb said. "Shake Medusa's ass past the south windows."

"Aye, Captain. I hope I guess the right floor. They all look the same from here."

"You'd better, because we aren't waiting for you to get here."

"What?" Atrice wheezed.

Caleb dropped the stun baton to grab his arm. Racing toward the window, he shot it out, one blast after another, weakening the glass until it melted.

Because of the angle, Caleb didn't know if he could make his idea work. There would be no way to tell how close Penn was before Medusa actually arrived, but he didn't slow or consider a new plan. They didn't have the time for any other options. He held Atrice tighter, forcing the pilot to keep running when every instinct likely told him to hit the brakes.

The Marines burst through the door behind them, eliciting cries of fear and surprise from the office workers as they opened fire. Their errant blasts peppered the wall around the window just as Caleb and Atrice hit the glass, punching through the weakened window.

Hanging in the air for what felt like a lifetime, Caleb found Medusa, two floors below them. He and Atrice fell, the air whistling by them as Penn used vectoring thrusters to quickly turn the ship sideways, a burst of thrust lining them up with the open hatch. Unfortunately, the hatch wasn't wide enough for them to fall through it side by side. Caleb pulled Atrice in front of him, wrapped his arms around him and turned them both so he would take the brunt of the landing inside Medusa.

I hope you know this won't be pretty, but the fear is delectable.

Medusa swallowed them up, but not before Caleb's right arm banged into the fuselage at the edge of the hatch, breaking on impact. An instant later, his back slammed into the blast door to Medusa's flight deck. Like being struck by a giant fist, the collision knocked the air from his lungs, and pain assaulted him everywhere. At least one rib shattered as he broke Atrice's fall, his right hip and leg also breaking from the blow.

"Got you!" Penn cried joyfully over the comms.

CHAPTER 33

"Go! Go! Go!" Johan shouted from his seat in the cabin.

Caleb groaned in excruciating pain as Atrice extracted himself and fell into a seat, quickly pulling on his harness. Caleb pulled himself up beside the pilot, only able to stand thanks to the chemicals Ishek had sent through his body. Instead of strapping in, he limped back to the flight deck and collapsed in the co-pilot seat.

"Damn, Cap," Penn said, risking a glance at him. "You look like hell."

"I feel like hell," Caleb replied. "Healing from this will be a real bear." He glanced at the sensor grid. Just like he thought, the RAF had sent everything they had available after them. Combat aircraft and starfighters clogged the airspace all around them, though most had yet to make it into firing range. "Ugly."

"And it's been a long time since I flew a ship like this."

"Are you kidding? You caught Cookie and me."

"I'm not even sure how. I was on the wrong floor."

"We survived."

Medusa rocketed skyward, aiming for a quick escape from the atmosphere. Multiple warning tones sounded, a few of the ships on the grid flashing to indicate they had a target lock. Penn rolled the ship over, banking hard to the left. "Cap, you may want to take over fire control."

"Right," Caleb said, selecting targets through the fire control system. He squeezed the trigger, the FCS perfecting his aim as he shot back at the chasing ships. The sky filled with projectiles criss-crossing one another, the guided missiles launched by the Royal Marines closing in fast. Switching systems, Caleb triggered countermeasures, using the wing-mounted turrets to blast the warheads. Further back, the RAF forces did the same, knocking out the rockets he sent their way before they hit anything.

Penn continued evasive maneuvers, keeping them ascending toward orbit. Caleb did his best to keep the trailing opposition honest, firing salvos of missiles back at them while mindful that the rockets would be difficult to replace. They continued gaining altitude, Medusa's powerful thrusters keeping them ahead of the Marines and making it increasingly difficult for the defense to catch up.

Meanwhile, Caleb opened a comms channel, trying to hail Gorgon. Burke had claimed they'd sent a Specter after the ship. No doubt Damian had seen it coming. But what had happened since then? The lack of response from Gorgon left him fearing the worst.

They continued their ascent; the sky darkening ahead of them, the Marine ships falling further behind. Unable to match the velocity of the shuttle, they finally gave up the chase while the handful of starfighters stayed on their tail despite their inability to catch up. The sensor grid reached out to orbit, painting the busy area just beyond the atmosphere. Fortunately, of the dozens of ships in their path, none of them were Specters.

Unfortunately, some of them were still military.

Three Navy patrol ships sped across space on an intercept course, already trying to get a target lock on them.

"Penn," Caleb said in warning.

"I see them," she replied. "I don't know if we can make it past."

Ish, I don't suppose they're piloted by Legionnaires?

Negative.

Are you sure?

I am more focused on separating the signal from the noise. But it remains challenging in this environment. I cannot be certain, but I also cannot target them if they are. Not without something to differentiate them, and you can't punch them from here.

"Just do your best," Caleb said to Penn.

"What's the point?" she continued, her morale sinking. "You can't reach Gorgon, and we don't have a hyperdrive on this boat."

"The point is we don't quit," he answered. "Knuckle-up Penny. We're going to make it."

His forced confidence was enough to break her from the momentary funk. As hurt as he was, if he could remain positive, so could she.

Her body language shifted as she changed Medusa's vector, reducing their approach angle toward orbit. Hoping to clear the patrol ships, the maneuver was enough to leave one of the Navy vessels too far away for it to matter, but that still left two tangos between them and freedom. Not to mention, the change in course had allowed the starfighters to gain. It was a risky gambit that might not pay off, but at least Penn was back in the game.

Caleb reset the fire control system, sending energy pulses blasting back at the chasing fighters as they flashed on the grid, firing additional projectiles. The FCS knocked down most, but two of the rockets slipped through, detonating against the shuttle's shields. The impact shoved them violently sideways, pulling Caleb hard enough against his restraints that his broken bones throbbed in pain. He gritted his teeth to keep from crying out.

Ish, why aren't you healing me?

I cannot while you're coming off the boost.

Penn righted Medusa and continued toward orbit. He kept firing at the fighters behind them, making them evade the energy blasts and reducing their chance to attain a target lock. Reaching the upper atmosphere, he switched targets to the Navy ships ahead of them. Closing from either side, they were already locking missiles on Medusa while opening up with their plasma cannons. Penn banked left and right to avoid the firepower. She wasn't nearly as good a combat pilot as Ham, but she kept Medusa from being instantaneously destroyed. One missile slipped past Caleb's countermeasures, detonating against the shields and again knocking them around. A few plasma bolts impacted their shields as well, the lack of kinetic energy making the hits less rough.

Even so, they couldn't take many more punches before the knockout came.

Caleb did the only thing he could do, putting pressure on the patrol ship by firing back. His shots smacked harmlessly against their shields, not even close to breaking through, but he kept firing anyway. The second patroller unleashed a fresh barrage of missiles. The FCS took out a few, but two more broke through, jolting them upward, disabling the shields along the bottom of the hull, and wrenching Caleb's broken arm. This time, he couldn't stop himself from grunting in pain.

"We aren't going to make it," Penn said.

"We're almost through," Caleb shouted. "Full speed ahead!" Of course, he didn't know what they would do once they were past. They would still be in range of the patrol ship's guns for several minutes more, with nowhere to run to.

Not without Gorgon.

"Gorgon, do you copy?" Hailing the ship on their encrypted frequency, Caleb demanded an answer. "Gorgon, come in."

The patrol ships were close enough now to be visible in the forward surround, plasma cannons belching fire. Penn did her best to evade the shots, her lack of experience showing as she unwittingly maneuvered into a few hits. Fortunately, none found the gap in Medusa's belly shields, allowing the ship to shrug off the hits.

"Gorgon, damn it!" Caleb shouted. "Come in!"

"Medusa, this is Gorgon," Damian said. "Surprise! We're getting out of here in one minute. You'd better get here fast."

"What?" Penn asked as the ship suddenly appeared on the sensor grid, closer than Caleb would have thought possible. "How?"

Ishek's laughter reverberated through Caleb.

They had been running completely dark and powered down. Risky, but genius.

And close enough to engage the patrol ships, Caleb realized as Gorgon's batteries came alive. Energy beams lashed across thousands of kilometers, spearing into the shields of one of the patrol craft. Aware it was outgunned, it stopped firing on Medusa, focusing instead on escaping Gorgon.

"Come on, Penn," Caleb growled through the pain. "We can make it."

"Damn right we're going to make it," she replied. Medusa streaked toward Gorgon, which laid down such heavy cover fire the enemy had no chance.

The Specter was a different story.

It appeared further away, moving out from behind the sun where it had apparently been searching for Gorgon. No doubt having picked the ship up on their sensors around the same time as Medusa had, the Legion ship approached at full burn, gaining velocity and racing into the fight. It fired on Gorgon, its energy beams slashing into the ship's shields. Rather than take evasive action, a hyperspace field started forming around Gorgon, the distortion spreading quickly.

"We need to get inside that field!" Caleb snapped.

"I know!" Penn shouted back. "We'll be there in twenty seconds."

"Do we have that long?"

"I guess we'll find out."

Gorgon maintained its heading and velocity, giving them the best chance at catching up and syncing with them. Caleb realized that overshooting the field might be more likely than actually ending up inside it. He admired Penn for her range of skills, but again, she wasn't Ham. Or even Atrice. They had one shot at this, and one shot only.

The Specter brought more guns to bear and continued firing on Gorgon to kill the ship before the hyperspace field could finish forming. Gorgon's shields flashed and sparkled, catching each beam that smacked against it. Caleb knew it could only take this kind of punishment for so long. Thankfully, Medusa needed just a short time to reach the edges of the hyperspace bubble.

"Eight seconds," Damian announced. "Come on, Medusa."

Penn had already cut the mains and hit the retro-thrusters, hoping to slow the ship a little before entering the field. She gave up on that approach now, pushing the throttle forward and cutting the retros. The ship skipped forward and pressed into the field as the countdown hit three seconds. Immediately, she flipped the ship over, the burn from the mains shoving Caleb back in his seat so hard he could barely breathe. The pressure, even with his lingering adrenaline high, tore at his broken rib, the pain excruciating.

The hyperspace field completed around both ships. Gorgon became a blip of light bursting away from Atlas, but the danger to Medusa wasn't over, their survival hardly assured.

"We're coming in too fast!" Penn shouted in alarm, her teeth clenched, eyes narrow, knuckles white on the controls.

"Extend the landers," Caleb replied. "Maglock to slow us down."

She did as he said, extending the pads and firing vectoring thrusters while rolling the ship. The pads smashed into Gorgon; the maglock taking hold, pulling at the hull and wrenching them even harder before snapping and sending Medusa toward the other end of the field.

"Come on, you snake-haired bitch!" Penn growled, hitting the rear-facing vectoring thrusters for more braking power.

Blackness closing in around the edges of his vision, Caleb watched the compression closing in, his good hand clenched on his armrest, his knuckles white. It neared ever more slowly, until finally, fortunately, the distance lengthened, their velocity less than Gorgon's.

"Yessss!" Penn cried, nearly forgetting to cut the mains and flip the shuttle back over before setting their heading to remain close to Gorgon.

Caleb smiled despite his pain. They had escaped capture. They were still alive. Caleb could hardly believe they'd made it.

But they had.

He smiled and finally passed out.

CHAPTER 34

Penn dropped the shuttle onto the deck of Gorgon's hangar bay. Without landing pads, the ship rolled over to one side, coming to rest on a wing. It jarred Caleb just enough to bring him out of the blackness into a half-conscious fugue.

"Captain?" Penn's voice barely cut through his stupor. Her hand jostled his shoulder.

I'll begin healing your damage now.

Oh, now you will? Caleb replied dryly. He was one big throb, the pain nearly unbearable. *Thanks so much, Ish.*

You are exceedingly welcome.

"Captain, can you stand?" Penn asked. She balanced herself on the tilted deck, holding onto the column in front of him to look into his eyes. "Are you with me?"

"I'm supposed to ask you that," Caleb mumbled, his voice barely loud enough to hear. "I have some broken bones. Arm. Ribs. Leg. Ish is working on it, But I could use a stretcher."

"Sarge, do you copy?" Penn said. "Cap needs a lift to sick bay."

"I copy," Damian replied. "Nurse Gillroy is en route with a gurney."

The flight deck hatch opened, and Atrice peeked in. "That was some incredible flying," he said to Penn. "Just don't learn how to cook, too, okay? I'll be out of a job."

"Don't worry," Penn replied. "You're a much better cook than I could ever hope to be."

"Where's Johan?" Caleb asked, noticing the engineer wasn't with Atrice.

"He passed out during the high-G maneuvers."

"Should I ask Sarge for a second gurney?" Penn said.

"Nah, he ought to wake anytime now." Atrice turned the other way, opening the side hatch. It was tilted toward the deck enough that they would have to crouch to get out. "Thank you again for getting me out of there, Cap," he said, turning back to Caleb. "I owe you my life."

"You don't owe me anything," Caleb answered. "As your Captain, I'm responsible for you. And I hate when people die on my watch."

"Well, I'm still grateful."

"You can owe me," Penn said, still on an adrenaline high. "I love those brownies you made six months ago for Sarge's birthday party."

"I'll see what I can do."

A head ducked through the main hatch. "Captain," Damian said. "Other than our nail-biting escape, how did things go?"

"Pretty bad. Fitz was our traitor. He sold us out to Crux."

Damian's face darkened, his face going slack with shock. "Son of a bitch. I should have known it was him."

"How could you?" Penn asked. "I was his SO, and I didn't have an inkling."

"He always seemed shifty to me. Like everything was a joke no one else was in on."

"It doesn't matter," Caleb murmured. "He's a traitor. If we ever see him again, he's a dead man."

"We got a lead on Lo'ane's daughter," Penn added.

"I call that a win, and that's what matters right now."

"Aye, Captain," Damian agreed. He looked back over his shoulder. "Gillroy is here."

"I'll need some help," Caleb said. Penn removed his harness as Damian made way for Nurse Gillroy, her floating gurney waiting beside the main hatch. A volunteer transfer from Duke Draco's medical team, the nurse was short and stocky, with dark hair and an easy smile despite her obvious concern at Caleb's condition. She gently helped Penn load him onto the gurney.

"You're in awful shape, Captain," Gillroy said, maneuvering the gurney out through the flight deck hatch.

"Ish is working on it, but it'll take a few hours to heal the bone breaks."

"You're lucky you didn't break your neck," Damian added, stepping out of the shuttle behind the gurney. "I don't know what maneuvers Penn put Medusa through back there, but I'm glad we had an excellent pilot in that seat." He smiled back over his shoulder at Atrice as he got out behind him. "No offense, Cookie."

"Hey, none taken," Atrice replied. "Penn saved our lives out there."

"She did indeed." Damian looked back into the shuttle. "Johan! You getting out or staying there?" he shouted, ducking inside to check on him when he didn't answer. A moment later, he returned with the still groggy engineer, who needed to hold on to him to walk.

"Am I dreaming," Johan asked, "or did we actually make it out of there alive?"

"You're not dreaming," Penn answered before Caleb could. "You're dead."

"What?" Johan cried, face immediately turning pale. The smiles on the surrounding faces left him with a sheepish grin as he realized the joke was on him. "Does the fact that you're making fun of me mean I'm an accepted member of the crew now?"

"More than accepted," Caleb replied. "Highly valued. We couldn't have done any of it without you."

"Thank you, Captain."

"Does anyone else need to go to sick bay?" Gillroy asked, giving Penn, Atrice, and Johan the once-over.

"I'll follow you down," Atrice said. "I imagine you want to run a blood test on me, since I was away from the team and under enemy control."

"That's a good idea," Caleb said. "We'll all get tested. We can't afford to take any chances."

"Let's get you all down to sick bay," Gillroy said.

They made quick work of getting Caleb to sickbay where Nurse Gillroy transferred him to a bed before leaving to retrieve their blood testing machine.

"I'm curious," Johan said, looking at Damian as he scratched his eyebrow. "Atrice told me we were running from a Specter and Gorgon was gone. Then I passed out. Where the hell did you go and how did we find you?"

Damian chuckled. "We didn't go anywhere."

"What?"

"It's an old pirate trick," he replied. "Graystone used it once before we came into possession of Gorgon. Give the ship a little push, take advantage of a gravity well, and shut everything down. Ship sensors won't pick you up unless you're within a few minutes of collision. They just see you as a random asteroid. You can float for as long as the current air remains breathable, and as long as you don't go crazy from zero gravity. We picked up the Specter approaching from the port side, so we went dark and drifted off to starboard. Kind of boring, really." He chuckled, clapping his hand on Johan's shoulder before dropping his hand, all levity leaving his expression as he returned his attention to Caleb. "So what was it that Penn said about a lead on Lo'ane's daughter?"

Nurse Gillroy returned just then with the testing machine. "Who wants to go first?" she asked, placing the machine on the counter, along with a box of syringes.

"I will," Johan volunteered, rolling up his sleeve and sticking out his arm. "I have to get back to engineering."

Gillroy collected his sample and ran it through the machine. "Negative. Who's next?"

Penn stuck out her arm. Again, the sample came back negative. Caleb expected Atrice to go next, but he hesitated, so Caleb offered his good arm, already certain of his results.

"Your turn, Cookie," Penn said after finishing with Caleb.

Atrice swallowed hard, eyes flicking toward the door. His hands shook, and his face paled.

No doubt, his heart is racing too. He reminds me of Colonel Campbell.

He sure does, Caleb agreed, suddenly nervous about the pilot. Had the enemy snuck a moiety into him while he was their prisoner?

"Are you okay?" Damian asked him.

"I just hate having blood drawn," Atrice replied. "Creeps me out."

"It was your idea," Penn pointed out.

"I know. That doesn't mean I enjoy being stuck with a needle."

As Gillroy turned toward him with a syringe, he looked like he was about ready to pass out. "Oh, come on, Cookie," she said. "It's just a little prick."

He finally nodded, rolling up the sleeve of his flight suit and holding out his arm. He turned his head away, eyes clamped shut while Gillroy took the blood.

"You're good to go," she announced. Atrice's relief was

obvious, as if he hadn't even been sure himself that he wasn't infected.

"That's a strange reaction," Caleb said, calling him out on it.

"I didn't want to say anything," Atrice replied. "The Royal Guard knocked me out when they grabbed me. I didn't think I was infected, but..."

"Unzip your flight suit," Caleb said.

I'm not registering any other khoron nearby.

You've said that a lot lately.

I admit that I was wrong about Atlas. But we aren't surrounded by Legion here. There's only me. I'm positive.

There's no harm in having him show us.

"What?" Atrice looked confused. "Cap, I—"

"Unzip your flight suit," he repeated. "Or Sarge will do it."

Atrice glanced at Damian. He slowly unzipped his flight suit, pulling his arms out of the sleeves and shrugging it off his shoulders.

"Undershirt, too," Damian said.

Atrice nodded, pulling it up over his head. No sooner had he raised his arms than Caleb caught sight of the Advocate beneath his left pit.

Okay, I was wrong again. But that's because it's dormant.

Penn reached for her blaster. Damian moved to grab it.

"Wait!" Caleb said, raising his uninjured hand. "Don't hurt it. Atrice, don't move."

"Don't hurt it? Are you kidding?" Penn said, gaping at him in sudden silence. "

"Ish, what should we do with it? Why is it dormant?"

I believe they wanted to use him as a host, but were not convinced you would rescue him. In which case, it would make sense for it to wait until it could inflict immediate harm to become active.

"Wouldn't Atrice have seen it in the shower or something?"

Perhaps it would have abandoned him and sought a different host, hoping to remain unseen both by me and Atrice.

"How can it do that if it's sleeping?"

I didn't say sleeping. I said dormant. It is aware of its surroundings, but it cannot move without becoming active on the Collective. As I know it exists, I will also know the moment that happens.

"Can it hear me?"

The Advocate shifted slightly.

It has just awakened. It is reaching out to me.

Reaching out to you?

Yes. It wishes to surrender.

Caleb's eyebrows went up. "I've never heard of a khoron surrendering before."

The consequences of such are dire. But it has heard of both me and Gareshk. It believes at this point its best hope of survival is with us. But we must provide a host soon.

Caleb stared at the khoron. He could hardly believe it. "The Advocate wants to surrender. It's asking us for a host."

"I don't want to host it," Atrice declared, his face stricken.

"So it's willing to be subservient?" Damian asked. "Why would it agree to that?"

"To survive," Caleb answered. "It doesn't have much of a chance any other way."

"At least that makes sense."

"I'll do it," Penn said.

"You don't have to—" Caleb started to say.

"I'll do it," she repeated. "Ishek strengthens you, heals you faster, and helps you fight against the Legion. There's no good reason for me not to do it." She shrugged out of her jacket and unbuttoned her blouse. "Besides, I'd like to think

I'm strong enough that it can't overpower me, even if it wants to."

"Sarge might have to shoot you," Caleb said.

"Go ahead if need be." She took off her blouse, leaving her in a sports bra. She looked over at the khoron, still lodged beneath Atrice's upraised arm. "Do you hear that, bud? I won't take any garbage from you."

The khoron shifted, turning its face toward Penn, its thin tentacles undulating, stretching as if seeking her out. She drew her head back, grimacing at Caleb in a moment of obvious uncertainty before her look of distaste vanished and she turned back to the Relyeh, extending her bare arm toward it.

It stretched out between her and Atrice like a caterpillar, latching onto her at the base of her hand and pulling itself up her forearm. Damian turned away, sickened by the display. The Advocate tucked itself up under Penn's arm, its thin tendrils sinking into her flesh and working their way toward her brain stem. She shuddered visibly, face paling, eyes momentarily rolling back in her head.

"Damian, cover her," Caleb said.

The other man pulled his blaster, keeping it aimed at Penn as her eyes slowly regained focus.

"Penn?" Caleb asked.

She nodded. "I'm here, Cap. Vraxis and I have come to a quick understanding. If he wants to live, he'll do what I say. He knows I'm not above killing myself to keep him in line."

"I don't doubt that," Caleb replied. "Ish and I will start training you on the Collective tomorrow."

"Aye, Captain."

"Since that's settled," Gillroy interjected, "I'm going to pretend I didn't see what I just saw. As for the rest of you, you should all get out of here and let Captain Card get some rest."

"Sound advice, if you ask me," Atrice agreed. "I, for one,

need a shower. Badly." He shivered, giving Vraxis one last disgusted look.

"I'm sure we'll talk again soon, Cap," Penn said, slipping her arms back into her blouse and buttoning it back up. "I thought this might take some adjustment, but it feels strangely natural."

"I know the feeling," Caleb said, laying his head back down on the gurney.

Penn and Atrice left sick bay. Damian stayed behind, turning to Gillroy. "I need a moment with the captain, in private."

She looked to Caleb, who nodded, before she left them alone in the med bay..

"What did you find out about Lo'ane's daughter?" Damian asked. "I can't wait to know."

"Lo'ane visited a hospital and orphanage on the planet Callus, in the…"

"Kallio Combine," Damian finished for him. "Talk about out of the way. If she had a child and wanted to keep it quiet, that would be the perfect place for her to go."

"Have Rufus drop us out of hyperspace and set a fresh course for the Combine," Caleb said.

"Aye, Captain. Now that we know Fitz was our spy, should I release Naya and Tae from the brig?"

Caleb nodded. "With my firmest apologies. Tell them I'll speak to them individually later."

"Aye, sir." He patted Caleb on his good leg. "Let's not make a habit out of these daring escapes from hostile territory."

"I can't make any promises. We made it; that's what matters."

Damian turned to leave, but paused halfway. "I take it Fitz knows about Callus, too?"

Caleb nodded. "Which means Crux knows. Sticking that

Advocate on Atrice could be a blessing in disguise. We needed another bonded pair."

"I can't believe Crux would be so reckless."

"I can. He's not accustomed to opposition, and he probably still feels invulnerable enough to take a lot of risks. He'll either adapt or die."

"My vote is for dying."

Caleb smiled. "Mine too."

CHAPTER 35

Three weeks from Atlas to Callus. A long trip, but Caleb was accustomed to long trips. After spending months in the cramped confines of Spirit with Ham and Jii, three weeks on the much more spacious Gorgon hardly seemed like a burden at all.

Unlike on Spirit, where off-duty hours were filled with games, movies, spirited political discussions, and otherwise trying to avoid going insane, Caleb had plenty of irons in the fire on Gorgon to keep himself busy. Foremost among them was teaching Penn the ways of the Collective and how she and Vraxis could work together to increase their capabilities within the Relyeh pocket universe. Being in hyperspace during the training was an immense benefit as any Relyeh who tried to ping them could never get a fixed position. With enough signal, the enemy could collectively assemble a path and guess the destination, not that they needed to guess.

Thanks to Fitz, Crux and Iagorth knew where Gorgon was headed. Caleb knew that the Spiral's false Emperor could likely get some kind of force there to meet them, but considering the distance from the galaxy's seat of power and the Kallio Combine, he had a feeling it wouldn't be much of a contingent. However, he'd been wrong before, and he was ready to be wrong again. If they had to fight tooth and nail for every step that took them to Lo'ane's daughter, then so be it. Right or wrong, Haas and Draco had decided that restoring the bloodline to the throne was an important step on the path to victory, and he'd accepted the mission.

Training Penn on the Collective had bled naturally into training with not only the Razor's Edge, but all the boarding teams. In the past, they'd always operated as individual units with individual goals, sometimes coming into direct competition with one another. According to Granger, prior to Penn and Caleb's arrival they'd even had one instance where a couple of Berzerkers had been killed by friendly fire when they fought over who had actually captured the booty. It was an ugly episode he never wanted to see happen under his command.

Fitz had turned out to be as much of a bastard as Damian had initially warned, though Caleb's second didn't waste his breath on a *told you so*. The one upside to the former Star Guard's involvement with the crew continued to be the training course, which Caleb found could be easily modified to suit different mission objectives. From capturing flags to running squad-level scrimmages, the pitfalls, traps, and machinations on the lower decks challenged all of Gorgon's fighters, and as the days passed Caleb could see the aptitudes of even the weaker crew members increase.

Beyond training, the time spent working with Penn turned into downtime spent together. They had so much in common, that even their war stories had similar tones and outcomes, their lives following somewhat parallel tracks though billions of light years apart. While Caleb insisted his energy and focus remain on defeating Iagorth, there was a part of him—the part that he often found at loose ends—that could envision something more when the Relyeh were finally defeated. To him, that meant ending the threat to Earth and Proxima and the threat to the Spiral. He couldn't help wondering if putting down his rifle and settling down with someone would ever be more than a dream for him.

Sometimes, he questioned if the Hunger could ever be defeated. Between Iagorth and Shub'Nigu, the strength of the Relyeh often seemed overwhelming. And yet, he knew from Sheriff Duke that beating the Relyeh was possible with the right allies, a little luck, and an endless supply of determination.

If nothing else, he had determination to spare.

He was alone in his quarters, reading through everything the ship's datastore had on the Kallio Combine when his comm's patch vibrated behind his ear.

"Captain," Tae said. "If you have some time, I've got something good for you. It's about the wormhole."

"Are you in your workshop?" Caleb replied.

"Aye."

"I'll be there right away."

Caleb stood up from his terminal and hurried out of his quarters. He had told Tae his temporary imprisonment wasn't personal from the beginning, and thankfully neither he nor Naya had held a grudge for their detainment. Naya reacted to her release with gratitude, both for Caleb's understanding in her failure to get into Graystone's accounts and for the opportunity to remain part of the crew. The first family she ever really cared about. Tae had never really changed from being Tae. He'd shrugged the entire episode off as a chance to get a little more sleep and practice his meditative tantras, whatever that meant.

Rushing around the corner, he collided with Orin.

"Captain Cayheb," Orin said as he caught Caleb

smoothly, turning him aside. "If you had Jiba-ki hearing, you would have heard me approach."

"You have ears like a Jiba-ki," Caleb replied. "Why didn't you hear me and step out of my way?"

Orin's high-pitch laugh drew Caleb into a grin. "You have a point. You look especially content this morning, Captain. It is true."

"All healed up, well rested, well fed. The training is going well, and we still have a week until we reach Callus. Not to mention, Tae just informed me he's uncovered something useful about the wormhole. I'm heading to his workshop now to see what he's discovered. In our line of work, times when things are going well are times we need to savor. They don't last."

"That is most definitely true," Orin answered, "although things have gone well for me since I landed on Aroon. I have made many new friends and found acceptance despite my non-human nature. I spent many years hunting alone. Now I hunt with a pack, and I am grateful for it. I am not even upset I have lost my standing on the Dark Exchange."

"I'm glad you didn't need to kill me," Caleb agreed.

"As am I. It is true. Do you mind if I join you on your journey? I would like to know more about this wormhole."

"You're welcome to come along."

Caleb and Orin boarded the captain's personal elevator, taking it down to Deck Twenty-four.

"Have you been to Tae's workshop before, Captain?" Orin asked as the cab doors opened.

"No," Caleb replied. "I know where it is, but I've never actually been inside. Have you?"

"No. I have heard that Tae rarely invites anyone to his workshop. Sarge says he is a secretive *cuss*. Does that mean he swears a lot?"

Caleb chuckled. "I think he just means that Tae has a

way about him that doesn't invite visitors. He likes his solitude and his secrets."

They walked side by side through the corridors of Deck Twenty-four until they reached a nondescript hatch near Gorgon's stern. It was unmarked and indistinguishable from the others except for the small, handmade wooden sign in Japanese kanji affixed to it.

"Do you know what that says?" Orin asked, pointing at the sign.

"According to Penn, it says *get lost*."

Orin laughed. "I feel lost being this far astern. I suppose I have followed the instructions of the sign. It is true."

Caleb was ready to knock when the hatch slid aside. He and Orin stepped into the workshop, looking around at a hoarder's mess. Tools and parts were piled on every surface in the compartment. Holographic posters of different vid streams lined the upper parts of the bulkheads, while the deck had vanished beneath multiple layers of different colored rugs. He thought he caught sight of a cat vanishing behind Tae's workbench.

A shirtless Tae stood there, his display offering the only light source in the room and casting a eerie frame around his face. A larger computer rested on the bench beside the display, the ancient model giving off enough heat to make the compartment's climate uncomfortable.

At least now we know why he doesn't like to wear shirts.

Tae's eyes fixed on Orin. "I didn't invite you here. You scared Duffy."

"Duffy?" Orin replied.

"My cat." Tae glanced around the space. "He's around here, somewhere."

"My apologies. I did not intend to frighten your pet. I will go."

"Nah. He's already hiding. You might as well stick

around. Just step forward so the door can close before he runs out."

Orin did as Tae asked. The hatch closed behind him.

"I don't know how you ever find anything in this mess," Caleb said, looking around for the cat. Before now, he hadn't known of any Earth species in the Spiral, other than rats. They seemed to go wherever people went.

"It's not a mess," Tae responded. "It's a system. Anyway, the reason I invited you down here is because I have the simulator running on Hellboy here." He tapped the top of the large computer. "And I can't show you what I wanted to show you without him. So kindly disregard everything else you see."

"Gladly," Caleb agreed. "What do you have?"

"If you'd circle around to my right," Tae said, motioning to the spot. Caleb and Orin both moved to join him there, but Tae put up his hand in front of the Jiba-ki. "There's not enough space for both of you. Sorry, Orin."

"It is not a problem. I am taller than you. I will observe from behind you."

Tae tapped on his screen, showing a translucent, static version of the spiral wormhole. "So if you remember, I said I had an algorithm that needed to be tweaked. Well, I did some tweaking, reverse-engineered some more of the mathematical variables and came up with this simulation. What you're going to see, Cap, is the movement of the wormhole through spacetime. It's also color-coded to show when parts of the tunnel phase in and out of different dimensions."

"Dimensions?" Caleb asked.

"Parallel universes. Or maybe out of spacetime altogether. All I can tell you is that parts of the tunnel vanish and reappear, according to the equations. It could all be garbage. I'm not an expert in any of that. Anyway, here's the output of the equations."

He tapped his control board to play the animation. The

wormhole spun like a corkscrew, but also expanded and contracted like a spring. It reminded Caleb of how Benning had referred to the wormhole as a Slinky. As Tae had mentioned, portions of it seemed in constant flux, appearing and vanishing like sunspots.

"That's amazing," he said.

"Curious," Orin said. Almost mesmerized by the pattern, he leaned over Tae's shoulder to get a closer look at the screen. "It is almost as beautiful as me. It is true."

"So you recreated the algorithm and built a simulator," Caleb said. "Does that mean we can traverse it in the opposite direction?"

"Absolutely," Tae answered. "Like I said earlier, the ship would have to be programmed ahead of time to match the algorithm and stay in the center of the wormhole. I don't know what happens to anything that falls out, especially in the phased sections. Death is likely. Or maybe worse. Timing is also important. It's easier to get through during a contraction, because you can go straight across when the center bunches."

"How do we sync our time with the simulation time?"

"Good question. I don't know yet. I'll have to figure that part out before you can attempt to cross."

"But Ham and I can cross?"

"Yes."

Caleb smiled. "This is excellent work, Tae. You're a genius."

"I know," he replied in all seriousness. "To be fair, I couldn't have done it without Naya and Johan. They brainstormed the tricky spots with me."

"I'll be sure to thank and compliment them, too." Caleb glanced at Tae, ready to leave, but there was something in the engineer's expression that held him back. It was probably the real reason he hadn't been that happy to see Orin. "There's more, isn't there?"

Tae's gaze flicked to and from the Jiba-ki before he answered. "It's a...personal matter," he said.

"Orin, I need you to wait outside," Caleb said, turning to him.

"Aye, Captain. It is a shame I did not get to see the cat. I have heard that Jiba-ki resemble that Earthian creature, but I do not believe any species can be more beautiful than a Jiba-ki. I will not be far if you require my services." He turned and left the compartment.

"What is it?" Caleb asked once the hatch closed behind Orin.

"I have something else I want to show you." He returned to his control board, minimizing the simulation and switching to another view. It looked like security camera footage from the compartment they were standing in, the camera pointed at the door. "I audited my own systems after I got out of the brig. It took some time, but I recovered this file. Someone remotely wiped it from my secondary system, which doesn't broadcast publicly on the network."

Caleb watched as the hatch slid open and Fitz walked in, a pad in one hand, a bag in the other. Duffy, who had been resting on the control board, immediately jumped off and hid beneath the mess. "He broke in?"

"Yeah," Tae replied.

Fitz placed the pad and the bag on the counter and opened the bag, removing a more powerful computer. Looking around the room, he found the data chip reader Tae had made and put it on the workbench, connecting it to his computer. A quick search for the chip ended when he guessed it was still in the reader. He did something on the computer before taking a seat at Tae's stool.

"He accessed the data chip," Caleb said.

"Yeah. Likely copied the whole thing. My best guess is that he transferred it to a modern data chip and slipped it to the enemy during your little jaunt to Atlas."

Caleb felt a sudden sinking sensation in the pit of his stomach. "So Crux knows all about the wormhole. Including its location."

"I'm afraid so, Boss."

He exhaled in resigned frustration. "Damn it. I never should have put you in the brig. I gave him the perfect opportunity to get in here and copy the chip."

"It's not your fault, Cap. You did what you thought was right."

"Which would be fine if we were talking about Callus, or some other bit of intel we hoped to keep from Crux, and Iagorth. But now, once they're done with this galaxy, they can move on mine."

Tae's lips pursed as he shook his head. "No, he'd still need to figure out the equation. He didn't get that because I hadn't finished it yet. It's bad, but it's not as bad as it could be."

Caleb nodded, though he felt little relief from the statement. The last thing he wanted was for Iagorth to have easy access to the Milky Way. He exhaled sharply, refocusing himself. "There's nothing we can do about it now."

"Nope," Tae agreed. "And if we somehow beat the bad guys here, this little piece of thievery won't matter."

"Then I guess my only question is, why didn't you want Orin to know about this?" Caleb asked.

"It's not my place to decide who to tell. It's yours. And how can you decide that without knowing the information beforehand?"

Caleb smiled. "Fair enough. You're right. There's no reason for anyone else to know about this. It won't mean much to anyone here and will just become a distraction."

"Consider the secret safe with me and Duffy, Cap."

"I do," Caleb replied. "Keep up the great work."

"Aye, Captain."

Caleb reconnected with Orin outside the compartment.

Orin took one look at him and frowned. "Captain Cayheb, is everything okay?"

"Yeah, it's fine," Caleb lied, clearing his obviously worried expression. "Are you hungry?"

"Always. It is true."

"Then let's head down to the mess," he said, clapping his hand to Orin's shoulder. "I think Atrice is cooking Taris flank."

Orin licked his lips. "I like that plan."

Everything isn't fine, Ishek groused as they walked back down the passageway to the elevator.

No, Caleb admitted. *Before we only had to worry about the humans on this side of the universe. Now all of humankind is at stake.*

Yeah. No pressure.

CHAPTER 36

Callus was a beautiful planet from orbit, covered in blue oceans and green land masses speckled by white clouds and brown deserts. Nestled between an active volcanic mountain range and a pair of major rivers, Acala occupied the eastern edge of the planet's primary continent. The positioning made the settlement nearly impossible to reach on foot, which was the only reason people had started a colony there. The rest of the land mass surrounding Acala was home to an abundance of wildlife so aggressive that the humans who'd first arrived on the planet had quickly determined it wasn't worth the loss of life to claim any of the interior lands beyond the natural mountain barrier.

And what a home Acala was. For all the sparkle of Haydrun's Glitz district, Acala's beautiful construction more than matched it. The entire place was a sea of glass and shiny metal tucked into a green paradise, population two million.

The source of Acala and the Combine's fortunes was in the stars. Or rather, the space between Callus and its star, which was twice the distance between Earth and the Moon. All he had to do was look into the shuttle's aft feed to see the asteroid belt supporting the abundant wealth of the Kallio Combine. Or rather, the wealth of the three dozen oligarch families who'd established the Combine and the mining operations. The belt was so large it remained visible from Callus' surface in the daytime as a hazy streak arcing across the sky.

While the Combine could hardly be called a major trade hub, it mined and sold enough minerals to keep the oligarchs comfortable and the miners desperate. A service industry had formed for both, providing for a still massively unequal but wider distribution of wealth across the population. The sparkling glass and metal was highly visible during the descent. But Caleb's research had revealed the existence of dingy steel and cracked stone hidden beneath it, literally composing the still functioning foundation of Combine society.

He wouldn't find the answers he was seeking down that far. Lo'ane had come to Acala as a princess, not a pauper. Acala Primary Hospital sat near the center of what the populace called the over city; a glass pyramid surrounded by a giant botanical garden. That was where he'd find his answers, if there were any answers to be found.

As Caleb hoped, just knowing where he planned to go next wasn't enough for Crux to position a sizable force in orbit around the planet ahead of Gorgon's arrival. There had been no Specters to reckon with when the pirate ship came out of hyperspace. In fact, there was no sign of the enemy at all, either in space or on the ground. Only a few dozen expensive looking yachts and two mining transports, both ancient hulks, circled the planet in geosynchronous orbit.

The transports, Caleb had learned, had spent over a century hauling equipment and personnel out to the mines, and minerals and personnel back. While the yachts and transports were hardly a threat, he had asked Elena to keep a close eye on them, suspecting one or more of them could be a Trojan Horse. Both haulers had unfettered access to Acala's spaceport and were easily large enough to hold a thousand Legionnaires each, more than enough fighters to overpower him and his away team, even with Ishek running interference through the Collective. Ishek had no sense of any khoron anywhere close, but he'd been wrong twice before. This was too important to fully trust his senses.

I deserved that.

At least you aren't making excuses anymore, Caleb replied, shifting his starched shirt collar so it would hopefully stop choking him. Dressed in black pants and a long black coat with a high-collared white shirt, he had begun to understand how clothing made Orin feel. While the look was typical for Acala's over city, it was anything but comfortable. He couldn't wait to get rid of it when this was said and done.

The spaceport sat on the outskirts of Acala's over city, a small facility with barely any traffic. Approaching their assigned landing zone without incident, it surprised Caleb to see an actual car, with four wheels planted on the tarmac, waiting for them just beyond the border of the LZ. A chauffeur stood next to the rear passenger door.

"What's with the overly warm welcome?" he asked, glancing at Damian. He would have preferred Penn, but they needed her and Vraxis free to engage immediately should the enemy make an appearance. Her three weeks of training had gone exceedingly well, leaving her in a sound position to challenge nearly any other Advocate.

I let her win.

Yeah, right, Caleb replied.

They had taken turns, each bonded pair attempting to break through the other's defenses at random times throughout the journey. While Caleb had never broken through, Vraxis had entered his mind. Only for a second, but it was long enough for Penn to pull out a few memories about his childhood. Fortunately, she hadn't grabbed anything too embarrassing. At least, not that she'd admitted.

Fitz would have been his next choice for a second on the away team if he hadn't turned on them, and as usual Orin stood out too much to tag along. The same went for Sparkles with his shimmering tattoos. Caleb believed Damian was a fine choice, and Haruka and Goldie made suitable replacements to round out the small retinue.

"Since you paid the entry fee," Damian said, "the ride is complimentary."

"Is service to the Nexus Orphanage included, too?"

"The car and its driver are at our service, wherever we want to go within the city proper, for as long as we're here."

"Which hopefully won't be long," Caleb said, again tugging at his stiff collar. "Give me utilities any day over this getup."

"I agree," Goldie said from his seat behind Caleb. "I'm itchy as all hell in these starchy clothes."

"Why do you get to wear pants?" Haruka complained. "If I need to kick anyone, it will reveal more of me than should be seen."

"Because none of the skirts we had on board fit me. Honestly, I'd be happy to trade."

The comment drew a smile from the group as Atrice gently placed a mostly-repaired Medusa on the tarmac. "We're here, Cap," he announced.

"Copy that," Caleb replied, undoing his harness and getting to his feet. "If anyone other than us tries to board, lift off and stay close."

"Aye, Captain."

Caleb led the away team off Medusa and across the landing zone to the car.

"Good afternoon, gents," the driver said, his eyes dancing across them. "And lady," he added when they reached Haruka. Goldie coughed, earning a second look. The driver's face reddened. "My apologies. Ladies. My name is Ettore. I'll be your guide and concierge during your visit to Callus. If there is anything you desire, all you need to do is ask." He turned his hand over, and the doors to the car opened. "Baroness Kagata also extends her warmest of welcomes to you. Might I ask, what brings you to our secret paradise?"

"There's no need to be coy," Caleb said. "I'm sure Baroness Kagata knows who I am, even if you don't."

Ettore's false smile vanished. His entire personality shifted. "I know who you are, Captain Card. But I doubt Kagata does or cares. The only people who see or hear anything from her are the ones she invites to her balls. Same goes for the rest of the upper crust. It's the reason you didn't run into any trouble landing. The Combine nobility is too busy showing off to one another to pay attention to much of anything beyond their own pleasures, no matter how important in the bigger scheme of things." He waved to the nearly empty tarmac of the tiny spaceport. "It isn't like the entire galaxy is pouring into our little corner of the universe. As long as the mining operations are running smoothly, it's business as usual for the Combine."

"You don't sound happy about it," Damian said.

"Usually, I have to keep up the joyful servant act, so I'm happier right now than usual." His genuine smile came out, somewhat stilted by tension. "You probably read up on the Combine before coming out here. The few visitors we get usually buy right into the hype. Truth is, Captain, unless you're a noble, a facility manager, or a recruiter, you're faking it if you look happy."

Caleb's chest tightened at the rough assessment. "I knew things weren't great for the miners and their families, but I assumed anyone who lives and works in the over city would do okay."

"That's what the nobles want you to think," Ettore replied. "They can't completely hide the under city, so they make it sound less awful than it is."

"What do you mean?"

Ettore motioned to the car. "Where are you headed? I can explain on the way."

CHAPTER 37

Caleb directed Ettore to Acala Primary Hospital without giving him any explanation for why he wanted to go there, and Ettore didn't ask. He guided the car across the tarmac in silence, fixing his false personality to his face before pausing at a guarded gate and rolling down his window. "Good afternoon, my good man. I have the Creb party requesting entry."

The guard leaned over to look into the rear of the car, smiling broadly. "Welcome to Callus," he said with a wave. Looking at Ettore. "Request granted."

"Thank you, good sir," Ettore replied, rolling up the window and pulling away. As soon as they cleared the gate, he wiped his face clean again, glancing at Caleb over his shoulder. "It'll be about twenty minutes to the hospital. There's never any traffic because there are only a hundred coaches on the planet, but we can't hit the same speeds as a local shuttle."

"I definitely didn't expect to see an automobile when we landed," Caleb commented.

"It's all part of the act," Ettore answered. "Airborne transports are for commoners, and the wealthy are rarely in a hurry unless there's a party at the other end."

"You really hate the nobility, don't you?" Haruka said.

Ettore put his eyes back on the road, a single lane cutting across verdant fields lined with wildflowers. Acala stood tall in the distance, the view from the vehicle admittedly idyllic. It didn't match the driver's attitude at all. "Hate is a strong word." He paused. "It's also a pretty accurate word. There's enough coin flowing through the mines to keep everyone in the Combine comfortable, but the nobility had to turn accumulating wealth into a competition, and everyone else suffers because of it."

"That's a story as old as humanity," Goldie said.

"Believe me, I'm not claiming we're unique. That doesn't make life any easier."

"You said the under city isn't what the hypernet claims," Caleb said.

"That's right. When we get to Acala, you'll see people dressed similarly to yourselves, only a bit more uniform in the details. They aren't advertising, but everyone who lives here knows them as recruiters."

"Recruiters. You mean they hire people to work in the mines?"

"If by hire, you mean an indictment for some random infraction with a mandatory sentence working in the belt, then yes."

The comment surprised Caleb. "You're telling me the miners are forced labor?"

"Not all, but most. The mining operations are essential to increasing the nobles' wealth. Mine workers are essential to those operations. It's damned hard work, and there are never enough volunteers to keep things running smoothly. There isn't even enough of a criminal element to send real lawbreakers out to the belt. So, the government passed a slew of confusing laws open to wide interpretation and sent out the recruiters to help enforce those laws. They watch everything we do, and have the power to accuse and convict at their own discretion. I could spend ten cycles in the belt just for breaking character and telling you any of this."

"That's ridiculous," Haruka said.

"I can't believe Empress Lo'ane would let that happen," Damian agreed. "The Combine is still part of the Empire."

"Yeah, well, she did let it happen," Ettore countered. "And her brother let it happen before she took over, and his father before him. As long as the nobles pay their share of the taxes, the Empire is happy to pretend the Combine barely exists. My father was a nurse. He worked in Acala Primary when I was a boy. He told me Lo'ane visited Callus once, a long time ago, when she was still a young princess. He used to tell me how he thought her visit meant things would change. That she would see how most of the people lived and do something about the way the nobility treated their people." He sighed. "Long story short, she came, she went, and nothing changed. Well, not nothing. My father was accused of defaming the Kagata name and sentenced to three terms in the belt. That's three separate one hundred work cycles with a thirty-day recovery cycle in between to regain bone density and strength. The first time he came home, he was gaunt and weak. Thirty days wasn't enough time to recuperate. He didn't come home a second time."

"No," Damian said. "I can't accept that. How could Lo'ane see what was happening here and do nothing about it?"

"Maybe she didn't know," Goldie said.

"She knew," Ettore countered. "She had to know."

"What makes you so sure?" Haruka questioned. "You just said the Baroness puts on a good show. You're part of that show."

Ettore fell silent, as if he had never considered that

option before. He shook his head. "She had to know. It's her job to know. Anyway, you're pirates. You've been robbing Royal Navy cargo ships for months. You're the last people I would expect to defend the Empire."

"You may have heard about us through whatever back channels you follow," Caleb said. "But believe me when I say that you don't know as much as you think you do. Even if you're right about Lo'ane and her family. Even if they weren't as above board as they seemed, I guarantee Crux is worse. That we could land here at all speaks to how much attention the Combine pays to the Empire, or the Empire pays to the Combine."

"I already told you, the only thing the Combine nobility cares about is that the mining operations are running at full capacity and that there's enough wine and cheese production to keep them fat and drunk."

"Which is the real reason Lo'ane came here all those years ago. She was trying to get away from her family, somewhere she could give birth and surrender her baby with no one knowing."

Caleb thought Ettore might crash the car, he reacted so strongly. "What?" he cried, swerving as his head whipped back over his shoulder. He caught himself, righting the car. "You have to be joking."

"It's no joke," Caleb said. "I risked my life getting into the Royal Archives to confirm it."

"But why? Why do you care about the Empress or her baby?"

"Because Lord Crux isn't the rightful ruler of the Spiral," Damian said. "He stole the throne."

"He won throne," Ettore countered.

"You're on the bastard's side then?" Goldie asked.

"I'm not on anyone's side except my family's. If Crux sent the Legion here to stop the oligarchs from sending innocent people to the belt as slave labor, I would support it one hundred percent."

"It's not that simple," Caleb said. "Crux is getting help from another race. One that will make the Combine nobility look like saints if given the chance. That's why I care. I don't intend to let that happen."

Ettore considered for a moment. "So you aren't attacking the Navy to hurt the Empire. You're trying to hurt Crux."

"While helping the resistance."

"I think I understand. You aren't who I thought you were, Captain Card."

"Is that good or bad?"

"I thought you were a pirate captain telling the system to go to hell. But you're part of the system. I wouldn't call it good."

"I'm not part of the system. And if I succeed, I'll do what I can to force change here."

Ettore glanced back. "Do you mean that?"

Caleb nodded. "Absolutely."

"I want to believe you, but—"

"Then you should," Goldie said. "I've only known Captain Card for a few months now, but I know him to be a man of his word."

"And he's earned the complete loyalty of Gorgon's crew," Haruka added. "Because he does everything he says he will."

"In that case, I'll do what I can to help you get the information you need. I assume you want to go to the hospital to search their records, so you can track down the heir."

"That's right," Caleb said.

"The stars are in your favor today. My sister is a doctor there. She can help."

"I can't ask her to do that. I don't want to be responsible for her being sent to the belt."

"I'll ask her to do it. And you don't need to worry. They

don't send doctors to the belt. They're too valuable. If she gets caught, it'll be my ass on the line for putting her up to it."

"I don't want to be responsible for you being sent to the belt either."

"Vicki's done well enough; she got us out of the under city. But I'll never forget the eight years we spent there after they sent Dad to the belt. There's so much needless suffering down there, Captain. If I can bring attention to it, never mind change it, then it's worth the risk."

"I'm not in a position to turn down an offer to help," Caleb admitted.

Ettore grinned. "Good, because I wouldn't take no for an answer, anyway."

CHAPTER 38

If anything, Ettore had downplayed the presence of recruiters within Acala. Driving through the downtown toward the hospital, it seemed to Caleb as if the men and women in dark coats, dark pants or suits, and white, high-collared shirts were on practically every corner, watching the many passersby like hungry sharks. The people in the over city were all well-dressed, though Ettore pointed out that, like the car, it was still all part of the act.

The pedestrian's clothes were like uniforms, each a reflection of their position within the over city. Many of them arrived and departed on small round elevators built into the massive foundations that kept the rich from collapsing onto the poor. Arriving elevators emerged from tubes marked with green lighting and departed via tubes marked in red.

It didn't take long before Caleb saw the recruiters wandered the under city, too, searching for a hint of trouble. Unsurprisingly, Ettore explained that bribery was common among the recruiters, and they often accepted all kinds of favors for security from being sent to the belt. The scene—the entire concept—thoroughly disgusted Caleb.

When they turned onto a simple road that cut through the gardens around the hospital, he couldn't help but notice how the patients seemed to be especially well cared for. Nurses had brought some of the healthier people outside, pushing them around the grounds in wheelchairs or leaving them resting on blankets or benches to read or listen to music beneath the trees.

Caleb wondered if maybe the Baroness and her ilk weren't so bad after all. Then Ettore explained the hidden costs involved in almost every commoner's healthcare. Most of these people had one or more relatives who volunteered for the belt to pay for their treatments, sacrificing part of their own lives for that of their loved ones. It was disheartening that the upper classes here could be so heartless.

Ettore pulled the car up to the curb just outside the front door, getting out and opening the doors for them before leading them into the building. They passed through a large lobby, the chairs and couches empty, to the front desk where four female employees sat. They were all dressed in stark white uniforms, their hair pulled back into the same tight buns.

"Can I help you?" one of them asked, her red painted lips stretched into a bright smile.

"I'm here to see my sister, Doctor Vicki Alonzo," Ettore said.

"What is this regarding?"

"She's my sister. I just wanted to say hello."

Caleb noticed movement out of the corner of his eye. Glancing that way, he spotted a recruiter sitting in the corner, positioned so he would be easy to miss on the way in.

The women at the front desk knew he was there, though. They were stiff, almost robotic, as they dealt with

Ettore. "I'm afraid Doctor Alonzo is occupied at the moment. Did you want me to leave a message for her?"

A flash of annoyance crossed Ettore's face before vanishing. "Yes, tell her I'll be waiting in the lobby until she's free."

"Are you certain? Don't you have anywhere else you need to be?" Her eyes flicked with warning toward the recruiter.

"Mister Creb and his associates are from off-world," Ettore replied, raising his voice so the recruiter would hear. "They specifically requested to speak with my sister regarding a new medical tool they'd like her opinion on."

"I see. In that case, I'll send her your message. You can have a seat anywhere you'd like."

"Thank you."

The recruiter stood before they could move, heading their way. "Good afternoon," he said as he approached. "I'm sorry, did I hear correctly that you're off-worlders?"

"That's right," Caleb answered.

"Welcome to the Kallio Combine, to Callus, and to Acala," he said with a smile. "It's always nice to have fresh faces in our fine city."

"Thank you," Caleb replied, returning a facsimile of the man's smile.

The recruiter turned away from him, looking at the woman who had helped them. "Maggie, I don't recall hearing you welcome Mister Creb to Callus."

Maggie's face paled. "I... uh... I—"

"I think perhaps you didn't hear her," Caleb said. "You were across the room, after all. I clearly heard her welcome, and I truly appreciate it."

The recruiter made a face, clearly unhappy to have his prey stolen out from under him. "I see. If you're happy, I'm happy, Mister Creb." He spun around to return to his seat.

When Caleb turned back around, Maggie mouthed a silent "Thank you."

Caleb nodded before he turned and took a seat on a sofa with Ettore and Goldie, while Haruka and Damian sat on flanking chairs.

"You just saved her from the belt," Ettore said so softly the recruiter wouldn't hear.

"I figured that much. All because she didn't welcome me?"

"They've convicted people for less."

Caleb shook his head. "I don't know how anyone lives having to walk on eggshells all the time, hoping not to slip up when a recruiter is around. It must be torture."

"We endure it when we must. There's no other choice. Some people crack. Those people never last long in the belt."

"How can you stand it?" Caleb asked. He looked back at Maggie behind the desk. "If they're willing to convict her for something like that, how long would you be sentenced to for helping us?"

Ettore shrugged. "If they catch us? The rest of my life. If my father couldn't survive the belt, then I won't make it more than a cycle or two either."

Caleb shuddered at the thought. Even surrounded by it, he could hardly believe a place like this existed.

The lobby remained empty while they waited for Vicki. The recruiter didn't leave either, remaining on the opposite side of the room, his eyes passing over them from time to time. A handful of people came and went, handled with the utmost care by the women at the front desk, their eyes always dancing over to the recruiter, waiting for him to find some fault. Watching it was painful for Caleb. He could only imagine what it must be like to live it every day.

On the upside, I can taste their fear. It is sublime.

Caleb did his best to ignore the scent of their pheromones, though he couldn't help being aware of their constant low-grade fear.

After nearly an hour, Doctor Alonzo appeared through one of the corridors leading deeper into the hospital. She looked similar to her brother in appearance but had a much more serious demeanor about her that made sense considering her occupation.

"Ettore," she said as he stood and the siblings approached one another. "What are you doing here? You know I'm very busy, and—" She cut off her complaints when she noticed Caleb and the others. Perhaps mistaking him for a recruiter, her expression became more guarded, her lips a tight thin line across her face.

Ettore introduced them."Vicki, this is Mister Creb and his business associates. I believe you had an appointment." He winked at her, signaling her to go along with his lie.

"Oh," she replied. "Right. I'm so sorry, Mister Creb. I don't know how that slipped my mind. My sincerest apologies."

"It's no trouble at all, Doctor Alonzo," Caleb replied, getting to his feet. "I understand you're very busy. We'll take up as little of your time as possible."

"If you'll all follow me, we can discuss your proposal in more detail," Vicki said, with a practiced smile.

They all trailed Vicki past the front desk to the bank of elevators in the lobby's rear. Vicki tapped the controls, and the doors opened to a cab already on the ground floor. She waved them inside, glancing toward the recruiter before joining them on the elevator.

"Ettore?" she hissed. "What the hell is this? Are you trying to get yourself sent to the belt?"

"Vicki, my sweet sister, this is important," Ettore replied. "Do you know who this is?"

Her gaze shifted to Caleb. "I don't know you from a hole in the wall. No offense."

"None taken," Caleb replied.

"Vicki," Ettore groaned. "This is Captain Caleb Card." He

lowered his voice. "The pirate captain from the news. You know, the one who's been attacking Navy cargo haulers? The Blue Demon?"

"Blue Demon?" Damian said.

"On account of his eyes," Ettore explained, pointing at Caleb's face. "I didn't make it up."

Ishek's laughter at the nickname rippled through Caleb's senses.

"You must be double crazy for bringing a wanted criminal here," Vicki exploded in a harsh whisper before looking at Caleb again. "No offense."

"Again, none taken," Caleb answered.

"Relax, sis," Ettore said. "Baroness Kagata has no idea he's here, and none of our people are about to rat out their newest hero. We're fine."

"Mmm hmm," Vicki replied unconvincingly, turning back to Caleb. "Why did you want to meet with me?"

"I'm looking for information about Empress Lo'ane. Princess Lo'ane when she visited this hospital about nineteen years ago. Ettore said your father used to speak about it."

"He did. What kind of information?"

"I need to confirm that she gave birth here."

"What? The ruler of the entire Manticore Spiral came to Callus nineteen years ago to have a secret baby? Are you crazy?"

"I have good reason to believe it happened."

"Yes, well, if it did, there is no way our records would be accurate on the matter."

"She likely went into the datastore with an assumed name, but that's why we need a list of births from that time period. We'll cross-reference it with a second datastore. As long as she didn't change her pseudonym, we'll be able to match her to identify the child."

"You sound like you have it all figured out."

"Hardly. But we know that much."

Vicki smiled. "If you get my brother in trouble, I'll kill you myself."

"If I get your brother in trouble, I'll get him back out of it. You have my word."

The elevator stopped, the doors opening. "Deal. We can search the datastore from my office. This way."

Caleb and the others followed Vicki to her office, nearly halfway down a short hallway to the rear corner of the building. Entering the room, the view from the pyramid immediately drew Caleb's attention. The gardens meshed with the city, colorful and serene, hiding the corroded truth.

Vicki circled her desk, tapping on the control board for her terminal and activating a holo-projector over the center of her desk. It still showed a scan of someone's insides, a small circle around a dark spot on the lungs. The image faded away, replaced by a more ordinary interface for patient records.

"Is he going to make it?" Haruka asked.

"Who?" Vicki asked.

"The patient with lung cancer."

"You know how to read scans?"

"I've seen one like that before. My father's."

Vicki shook her head sadly. "Unfortunately, no."

"All these years, and we still can't cure cancer?" Caleb said, shaking his head.

"What do you mean by all these years? It's not as much a matter of can or can't. The medical community has chosen not to pursue a cure."

"Why not?"

She shrugged in response. "I honestly can't tell you, Captain Card. The investment just isn't there, I suppose."

Or certain factions repressed it. Medical technology is still technology.

Ishek's answer chilled Caleb. He had only considered

the Relyeh meddling in terms of warfare. But Ish was right, advances in any area could apply to other things, and the enemy needed to keep humankind weak.

"I'll need something to query the datastore. A name or dates."

Caleb gave her the dates for the last four weeks of Lo'ane's visit to Callus. The range might be too large, but he had little else to go on, and he didn't want to narrow the range too much. Vicki ran the query, which quickly returned a list of results.

"There were two hundred eighty births in that period," Vicki said.

"Can you filter out addresses in the under city?"

She nodded, doing as he asked. "One hundred and four results," she replied, narrowing the list by more than half.

"Not bad," Damian said. "What about gender? We know Lo'ane had a daughter."

"Good idea," Caleb said as Vicki entered it in.

"Sixty-seven," Vicki answered.

"Can you send that list to his pad?" Caleb asked, pointing to Damian. Vicki nodded again, tapping her control board to send it.

"Got it," Damian confirmed.

"Thank you for your help," Caleb said. "Both you and your brother. That's all we needed here."

"I'm glad I could help," she replied. "But just how were you planning to get this data if Control hadn't assigned Ettore as your concierge?"

Goldie laughed. "You don't want to know."

"You would hurt people over this?"

"Only bad people. But no, we're using stun rounds."

"We planned to get access to a terminal and create a network between it and our ship so our engineers could hack into the datastore," Caleb corrected. "The guns are our backup plan, and I'm glad we don't need to use them."

"I see. Well, I'm glad too. If you have what you came for, I need to get back to my scheduled duties. I hope Ettore is right about you, Captain, and that you're truly planning to help the common people of the Combine."

"I gave him my word," Caleb answered. "And I give it to you, too. As long as I don't die before this is over, I'll see that things change around here." He turned to the others. "Let's go."

They filed out of the room, with Ettore and Caleb in the lead. They were nearing the corner when the recruiter from downstairs appeared around it, flanked by two more recruiters and a handful of hospital security guards. The two groups froze at the sight of one another.

"You," the recruiter said, thrusting a finger at Ettore. "Stop right there."

It seems we may need to use the guns after all.

CHAPTER 39

"What's going on?" Caleb asked, resisting the urge to go for his weapon. "Is there a problem?"

The recruiter smiled wickedly, pleased to have someone to target for incarceration to the belt. His gaze shifted from Caleb to Vicki, who had moved to her office doorway. Her face paled in response to his attention.

"The datastore triggered an alarm," one of the other recruiters said. "We traced an illegal records access back to your office, Doctor Alonzo."

"What are you talking about?" Vicki shot back. "None of the patient records on the hospital server are off-limits to me."

"That's where you're wrong," the first recruiter said. "You may have permissions, but records from the time period you selected are not to be accessed."

"And how was I supposed to know that?"

"The records in question are nearly twenty years old. What reason would you have to go back that far?"

Vicki looked stricken. "I'm a doctor. You can't send me to the belt."

"No, we can't." His gaze shifted back to Ettore. "But he's your blood relative, correct?"

"Wait a second," Caleb said, no longer able to keep his mouth shut in the face of such insanity. "You can't arrest someone for running a database search they didn't know they weren't supposed to run. That's crazy."

"I understand you're a visitor here, Mister Creb, so I apologize if any of this is distressing to you. The nobility has enacted certain rules and regulations to ensure the peace and security for all citizens of the Combine, as well as all our visitors. Unfortunately, Doctor Alonzo has broken one of those rules."

"She didn't know she was breaking it," Caleb pointed out.

"That's beside the point," the recruiter insisted, his arrogant smirk proving how much he enjoyed the power he held over Vicki. "Rules are rules, and infractions result in punishment."

"This is total crap," Goldie growled, equally angered by the situation but with less emotional control. "You can take your rules and shove them up you—"

"Goldie!" Damian warned.

"Doctor Alonzo," the third recruiter said. "Did you transfer the data you retrieved to an external device?"

Vicki hesitated for a moment before nodding. "I sent a copy to his pad." She motioned to Damian.

"Sir, I apologize, but I'll need to see your pad," the recruiter said to him.

Damian smiled. "There's no way in hell you're touching my pad. If you didn't want the data to leave the datastore, you should have blocked its access."

The recruiters' smiles vanished, their faces hardening at Damian's defiance of both their authority and their request. One of the hospital guards tapped on an earpiece, activating his comms. "We're going to need backup on sixty-one. Doctor Alonzo's office."

"Since you're a visitor to our planet, I'll permit you one misstep," the recruiter said slowly, emphasizing each word. "I'll ask you again, sir. Please allow me to access your pad and delete the offending records."

Damian sighed, opening his coat and feigning a reach for his pad. Only his pad wasn't inside his coat's interior pocket. Instead, he withdrew his blaster, pointing it at the man. "I'd like to see you try to take it."

The recruiter didn't move, he just became more angry. "Pointing a weapon at a recruiter is punishable by life in the belt!" he growled. "You have three seconds to—"

A group of stun blasts traced over Caleb's shoulder, each striking a recruiter, followed by the guards. The entire entourage of eight shuddered at once, their muscles spasming and losing strength, dropping them to the floor.

"Oops," Goldie said, drawing a laugh from both Haruka and Ishek.

"Ettore, we need to get to the Nexus Orphanage asap," Caleb said.

"It's a six-hour drive from here," he replied. "We'll never make it ahead of Planetary Defense."

"We might," Vicki countered, stepping up to them. "We can take an emergency shuttle."

"We?" Ettore said. "Sis, you belong here. Don't get mixed up in this."

She made a face at him like he'd lost his mind. "I'm already mixed up in this, Etty. It isn't your fault. You didn't know. We need to hurry, before they fully revoke my access."

"Toodles," Goldie said, waggling her fingers to the helpless recruiters as the group stepped over them. Hurrying back to the elevators, Vicki hit the call button to go up. When a set of doors opened, it was to a cab filled with more guards. A shout from behind revealed even more guards rushing them from the other side of the floor.

Can I take over? Ishek asked.

Not this time, Caleb replied, pulling his blaster and stepping aside to allow Goldie and Haruka to fire into the elevator. He and Damian shot back at the guards coming down the hallway, dropping them in a matter of seconds.

"Stairs," Vicki said as the doors closed on the paralyzed guards in the elevator. They followed her through a door near the elevators and into the stairwell.

"How many flights do we need to climb?" Ettore asked.

"Only twenty," she replied.

"Twenty?" he cried.

"Stop complaining and move it," Caleb growled.

They continued up the steps, quickly at first, slowing less than ten levels up when Ettore ran out of steam. He trudged up the steps as Goldie and Haruka went ahead, hoping to secure the emergency shuttle before the others arrived.

"Do you want to go to the belt?" Vicki snapped back over her shoulder at her brother.

"This is why I don't want to go to the belt," he replied. "I wouldn't last a month there."

"Cap, we've reached the shuttle bay," Goldie said over the comms. "Guards are out of commission, just don't trip over them when you come through the door."

"Copy that," Caleb replied with a smile. "Is there a shuttle for us?"

"Aye, Captain. And the skies look clear for the moment. I'm sure that won't last, though."

Caleb glanced at Ettore. "Pick up the pace, or we'll have to leave you behind."

"You wouldn't. You need me to fly the shuttle."

"I can fly the shuttle," Vicki countered.

"You wouldn't leave me; I'm your little brother."

"I'm not spending the rest of my life rock-hopping because you're a lump, little brother."

Ettore growled, finding a second wind to regain a more speedy pace. They reached the top floor of the stairwell less than a minute later, spilling out into the shuttle bay. Painted bright white with red stripes and a band of lights across the front, the half dozen emergency shuttles looked more like bricks resting on gravity coils.

The hatch to the shuttle Haruka and Goldie had picked was already open, with Haruka on the threshold and Goldie just outside. They waved the others forward at a run, but then Haruka suddenly jumped out of the shuttle, she and Goldie firing through the gaps between Caleb and the others. Glancing back, Caleb watched the first two guards who had chased them up the steps convulse and collapse.

They never learn, Ishek commented.

"Hurry. Get in," Goldie pressed, prompting Caleb to push Ettore toward him. Caleb stepped aside so Vicki could go next. Then Goldie followed her inside.

Caleb waited until everyone else was clear before climbing into the shuttle. The interior was mostly bare bones, with space for a gurney on one side, and shelves holding medical supplies and equipment along the other. An open arch in the front led to where Vicki and Ettore had already taken position—Vicki at the controls, Ettore riding shotgun.

Caleb was swinging the hatch closed when a stun round snuck through the opening and sizzled against the seat just behind and off to his right. None of the hospital guards had been armed, meaning the shots had likely come from law enforcement or planetary defense. It didn't matter. They were too late.

"Hold on back there!" Vicki shouted, the shuttle vibrating as it lifted off the deck. "I'm going full throttle."

With no more open seats, Caleb stepped forward and grabbed both sides of the archway leading to the flight deck. The power source whined, and the shuttle jerked forward, rapidly gaining speed. Escaping through the small open face of the pyramid's upper reaches as if they really were responding to an emergency, Vicki added sirens and lights a moment later, sending them hurtling at top speed over Acala.

"Are we clear?" Caleb shouted over the screaming engine.

Ettore looked back at him. "We made it for now, Captain. PD won't scramble assets to intercept us. Not when word of it might reach back to Baroness Kagata. And not when they can track the shuttle wherever we go. They'll wait until we've landed to pin us down."

"Understood," Caleb replied. *Ish, contact Vraxis. Have him tell Penn to send Cookie to the orphanage. We'll move out directly from there.*

Consider it done.

"Are you sure you still want to go to Nexus?" Vicki asked.

"I'm not leaving Callus without at least the name of the Empress' daughter."

"Even if it means my stupid brother and I end up mining asteroids?"

"I'm sorry you got mixed up in this, but yes. There's too much at stake to give up now."

He heard her exhale, obviously resigned to whatever her fate was destined to be. "We'll be there in fifteen minutes."

CHAPTER 40

Vicki guided the emergency shuttle down toward a small landing pad just outside the Nexus Orphanage grounds. While the landscape surrounding the grounds approached idyllic, with a crystal clear river flowing just beyond the one wall and a thick, verdant forest flanking it, the facility itself was unimpressive. Two smaller wings surrounded a large main building, creating an almost perfect square around a muddy courtyard. A handful of dirty children of different ages were busy kicking a weathered and no longer round ball through the muck. There were no adults watching over them, but Caleb could see why that wasn't necessary. A tall wall surrounded the entire facility, topped with what appeared to be razor wire. To keep trouble out? Or to keep the kids in?

Atrice is on his way. He's going to feign launching back to orbit before cutting a wide path around the wilds beyond the Strophos Volcano and circling back. Twelve minutes.

I'd prefer less than ten, Caleb replied.

I'm not trying to relay that. Knuckle up, Marine.

Caleb almost laughed out loud at Ishek's comment despite himself.

The shuttle settled onto the landing pad, the vibration in the deck finally subsiding. They had made the trip without incident, though Caleb knew planetary defense would be along soon enough. Ettore had explained during the flight that most of the PD enforcers were likely on his side or would be if they knew about his promise to help, but to take no action would equal a guaranteed trip to the belt. It meant they had fifteen minutes to dig into the orphanage's datastore and hope they found a match to the list of names on Damian's pad, plus the name of the child that match had put up for adoption.

"Let's get this done," Vicki urged in a no-nonsense tone that Caleb appreciated.

"Goldie, stay with the shuttle," he ordered.

"Aye, Captain."

Caleb and the others followed Vicki out of the shuttle. They hurried across the landing pad toward one of the two smaller buildings where a pair of nurses in dark uniforms had emerged, likely curious why an emergency shuttle had landed at the facility. One woman was short and thin, the other tall and broad. Both wore curious looks as Caleb approached. The taller nurse looked past them at the shuttle. "Is there some sort of emergency? No one informed us of anything."

"I'm Doctor Alonzo from Acala Primary Hospital," Vicki replied. "This is my brother Ettore. We need to access your datastore immediately."

The two women exchanged glances before looking back at them. "We don't have any record requests on file for today," the shorter nurse said.

"There's been an incident at the hospital," Vicki continued, impressing Caleb with her acting skills. "Its possible records were damaged or destroyed." She pointed at Caleb and Damian. "I brought two recruiters with me to verify my credentials. This one also has a list of names and dates he needs to cross-reference with your datastore."

The taller nurse nodded, wary of Caleb and Damian now that Vicki had called them recruiters. "Yes, of course, doctor. Right this way."

Haruka was already busy scanning the area around them for threats. The only thing Caleb saw were children, most of them having rushed over to get a look at the strangers. Covered in mud and dirt, their expressions filled with hope, he couldn't help the pang of compassion for them. He was hardly the fatherly type, but he wished he could whisk them all away from here. Anywhere, except the belt, had to be a better home than this place. Ettore had told him what happened to orphans who weren't adopted by their fifteenth birthday.

"Hi," one child said to him. A girl, no older than seven or eight.

"Hello," he replied.

"Do you have any candy?"

"I'm sorry, I don't."

"Can you get some candy?"

Caleb opened his mouth to answer.

"Leave them alone," the short nurse snapped at the girl. "Nobody wants to adopt a loudmouth."

All the children clamped their mouths shut, not wanting to risk their chances at getting adopted.

"They didn't come here for any of you," she continued. "And can you blame them? You're all a mess. Head inside and get yourselves cleaned up. If you're still dirty when I come to your dorm, you'll spend the night cleaning the toilets."

The children all rushed off into the building ahead of them, desperate to avoid punishment.

"You don't need to be so mean to them," Haruka said.

"Who the hell are you to criticize how we treat these

children? They're all lucky to have a roof over their heads and food in their bellies," the short nurse snapped.

Haruka looked like she wanted to punch the nurse in the teeth. She settled for clenching her hands into fists while remaining silent.

"This way," the tall nurse said, leading them toward the building on the other side of the courtyard and into the building's simple foyer. From there, the nurses escorted them down a short hallway to an office door that opened when the tall one waved her hand across the sensor beside it. They entered a nondescript office without a window or even a picture hanging on the wall to break the beige monotony. She sat behind the desk in the center of the room. "I'll need your list of names," she said as she began tapping on the control board for the computer terminal on the desktop, the surface otherwise bare except for a small comm device.

Damian retrieved his pad, holding it out to transmit the list to the terminal. The nurse quickly scanned the names, her helpful demeanor abruptly turning dark. "These records are nearly twenty years old," she remarked. "What could you need them for?"

"I told you," Vicki said. "Some of the hospital records were destroyed."

"I know, but why these, and why are you so desperate to get them?"

"Doctor Alonzo requested your help," Caleb said, taking on the affect of the recruiter they'd encountered in the hospital. "It's in your best interests to comply without argument."

"Cap, you have eight minutes," Goldie informed Caleb through his comm.

"Run the names against your records," Caleb continued. "Now!" He barked the order like a drill sergeant. The nurse flinched in response, tapping furiously on the control board.

The comm device on the desk beside her beeped. She tapped on it. "Hello?"

"Nurse Troyer?" a voice asked.

"Speaking."

"This is Captain Jurson Kane with Planetary Defense. We tracked a stolen hospital shuttle to your location. Are its occupants there with you now?"

Nurse Troyer's eyes shot up to Caleb's, her expression filled with alarm. She looked like she was about to reply when Haruka pointed her stunner at her forehead and shook her head in silent warning.

"Yes. Everything's fine here," Troyer replied in a quivering voice.

Yesss. I hunnngeerrrr.

"Are you sure, ma'am?"

"No," she snapped, making her decision. "We're under at —" She shuddered when the stun round hit her, the comms device clattering to the floor and breaking. Damian quickly grabbed the other nurse, restraining her while Vicki circled the desk.

"Did she run the names?" Caleb asked.

"Yes," she replied. "There's only one match. Genevieve Ling, age nineteen surrendered a newborn baby girl to the orphanage named Castra."

"Ling?" Caleb said. "That has to be her." He turned a hard, tenacious expression on the nurse. "Castra," he barked. "What happened to her?"

She jerkily shook her head, her eyes wide with panic. "I...I don't know. I don't know anything about anyone named Castra. I've only been here for two years. N...Nurse Troyer, she's been here for nearly thirty. She...she would know."

Caleb glanced at the other woman, silent and unmoving

on the floor. She wouldn't recover in time to be of any help. "Some children must have known her," he said. "Where can I find the older kids?"

The nurse hesitated. "What is this ab—"

"Where!" he shouted.

"Building C, the east corner."

"The rest of you, go back to the landing pad to wait for Cookie. I'll meet you there."

Caleb burst out of the room, running down the hallway and out the door. He crossed to the dorm, the door into the building locked. A hard kick sent it crashing open, and he rushed inside, quickly locating a group of surprised teenagers.

"A girl named Castra," he said, hearing Medusa's engines as she landed. "Did any of you know her when she was here?"

"We all did," a boy answered. "She left four years ago. Aged out."

Caleb froze. He had always assumed Lo'ane had brought her daughter here expecting she had planned for a noble to adopt her daughter. But the Empress had apparently done no such thing. She had truly abandoned her child here and let the stars have their way with her. Considering she'd been sent to the belt, it was no wonder she didn't want her long-lost offspring to be found, much less gain the throne. Even if Castra was still alive, she was probably everything they had feared she'd become.

"Cap, Medusa is here," Goldie said. "And PD isn't far behind."

Caleb didn't answer right away, still trying to process the truth of the situation.

We need to go.

Ishek's prodding didn't help. He had come all this way to find Lo'ane's heir. He couldn't just give up now.

She is a miner, if she is even alive. She is useless to us.

Caleb's eyes slid across the teenagers gathered in front of him. They wore threadbare clothes and no shoes, passing the time playing a card game that looked as if Lo'ane had brought it to the orphanage twenty years ago. The galaxy considered these kids useless, too.

"I don't accept that," he growled. "Can you tell me anything about her? What does she look like?"

"She has light brown hair," an orphan replied. "Pale skin and lots of freckles."

"Her eyes are green," another said.

"They're blue," the first countered.

"No, they're green."

"Hazel," the third interjected.

"Cap," Damian said. "Everyone's on board. We need to go, now."

Cal, why are we still standing here?

I have a plan.

I hate when you say that. And like always, hate your plan.

"Cookie," Caleb said, tapping his comms patch. "Go without me."

"What?" Atrice replied. "You didn't leave me behind. I'm not leaving—"

"Go!" Caleb barked. "Lo'ane's daughter isn't here, but I'm going to find her."

"How?"

"I'll stay in communication with Penn through Ishek. You need to go, now. That's an order."

"Aye, Captain," Atrice reluctantly replied. Moments later, the sound of Medusa's engines ramping up to take off rent the air.

This is really a bad idea.

I have to know if she's still alive. And if she is, I need to meet her for myself. I'm not just discarding her because she's had a rough life. Not when so much is at stake.

Don't you think rough is an understatement?

Caleb turned away from the kids, still distracted arguing over Castra's eye color. He could feel their eyes on his back as he left the dorm. Looking up, he watched Medusa's thrusters flare; the shuttle rocketing toward orbit. To his right, a group of PD ships approached the orphanage. Spotlights suddenly locked onto him, and he slowly raised his hands.

Two of the ships kept him bathed in bright light while the others landed. Within a minute, an entire retinue of planetary defense guards rushed into the courtyard, rifles aimed at him. A single recruiter cut through them, his uniform crisp, the fit perfect. He regarded Caleb with an air of arrogance and disdain.

"It seems your band of miscreants left you behind." It was obvious from the way the recruiter looked at Caleb, he had no idea who he really was. In his eyes, just another law-breaker.

"Bastards," Caleb growled before spitting on the recruiter's polished shoe.

The man scowled as he looked down at the spittle. "You'll spend the rest of your life in the belt for that. Grab him."

Two of the guards grabbed him by his biceps, holding him tight as he faked resistance, acting as if he were afraid of what would happen next.

If Castra was alive, he would find her in the belt.

He couldn't get there soon enough.

———

Thank you so much for reading Galaxy Under Siege! For more information on the next book, please visit mrforbes. com/forgottengalaxy4. Also, please continue to the next page for more information on Caleb and other books by M.R. Forbes. Thank you again!

THANK YOU!

Thank you for reading Galaxy Under Siege!

Did you know there are more books that take place in the Forgotten Universe, including Caleb's origin story?

A lot more.

Want to read them, but don't know where to start?

If you're looking for Caleb's first series, go here: mrforbes.com/forgottencolony

Otherwise, head on over to mrforbes.com/forgottenuniverse to see a list of all the books.

Looking for something outside of the Forgotten Universe?

I love writing, and release a new book every 6 weeks or so. I've been doing it for over ten years now, so I've got a pretty decent-sized catalogue. If you love sci-fi, you're sure to find something you'll enjoy. Flip to the next section in this book or head on over to mrforbes.com/books to see everything on my web site, or hit up mrforbes.com/amazon to look at my stuff there, including most popular titles, reviews, etc.

By the way, you can also sign up for my mailing list at mrforbes.com/notify to be alerted to all of my new releases. No spam, just books. Guaranteed!

OTHER BOOKS BY M.R FORBES

Want more M.R. Forbes? Of course you do!
View my complete catalog here
mrforbes.com/books
Or on Amazon:
mrforbes.com/amazon

Forgotten (The Forgotten)
mrforbes.com/theforgotten
Complete series box set:
mrforbes.com/theforgottentrilogy

Some things are better off FORGOTTEN.

Sheriff Hayden Duke was born on the Pilgrim, and he expects to die on the Pilgrim, like his father, and his father before him.

That's the way things are on a generation starship centuries from home. He's never questioned it. Never thought about it. And why bother? Access points to the ship's controls are sealed, the systems that guide her automated and out of reach. It isn't perfect, but he has all he needs to be content.

Until a malfunction forces his wife to the edge of the habitable zone to inspect the damage.

Until she contacts him, breathless and terrified, to tell him she found a body, and it doesn't belong to anyone on board.

Until he arrives at the scene and discovers both his wife and the body are gone.

The only clue? A bloody handprint beneath a hatch that hasn't opened in hundreds of years.

Until now.

Deliverance (Forgotten Colony)
mrforbes.com/deliverance
Complete series box set:

The war is over. Earth is lost. Running is the only option.

It may already be too late.

Caleb is a former Marine Raider and commander of the Vultures, a search and rescue team that's spent the last two years pulling high-value targets out of alien-ravaged cities and shipping them off-world.

When his new orders call for him to join forty-thousand survivors aboard the last starship out, he thinks his days of fighting are over. The Deliverance represents a fresh start and a chance to leave the war behind for good.

Except the war won't be as easy to escape as he thought.

And the colony will need a man like Caleb more than he ever imagined...

Starship For Sale (Starship For Sale)
mrforbes.com/starshipforsale

When Ben Murdock receives a text message offering a fully operational starship for sale, he's certain it has to be a joke.

Already trapped in the worst day of his life and desperate for a way out, he decides to play along. Except there is no joke. The starship is real. And Ben's life is going to change in ways he never dreamed possible.

All he has to do is sign the contract.

Joined by his streetwise best friend and a bizarre tenant with an unseverable lease, he'll soon discover that the universe is more volatile, treacherous, and awesome than he ever imagined.

And the only thing harder than owning a starship is staying alive.

Man of War (Rebellion)
mrforbes.com/manofwar
Complete series box set:
mrforbes.com/rebellion-web

In the year 2280, an alien fleet attacked the Earth.

Their weapons were unstoppable, their defenses unbreakable.

Our technology was inferior, our militaries overwhelmed.

Only one starship escaped before civilization fell.

Earth was lost.

It was never forgotten.

Fifty-two years have passed.

A message from home has been received.

The time to fight for what is ours has come.

Welcome to the rebellion.

Hell's Rejects (Chaos of the Covenant)
mrforbes.com/hellsrejects

The most powerful starships ever constructed are gone. Thousands are dead. A fleet is in ruins. The attackers are unknown. The orders are clear: *Recover the ships. Bury the bastards who stole them.*

Lieutenant Abigail Cage never expected to find herself in Hell. As a Highly Specialized Operational Combatant, she was one of the most respected Marines in the military. Now she's doing hard labor on the most miserable planet in the universe.

Not for long.

The Earth Republic is looking for the most dangerous individuals it can control. The best of the worst, and Abbey happens to be one of them. The deal is simple: *Bring back the starships, earn your freedom. Try to run, you die.* It's a suicide mission, but she has nothing to lose.

The only problem? There's a new threat in the galaxy. One with a power unlike anything anyone has ever seen. One that's been waiting for this moment for a very, very, long time. And they want Abbey, too.

Be careful what you wish for.

They say Hell hath no fury like a woman scorned. They have no idea.

ABOUT THE AUTHOR

M.R. Forbes is the mind behind a growing number of Amazon best-selling science fiction series. He currently resides with his family and friends on the west cost of the United States, including a cat who thinks she's a dog and a dog who thinks she's a cat.

He maintains a true appreciation for his readers and is always happy to hear from them.

To learn more about me or just say hello:

Visit my website:
mrforbes.com

Send me an e-mail:
michael@mrforbes.com

Check out my Facebook page:
facebook.com/mrforbes.author

Join my Facebook fan group:
facebook.com/groups/mrforbes

Follow me on Instagram:
instagram.com/mrforbes_author

Find me on Goodreads:
goodreads.com/mrforbes

Follow me on Bookbub:
bookbub.com/authors/m-r-forbes

Made in the USA
Las Vegas, NV
28 November 2023

81738674R00187